LUCIENNE DIVER

I0587245

RISE OF THE BLOOD

The Latter-Day Olympians #3

WFP
WORDFIRE PRESS

QUOTES

"There's a lot going on in this story. It's really pretty much non-stop action of one type or another from beginning to end. Along with it you get a smooth plot flow, nice imagery, a unique locale, lots of interesting characters and great bantering dialogue."

—*Literary Nymphs Reviews*

"Wow! What a wild and crazy roller coaster ride of a story! Author Lucienne Diver has another amazing hit on her hands with this, the third installment in her wildly popular Latter-Day Olympians series ... This is a fantastic novel that will enchant readers of all ages."

—*Night Owl Reviews*

"I've said it twice now in my previous reviews of this series, but I'll say it again: if you're looking for an action packed Urban Fantasy with the perfect blend of Greek mythology this is the read for you! Tori is without a doubt one of my most favorite heroines

now! ... I look forward to reading more of her adventures and whatever mischief she gets herself into!"

—Jessica at A Great Read, 5/5 Stars

ISBN: 978-1-61475-610-1

Cover design by Janet McDonald

Cover artwork images by Kanaxa

Kevin J. Anderson, Art Director

Published by
WordFire Press, an imprint of
WordFire, LLC
PO Box 1840
Monument CO 80132

Kevin J. Anderson & Rebecca Moesta, Publishers
WordFire Press Trade Paperback Edition January 2018
Printed in the USA

Join our WordFire Press Readers Group and get free books,
sneak previews, updates on new projects, and other giveaways.
Sign up for free at wordfirepress.com

 Created with Vellum

DEDICATION

This one is for my husband, Pete, the most amazing man in the world.

CHAPTER ONE

"Sometimes you're the bug and sometimes you're that sticky tape they get all stuck on.
I'm pretty sure that's worse."
—Pappous, the strongman with the weak heart

D iminutive. *Diminutive?* You've got to be kidding me. I'm five seven, for gods' sake."

I was staring down at a national tabloid "newspaper" that Jesus (pronounced *Hey-Zeus*)—part-time office assistant when no auditions demanded his attention and full-time diva—had just thrown onto my desk. My very own face stared back at me. Or, more accurately, gazed across a dinner table at Hollywood hottie Apollo Demas. The photographer had used some kind of filter or something to make the whole thing appear dreamy. A filter or magic, because I knew exactly where and when the pic must have been taken, and I'd been mad as hell at the time.

"Really?" Jesus asked wryly. "*That's* your take away from this?"

"My take away is that if the rumors about me and Apollo won't die, *someone* has to. I'm perfectly willing for it to be him."

Jesus looked at me in horror. He lived in hope that he could match-make the two of us and that, in gratitude, Apollo would launch his acting career ... at which point he'd bid me a "say-onara, sister" and leave me entirely without office support. It was a terrifying thought, considering he was the only one who understood his filing system.

"You think this was his doing?" he asked.

I took a huge swig of the coffee from the to-go cup sitting on my desk to give myself time to think. The coffee was a lot more palatable than the headline, even with the scalding.

"I don't know," I said finally.

"You could call him and find out."

"You know I can't do that."

"I know you won't."

But he didn't know why, and I wasn't about to enlighten him.

"Anyway, the damage is already done. Do you suppose Armani has seen—" On that note, all three of our phone lines lit up at once.

Jesus snagged the phone on my desk. "Karacis Investiga-tions," he said, putting on his professional voice—one-third less ennui than his norm. "Hold please." He punched another button. "Karacis Investigations," he repeated for the benefit of whoever was on line two.

"No," he said as I crooked an eyebrow at him for a sign as to our sudden popularity. "Miss Karacis is not available for comment."

My head fell back against the headrest on my chair. I couldn't wait for the universe to rescue me. I was going to have to kill Apollo myself.

"Italian stallion on line three," Jesus said, making me realize

I must have missed something while I was plotting Apollo's death.

Armani. Crap.

I shooed Jesus out to his own desk to deal with the lit up lines and answered my phone, punching the button for line three.

Quickly, before Armani could get a word in, I said, "Listen, whatever it looks like, it's not what you think."

Dead air.

"Armani."

"*What's* not what I think?" he asked, voice tight and contained.

"Uh, that's not why you called?"

"*What's* not why I called?"

"The article."

"*What article?*" he asked in a strangled voice that indicated how hard he was working to stay patient with me.

I swallowed hard. "The one in the *National Informer.*" He was silent again.

"Someone get me a copy of the *Informer,*" he suddenly roared, which told me that he was at the station. Whoever got their hands on that copy would know even before he did what the ruckus was all about. It would spread through the station like wildfire. The whole police force would know by noon. In LA that was no small thing. I pulled the receiver away from my ear to bang it against my temple.

"Tori," he said loudly, calling me back to the conversation before I could give myself a concussion, "that's not what I called about, though you *will* tell me everything." The speed with which he got back to business told me that it was serious. "Zeus and Poseidon have escaped."

My heart stopped. My own gorgon glare couldn't have turned me to stone any more effectively.

"Hephaestus?" I asked.

"Still behind bars. The other two called up a humungous

storm. The prison had to be evacuated. They escaped during the transfer. Hephaestus wasn't so lucky."

"So they're ... loose?"

"Yeah."

"Since when?" The facility was hours away, but with gods that could be the blink of an eye. "Do I need to be worried?"

"No, we can take you into protective custody, get you to a safe house until they're caught. With any luck, it won't be long."

My precognition kicked me in the gut at that statement, and I knew otherwise. They weren't going to be caught within the next few hours or even days ... maybe not at all by conventional methods.

"No," I answered, before I could lose my nerve. "I'm not running. If they want to, they'll find me anyway, and I still haven't finished packing for the wedding." Or started. "Wait—" For a second I wondered if a threat to my life would be enough to get me out of the whole thing. Watching cousin Tina star in the role she was meant to play—Bridezilla—was so not my idea of a good time. But in my crazy clan, weddings were sacred, and Yiayia's wrath was a little more terrifying even than the greater gods. "No, never mind. Yiayia would kill me if I didn't show." And she'd talk me to death first. Zeus and Poseidon would probably just kill me outright.

"Still, you weighed the risk, didn't you?" he asked.

"Wait until you meet my family, then you'll understand." Armani was my date. Poor man.

"If they're all as ... wonderful as you ..."

I snorted, one of my more graceful habits. "What word were you really going to use?"

"Quirky came to mind."

"Well, they are that."

There was a pause, during which I heard the distinctive sound of newspaper crinkling, and then, "Um, do you want to tell me about your intimate little dinner with Apollo?"

I let my head hit the desk. It hurt.

"What was that?" he asked.

"I'm trying to brain myself."

"You sure you're equipped for that?"

"Some boyfriend you are."

"At least I don't make headlines with other men."

"You knew all about that dinner. I called you from the porch, remember, asking if murder was still a crime."

"You don't look ready to kill him here."

But I could tell he wasn't seriously concerned. He had far bigger worries.

The second we hung up, my buzzer sounded again. "*E! News* on line one," Jesus said gleefully.

"I thought you took care of that."

"Honey, that was line two. Some rinky-dink San Fernando Station. This is *E!*"

"Tell them they have the wrong lady."

"*Chica*, I'm fairly certain they have better facial recognition software than the LAPD. I don't think they're going to believe me."

"You're an actor ... act. Make it convincing."

He huffed. If *E!* had been calling for Jesus, I was sure *he* wouldn't be dodging the call. I just hoped they wouldn't offer him enough to sell me out. Maybe I ought to rethink that bonus he kept hinting about.

Lines two and three lit up *again* while he was dealing with *E!* I was considering my escape when Jesus's voice suddenly rose, and I heard his composure slip.

"Come again?"

There was a pause as he listened to the person on the other end of the line before he sputtered, "Well, you ... you just ... Hello? *Hello?*"

I didn't worry too much until Jesus flew into my office, ignoring the still-ringing phones. He *never* did that, lest it be his big break calling, unable to reach him on his cell. He looked pale, his eyes were wide and, even more shocking, I didn't think he was acting.

"Tori," he said. Not *boss lady* or *chica* or even his signature sniff. "I think we've just received our first death threat."

It wouldn't be my first threat, actually, but I hadn't seen fit to worry him.

"We?" I asked, more curious than alarmed. I already knew that Zeus and Poseidon would probably come gunning for me. It was actually fairly considerate of them to issue a warning. Maybe Armani could trace the call.

"Well, *you*, really, but who knows who he might go through to get to you?" He clutched his hands to his chest. "I'm too young to die."

I ignored the histrionics. "Calm down. What did the caller say?"

"Well," he said, rolling his eyes to the heavens as if it helped him remember, "the connection was horrible, mind you, so I didn't catch everything, but the gist of it was, 'Tell her there's nowhere she can run that we can't find her.'"

I blew out a puff of air. "You call that a death threat?" I'd had worse. The god of the dead, now *there's* a man who knew how to issue a threat. As for Zeus and Poseidon, why bother warning me? Wouldn't it be easier to ambush me if I wasn't on my guard? Not that I wouldn't be after their prison break. But there had to be more to it. To convince me there was no point in protective custody? They couldn't know I'd already come to the same conclusion. Reverse psychology? Wanting me running scared? In the end, it didn't matter. I was going to do what I was going to do. I'd have to fight them either way, I might as well do it on my own terms.

"What would you call it?" Jesus asked. I passed on that one.

"Call Armani. Let him know about the call in case he can track it." I picked up the phone myself.

"Who are *you* calling?" he asked.

"Apollo. You happy now? I'm pretty sure that call was about

a case we worked on together. I may want to kill him myself, but he deserves to know I won't be the only one gunning."

"Be gentle with him," Jesus said, leaving and closing the door behind him like I might actually want privacy while I gave Apollo hell. Because that's what I was planning to unleash.

But all I got was his voicemail.

"*Kalimera*. Please leave me a message. If this is the press, lose this number. If this is Tori, I'm on it."

Well, so much for that, except that he'd now given my name to anyone who didn't already have it. I left him a message about Zeus and Poseidon. I didn't bother reading him the riot act. He was one step ahead of me there. If I was lucky, which didn't seem terribly likely given my morning so far, he really was on it and all I'd have to worry about was two escaped gods with a grudge.

Lucky me.

CHAPTER TWO

"Beauty is in the eye of the beholder. Lucky for me your Pappous has a 'stigmatism."
—Yiayia

An hour later I hesitated in the entrance to Chi Chi's, the upscale spa Christie insisted on taking me to for wedding prep. I gave it one last try. "You do realize that the last time I set foot in one of these places, someone got killed."

Christie, my BFF and absolute polar opposite, gave me a *look*. "Your point being?"

"I'm just saying, there's precedent."

"So you want me to believe you're superstitious about spas?"

I shrugged. "It could happen again, you don't know. Might even be me who snaps."

I wasn't a mani-pedi sort of girl. I wasn't *any* sort of girl. Somehow, I'd managed to achieve total womanhood without any of the LA rites of passage—no wax on or wax off, no shellacking, seaweed wrapping or other creative forms of torture in the name of beauty. I believed firmly in "don't file what ain't broke."

"It's a risk I'm willing to take," she said wryly. "Tori, you're going to be a bridesmaid in a destination wedding in one of the most romantic places on Earth. What kind of friend would I be if I let you go with raggedy-ass nails and pores the size of champagne bubbles?"

"Champagne bubbles, really?" I asked, pleased.

"Honey, that's not a good thing."

My smile fell. "I did mention there've been death threats, right? Armani wants to put me into protective custody. I probably shouldn't be out in public at all."

"I thought it was *Nick* these days. Anyway, the man just wants you in *his* custody, probably with handcuffs and other restraints. Safest place for you is in public with lots of witnesses. And before you start in on the expense, don't. Just don't. It's my treat."

"But—"

"No buts." She put her hand to my back and virtually propelled me through the doors, knowing I wouldn't dare hip check her after she'd helped me take down a killer cult and rescue Uncle Christos just last month.

A woman with the longest, straightest, whitest-blonde hair I've ever seen rushed out from behind a counter at the sight of Christie, gripped her by the shoulders and gave her an air kiss to each cheek, which Christie returned. Me, I was too busy watching to be sure she wouldn't accidentally puncture Christie's flesh with her dagger-like nails—gold swirled with black.

"Chi Chi," Christie said, stepping back and turning talon-lady toward me. "This is my dear friend Tori. She's a blank slate. I want to give her the works."

Chi Chi eyed me, her brown eyes as dark as her hair was light. It was a striking combination, but her diamond-studded nose ring distracted from it all, focusing attention on the wrong part of her facial landscape. Apparently, I had my own pause button—Chi Chi's gaze hadn't dropped any lower than my brows.

"We have a lot of work ahead of us," she said to Christie. "I think we start with the threading."

"Threading?" I asked, but not with actual fear. Absolutely not.

"Of the brows," Christie explained. "They're a little … untamed."

I imagined whips, Chi Chi in full lion tamer regalia. I suspected she could take me in a cage match.

"Um, okay." *Show no fear*, I reminded myself. "We'd better get started."

As she led me away, I looked over my shoulder at Christie for reassurance. She gave me a double thumbs-up and turned toward another … stylist? masochist? glamscaper? … who was coming to take her away, ha, ha. I wondered what Christie was having done, then decided I didn't really want to know. She was due for some kind of swimsuit shoot in the French Riviera around the time I'd be in Greece enduring Bridezilla and my crazy clan. I assumed scary words like Brazilian were in order. The fact that I even knew a Brazilian wasn't just someone from Brazil meant I'd been associating with Christie for far too long.

I survived the eyebrow threading, but the *facial* … I wondered why the guys at Guantanamo Bay bothered with waterboarding when extractions seemed so much easier and, apparently, less controversial. Having a young thing with too much bosom leaning over me with a telescopic lens that made molehills into mountains on the level of Vesuvius was not my idea of a good time. Then she *squeezed*. I nearly erupted right out of my chair.

"Ow! What did you do, file your nails to points?" I asked, batting her hand away when she came back for another round.

"Some of your pores are impacted. When was the last time you had a facial? Do you exfoliate?"

"Exfoliate? Do I *look* like a tree? Wait, don't answer that."

With my hair, I definitely tended toward bushy.

Brittany, as she'd introduced herself when I entered her lair, pushed me back into the rack ... er, chair ... with a strength that said she could probably bench press me and the horse I rode in on. I'd fought gods and goddesses, but Brittany ... clearly she was a force to be reckoned with.

"It will go faster if you stay still."

Don't struggle, said the spider to the fly.

I crossed my arms over my own much smaller chest and tried for stoicism. I failed miserably.

Afterward, I lay there with cucumbers on my eyes and some sort of soothing or detoxifying or gods-knew-what-kind-of balm on my skin when Katy Perry's "California Girls" suddenly blared right in my face. See, torture. I was pretty sure Chi Chi's had cornered the market.

Then I realized that all the music I'd heard so far had been low key and new-agey. This was definitely not on the menu. It wasn't coming from my phone, which would melt to slag if I'd ever made it ring out a Katy Perry song. Any self-respecting phone would.

I peeled a cucumber off one eye and squinted around me. An eye stared back—huge, golden brown, long lashed. I jumped out of my chair, and there was no Brittany to hold me back. The other slice of cucumber flopped to the floor.

The music squealed to a halt and a "Whoa!" issued from the magnifying lens that had been right above my head. The eye pulled back to reveal brows, hairline, cheek and, finally, a full face—*Hermes*, god of mischief.

"So not a good look for you, *agape*," he said, eying me top to toenails. "Your pores are the size of—"

"Would everyone *stop* obsessing about my pores?" I nearly shouted.

"Sorry, I didn't realize I'd hit a sore spot."

I forced myself to breathe slowly and count to five. Bashing the magnifying glass would only hurt my hand. Hitting Hermes himself would be so much more satisfying. He'd scared me half to death.

"What do you want?" I asked. "And get to the point? I'm relaxing here."

"Yeah, you look really relaxed. Maybe a nice massage?"

He waggled brows at me that not only hadn't been threaded, but were threatening to merge and mate with his hairline.

"Pass." For all I knew that was next on Christie's menu of masochism. "The point?"

"Oh, you're no fun. The point is, you owe me. I'm here to collect."

"I owe you for what?"

"Keeping your friends safe during the last battle."

"You mean locking them in the bathroom?"

"Did they escape unscathed?"

"Yes," I answered reluctantly.

"Then I did my job."

Crap. It was impossible to win an argument with the god of mischief. By the time I was born he'd already had thousands of years of talking his way into and out of trouble.

"*Fine*. What do you want?"

"Her number."

"Whose number?"

"Your friend."

"Tori," Christie's voice carried from outside the room Brittany had tucked me into, far enough back, I'd have thought no one could hear me scream, let alone converse with ancient pains in the butt. "You all right? I hear voices."

Cerberus crap. A big steaming pile.

"I'm okay. Just … watching a video on my phone."

"You're supposed to be relaxing."

"Let her in!" Hermes said gleefully. "Three's a party." Then he gave me that all-over look again. "Hmm, maybe not. Though you do clean up pretty well."

"Gee, thanks," I mumbled.

"What's that?" Christie asked.

"Nothing. I'll shut it down."

"Uh, okay. It's just … the girls thought you might be talking to yourself. They were worried."

Great, I was a crazy talking, walking disaster with pores the size of volcanic craters.

Could the day get any better?

"How about that number?" Hermes asked.

I glared at his face in the magnifying mirror. "I don't pimp out my friends," I said in a hush.

"So who's asking you to?"

"You're a *god*. You can't get her number for yourself?"

"She's unlisted."

I wanted to smack my head on something—hard—but it would probably leave a mark Brittany would feel compelled to fix. I didn't think I'd survive it.

I thought about Hermes's request. If I denied it, would he turn up in Christie's bathroom mirror as she stepped out of the shower? It was exactly the sort of thing he'd do. Maybe the fact that he wanted to start out a little more conventionally was a good sign, something to be encouraged? As if Hermes needed encouragement.

"Tell you what," I said, "I'll give her *your* number. If she calls, she calls."

"*That's* the kind of tit for tat I can expect? Honey, I credited you with much better tits."

I looked down at myself. "Really?"

"Well, perhaps not. Anyway, this will barely touch your debt."

"Fine, whatever. Are we done here?" *Before the spa folk come at me with straightjackets.*

"Unless you want to hear about—"

"I don't," I said quickly, slapping at the mirror to torque it away and break our connection.

"—the plot—" I heard as he spun away from me. I rushed to

grab the mirror back into position again, but he was gone.

There was a knock at the door, followed almost immediately by it opening. "Everything okay in here?" Brittany asked, looking around like I was a babysitter who might have snuck my boyfriend in after hours.

"Sure, except I think my face might be starting to crack."

She smiled at the thought. *Great.* "That just means you're done! You lay back down and I'll clean you up and turn you over to Valencia."

"Oh goody."

If there was more torture, I didn't even notice. I was too busy thinking about Hermes's last words. As soon as Torquemada here was finished with me, I was going for the cell phone I'd actually left in my spa locker along with my clothes. Then I was going to blackmail Hermes into telling me what I'd missed.

But Hermes wasn't taking calls—at least not mine—and Valencia waited outside the locker room door to take me to some fresh hell, pacing and looking in impatiently while I tried my call again, as though her time was more precious than mine. Probably it was, if we were talking hourly rates.

I left a message and surrendered myself.

Christie was already sitting in what looked like a dental chair, her feet soaking in a solution tinted by the Tidy Bowl man.

"Polish," Valencia said.

It was like she was speaking Greek, only *that* I'd have understood. "Um, no, I'm good."

She snapped a finger toward a wall rack of nail color. "Pick your polish," she ordered.

"Oh." I'd been afraid that after all of Brittany's work, she'd been talking about some kind of buffer or something that would shine me up to a high gloss. "Uh, you pick."

"What color is your bridesmaid's gown?" Christie asked.

"Puke green."

She lowered the magazine she was holding—the one with

the star who cheated on the other star, making their new movie promo a study in awkward. "Seriously?"

"For reals. Only I'm sure they call it something a lot fancier."

Christie canted her head like she was trying to envision me in puke green. "Val, give her the crushed shell shellac."

"Wait, shellac?" I asked. But clearly I had no power here; Val was already off to do Christie's bidding.

"The way you live, yeah. It lasts for, like, *ever*, and I know you won't just go home and take it all off with nail polish remover."

"How do you know?"

"It doesn't work like that."

"How does it work?"

"That's for me to know and you to find out."

"You know, lady, you have an evil streak. I have a friend who would be just perfect for you. And by perfect, I mean that you two together would be truly terrifying."

"Sounds intriguing. Is he cute?"

"Why don't you call him and find out for yourself?"

Then I proceeded to tell her all the reasons why it was a very bad idea. The warnings were barely out of my mouth before I realized they were like waving a red cape at a bull or a flame before a moth. Christie had terrible taste in men. Hermes was just her type.

I'd have felt a lot worse if Christie a) wasn't a grownup, and b) hadn't just had me shellacked against my will.

We were followed when we left the salon. With plots afoot and escaped enemies on the loose, I didn't think I was being paranoid at my concern when a black SUV with tinted windows followed us out of the parking lot.

"Christie, I'm going to pull over here," I said, keeping an eye on the SUV in my rearview mirror.

She looked where I indicated. "This grease pit? Are you kidding me? You can have a heart attack just breathing the air."

"They only gave us rabbit food back at the salon. I'm starving. And anyway, I'm testing a theory."

"How much the seams of your bridesmaid's gown are likely to hold? Do you hate it that much?"

I did, but that was beside the point. At the last possible second, I cut across two lanes of traffic to take the turn into a fast food drive thru. I checked the rearview mirror as I switched to see the front of the SUV jerk suddenly into the nearer lane, leaving the back still sticking out. Next came a brake squealing, metal-crunching impact as another car struck the back of the SUV, causing it to rock on its wheels. I was recalled to my own driving by my front wheel thumping over a concrete piling. I righted our trajectory, pulled into the drive thru line and grabbed my phone out of the car's cup holder to report the accident. It was still ringing when the SUV raced off, leaving the scene and the driver of the other car staring stunned after it, half out of her own vehicle. She looked around then, as if to see if anyone else planned to report the rear ending, shrugged and got back into her car. Just another LA day.

I ended the call and relaxed back into my seat. "What was that all about?" Christie asked.

But, crisis averted, the munchies had kicked in with a vengeance, and I was totally focused on the drive thru menu board. "They serve sweet potato fries now? Awesome!"

"*Tori.*"

"Oh, sorry." I turned a sheepish grin on her. "I don't know. It might have been those enemies who escaped. Or someone they hired to follow me. Or …"

"Tori!"

"Don't worry, I've got it covered."

"How?"

"Tomorrow, I leave for Greece."

Where the old gods would have the home court advantage.

CHAPTER THREE

"Is it bad or is it Tornado Tori bad?"
—Tori's father, assessing a messy situation

I surveyed the wreckage of my apartment. Well, the apartment I was housesitting for Detective Helen Lau, Armani's former partner, until her return from traveling with honest-to-gods dragons. I knew I'd forgotten something. I just couldn't think what it was. "It's not like they don't have stores in Greece," Armani said, frustrated. He'd been fully packed before we went to bed last night. That's right, I said "we" and "bed." Couldn't wait to see the look on my mother's face when she heard we were sharing a room or the inquisition my father was likely to unleash on Nick. *Nick*, I had to practice that. Bad enough we'd be shacking up. If I couldn't even convince my family we were on a first name basis ...

"I can't kick the thought that I'm forgetting something important."

Then it came to me. *Oh, Hermes's hairy arse*—it wasn't the thought I had to kick, it was the habit. *The ambrosia.* I still hadn't thought of a way to take it with me. Without it—sweats, shakes, loss of concentration, cramps, pain and a better than average chance of death. So, nothing serious then.

"Me!" Came an announcement from the doorway to the apartment. "You're forgetting *me.* But now I am here, and all's right with your world."

Oh *hell* to the no. *Jesus?*

I stared at him and his flaming red luggage. "How did you get in?"

"Nick buzzed me up." I looked at Nick.

"I did ask first, but you were sort of … frantic at the time."

"But … but …" I stopped, took a deep breath and said, "Jesus, you are *not* going to Greece with us. I'm fairly certain you wouldn't fit in my carry-on. Hell, I'm not even sure your personal items would fit in my carry-on."

"Not to worry." From the man-purse slung over his shoulder, he produced a colorful piece of paper with a barcode. It looked suspiciously like a boarding pass. "I have my own ticket."

"But—"

"You said that."

"But—"

"*Chica*, it does not bear repeating. Apollo said that he had it covered, and he does. I am here to run your interference."

"*What* interference?"

"At the airport."

I could feel steam about to come out of my ears. If I built up any more, I could power my *own* way to Greece. I gave him my dead stare, the one that brooked no resistance … if only my power ran that way. "Why would there be interference at the airport?" I asked through clenched teeth. One more evasion and I was going to blow.

Jesus cut his gaze to the side, a sure sign that he was about to prevaricate.

"Tori," Nick cut in, "I think he's going to have to explain on the way. Our cab's here." He looked up from his phone to me. I hadn't even heard the alert, I'd been so focused on Jesus.

"Fine, but this isn't over," I said, trying to impress it on him with my *look.* Hard to do when he wouldn't meet my eyes.

I nearly gave myself a hernia swinging my carry-on over my shoulder. I was no wilting flower, but somehow by the time I was through loading it up with all my electronics, enough books to get me through umpteen excruciating hours spent in airports and on planes, and things like jewelry I couldn't risk putting in checked luggage, it weighed a ton. Armani—*Nick,* dammit— didn't risk a direct hit with it by offering his manly muscle.

He did, however, hold the door for us, and I allowed it. After all, I'd have done the same for him, only he got there first.

I held my questions until we got into the cab—Jesus chose to sit up next to the driver, so my laser-like stare had no effect on him. I had to make do with my words. "Spill," I ordered.

He looked back at me over his shoulder. *"This* is your interrogation technique? *Spill?* I think I deserve a bit more effort." He crossed his arms over his chest and turned back around.

"Would you like me to move on to threats? I can, you know, starting with your job."

Jesus gasped and gave me the stink-eye in the rearview mirror. "You wouldn't dare."

I nudged Nick, who sat beside me in the back merely watching with amusement. The cabby, for his part, was still trying to fit our luggage into the trunk. The car rocked as he finally slammed the trunk shut and climbed into the driver's seat.

"Oh, I don't think there's much she wouldn't dare," Nick said, catching on to his cue. "You'd better tell her. You know she won't leave it alone until you do. She's like a … um … a PI with a lead."

He'd been about to say "a dog with a bone," I just knew it. Lucky for him he'd held back.

Jesus sighed dramatically, the way he did everything. "Okay, but if he asks, you beat it out of me."

I grinned. "We could make it *very* convincing."

Jesus stuck his tongue out at me. Then he made me wait. He adjusted his seat, his belt, his cuffs, he cleared his throat, and just as I was about to launch myself over the center console and throttle him, he finally condescended to answer. "You know how Apollo said he was going to put to rest those rumors about you and him being you and him?"

"Yes," I said, wondering what that had to do with Jesus and Greece.

"Well, he has a plan."

A public affairs rep from the airline descended on us the second we set foot out of our cab. She snapped her fingers at someone behind her before we could so much as wrestle our luggage to the curb. I glanced over at Jesus, sure I saw Apollo's fingerprints all over the suspicious red carpet treatment, but he only smiled and shrugged. Goldilocks, because that was how I was going to think of the blonde in the shapeless blue suit, seemed in a horrible hurry to get us off the sidewalk, past the crowd I could see gathered just inside the doors, and through security.

When the mob shifted, I understood exactly why.

Apollo's plan apparently involved nearly six stunning feet of brunette bombshell. Only part of that height came from her sky-high rhinestone heels ... or were those diamonds? Surely not *diamonds*. Whatever they were, there was no question about the breasts currently defying gravity in her strappy silver gown more suited for walking the red carpet than catching a flight. Although, perhaps that was what one wore in first class. I wouldn't know.

Most stunning of all, she wore the ultimate accessory—Apollo Demas, looking more gorgeous than I'd ever seen him before, and that was saying something. He was dressed all in black—shirt, tie, suit, wingtips. His leonine golden hair stood out against it like the rays of the sun. His turquoise eyes were even bluer in contrast. And the glint in them as they gazed down on the bronzed beauty beside him and up again at the cameras flashing all around was luminous. Not to mention devastating.

I looked to Jesus. "Tell me they're not on our flight," I growled quietly, trying not to attract any attention as we veered very widely around the paparazzi pileup.

He avoided my gaze. *"Tell me,"* I repeated.

"I can't," he said. To his credit, he sounded like he felt badly about that. "He's apparently coming out of retirement to do a very special film. There's some wealthy financier putting up a lot of the money for it, hoping it'll help revitalize the Greek economy. I think maybe you know him—Hector Papadopolous."

"Uncle Hector?" I asked, stunned.

"Is he?" Jesus asked disingenuously.

"Let me guess," I continued, "Brunette Barbie is Apollo's costar."

"Serena Banks," he said, with something like awe in his voice. "Hottest thing to hit Hollywood since … since maybe ever."

He blushed at the glare I sent him. "I'm just saying," he continued lamely.

I felt a pang of envy, which was as selfish as it was stupid. I'd wanted Apollo to move on, and yet … And yet what? There was no *and yet*.

I shot a sudden glance at Nick and caught him looking back over his shoulder, even though Apollo and Serena were now well out of sight. He jerked guiltily when he noticed me watching.

"What?" he asked.

"You tell me."

"Just wanted to be sure none of the paparazzi had caught sight of you and that we were in the clear."

"Uh huh."

"Really."

I let it go. After all, I'd ogled Apollo a time or two, so I had no moral high ground here. Our airline rep escorted us straight to the gate, where we got to board with the first wave, passing cushy first class seats where Serena and Apollo would probably be sharing champagne and caviar. Served them right, being faced with fish eggs.

"You okay?" Nick asked me as we got seated ... back in coach.

"Sure, why wouldn't I be?"

"You tell me."

I gave him my very most level look. "I'm fine."

"Fine."

"*Fine.*"

And with that, I snapped open the SkyMall magazine and prepared to mentally spend money I didn't have on things I didn't need. Mental retail therapy.

Nick sighed and pulled the airline magazine out of the seat pocket in front of him. I glanced sidelong as he did it and came face to face with green cat's-eyes staring at me from the cover. Serena Banks. Of course. She had the feature story.

I buried myself in SkyMall, trying not to care as Nick, I was certain, turned straight to the article.

I *did* care when the rumbling started.

Despite the fear of heights that kept me out of the Karacrobats, my family's acrobatic troupe, I wasn't generally phobic about flying. Oh sure, my heart raced and I white-knuckled the armrests on takeoffs and landings, but I had a really advanced case of denial for the intervening air travel. My best guess was that it was a control thing. When I was close to the ground, I had the illusion of some sort of control. Sitting still while the plane jittered and banked and got underway took monumental amounts of willpower. Once we hit cruising altitude, I figured my only options were live, if things went well, or kiss my ass goodbye if they didn't. But I had a bad, bad feeling about this flight. I hoped it was just nerves and not my Apollo-granted foresight, because we'd already taken off, and the control I'd never actually had was well out of my reach. But the feeling grew and grew as the sky darkened around us and seemed to charge with some ominous energy. I stopped paying attention to the SkyMall and took to staring out the window.

Rumbling rattled the windows and a flash fork of lightning chased itself from one bank of clouds to another. The plane veered sharply away, trying to escape the storm, but gale-force winds pushed at our tail in hot pursuit.

An announcement came on about turbulence and returning to our seats. It was getting harder and harder to stay in mine. My internal alarms were now blaring full force, and I wanted to shout for the crew that the plane needed to be brought down now, *now*, NOW for an emergency landing while there was still a chance to control our descent. This was no natural storm. There'd been no warning before takeoff about rough weather ahead, and a storm like this would have been hard to miss on the radar.

Paranoia? Maybe, if not for my internal alarms and the fact that Poseidon Stormbringer and Zeus, of the fateful lightning, were on the loose and that the people most responsible for their incarceration were all on this flight. Coincidence? Didn't seem likely, but there was no time to think about that right now.

To our left came a sudden crash like two monstrous hands clapping together and then bursting apart. The resultant shock-waves buffeted the airliner like a kite. Panic had me reaching for the armrest, but since Nick's hand was already there, I nearly shredded him with my newly manicured nails. He hissed with pain, but didn't draw back his hand. Instead, he turned it over to take mine. He looked into my eyes. I stared into his, and thought *well, if the world ends, at least we'll go out together*. It was a shockingly romantic thought for me, and that, more than anything, snapped me to. We were *not* going to die. My cousin Tina would kill me. It would make her wedding party lopsided.

I unbuckled my seatbelt and started to rise, to demand that we make an emergency landing or something, not caring how crazy I'd sound, when the lightning flashed again, cracking across the sky like a whip. The plane flinched as it struck, bucking like a thing alive desperate to escape the pain. I was flung forward, bashing myself on the overhead bin and falling into Nick's lap. He gripped me close and held on tight.

"Stay put," he ordered. "There's nowhere to go. We'll get through this. It'll be okay."

But I knew he was wrong. I struggled against him as the plane banked sharply. No, not *banked*. Sheared off, beginning to fall, as if something was off on one side … like an engine.

"We have to land," I yelled. "Now!" As if this was a newsflash.

There was so much screaming going on—babies crying, grown men and women praying or wailing or whatever—that no one heard.

Another crash of thunder came from the side of the plane, and punched into us like a fist, knocking us even farther off-kilter. The metal of the plane groaned in defiance, but it wasn't a victorious sound. It was more like, "You'll never take me alive." And that's exactly what I was afraid of.

"We have to do something!" I shouted at Armani. *Nick, dammit, Nick.* Even as we rushed toward death, I couldn't get it right. But that's how I'd thought of him when I'd first met him, a defense mechanism against my attraction, one I'd never gotten over.

"Like what?" he shouted back.

I didn't want questions, I wanted *action*, but I didn't have any to suggest.

Oxygen masks fell from the ceiling as the plane continued to drop altitude and the pilot was too busy, I supposed, trying to stop it to comfort his panicking passengers … as if an announcement would have made any difference. As if they, like me, couldn't feel the ground rushing up to meet us.

Armani lifted me off him to grab two masks before pushing me down into a seat and manhandling me to get my mask into place. I didn't fight him, only because the sooner he knew I was okay, the sooner he'd see to himself and I could lunge past him.

The second he was distracted, I did just that, avoiding his grabbing hands to lunge down the aisle. Down was the operative word. We were now at a forty-five-degree angle, nose to the ground—falling, falling.

I canted left and then right as the plane lurched, the pilot battling to level off. I apologized as I went, gripping a man in a very personal place when a really bad thunderclap threw me off balance and I had to catch myself.

I hit the curtain between us and first class to the curses and cries of my fellow passengers. A flight attendant strapped down into her jump seat and counting off frantic prayers on a rosary tried reflexively to stop me from crossing the sacred threshold, but I stopped her with a look. *The* look. I froze her in place. She'd space right through at least a few minutes of panic, long enough for me to invade first class.

Apollo was already out of his seat and met me halfway down the aisle. "You okay?" he asked. It was a silly question, so I ignored it.

"What do we do?" Scratch the *we*. If there was anything I could do, I'd have done it. "Don't you have some power to stop all this?"

But I knew the answer before I heard it from his lips. I could see it in his eyes.

"I'm the god of the sun, and they've cut me off from it. Even if I could harness it still, I have no control over storms. There's nothing—"

"Screw nothing!" I said. I looked around frantically for

something, anything. But there was nothing physical to fight or fight with.

A male flight attendant risked life and limb to close in on us, coming from the front alcove.

"Sir, ma'am, you're going to have to return to your seats!" he yelled over the noise of the screaming plane and howling passengers.

The aircraft bucked again, and I screamed myself. Apollo's arms went around me, and we fell hard into the seat beside us, into the laps of an elderly man and woman who looked dumbstruck. The armrest between them dented my side. As we scrambled to right ourselves, the plane started to roll. I screamed again and gripped Apollo for dear life. If only I could freeze the air like I could people, but I couldn't stare it down. *Eye of the Storm* was just an expression and anyway, we were locked tight in its abusive embrace.

Thunderclaps crashed to our left and right as if trying to crush us between them. The plane was blown forward and shot ahead like a torpedo, momentum giving it momentary stability.

Then the miracle happened…. We stayed that way. The plane rocked from side to side, but the gut wrenching roll had halted, and we started to level off.

Apollo and I looked at each other, as close as lovers on the bony knees of the old couple we'd crashed into. The man bounced his knees upward at that moment as a prompt to move, and Apollo helped me stand. We both held to the back of the surrounding seats, sure the reprieve was only temporary.

Someone snapped a picture with a cell phone camera, which I knew only because it took the pic with the totally unnecessary shutter sound. I whipped my head around to look for the source and was stopped by Serena's death glare. She was turned around in her seat, glowing green eyes taking us in.

Glowing green. Crapcakes.

I turned back to Apollo. "Um, about Serena … is there anything you want to tell me?" Apollo looked toward the woman in question, but the glow in her eyes was gone. Now she looked more miffed than outright homicidal. Had I truly seen what I thought I'd seen or was I now imagining monsters where none existed? Was my mind playing tricks on me, turning simple jealousy into a literal green-eyed monster?

"Serena?" he asked, "What do you want me to tell you? You wanted the press off your back, the new film's PR guy wanted a little off-screen romance to help sell the movie ... it seemed like a win-win. Surely you're not jealous." He was watching me closely. Too closely. "I thought this was what you wanted."

He was right. It was what I wanted. Maybe. Possibly. Anyway, it was what had to be. There was Armani. And besides, Apollo would swallow me whole. With those turquoise eyes and that toned ... everything ... and the sparks that flew between us ... It was amazing the oxygen in the air hadn't ignited on our spark. But he was also a *god*, and even if ancient history wasn't full of cautionary tales about trifling with gods, my own experience would have been enough to warn me off.

"Yes," I lied. "That's what I want."

"Good."

"Good."

"Fine."

"Great," Serena cut in, rising from her seat. "Then if everything's back to normal, perhaps you'll unhand my costar and return to your ... class."

I ignored her, especially since I hadn't "handed" him to begin with, and turned back to Apollo.

"What do you think happened?"

He gave Serena an *in a second* look before answering. "I'd guess we flew out of range or they ran out of power. I think that last thunderclap was meant to be the coup de grâce."

"But they missed."

"They'll try again—themselves or ... well, they have adherents still in the old country."

"Oh joy."

"I have to go," he said, as Serena's glare seemed to gather force.

He started to move past me, and it hurt, even though it *shouldn't*. I was with Nick. He had the right to be with whoever he wanted, for real or for show. "Thanks for ..." What? He hadn't done anything. But then, neither had I. "For being there," I finished lamely.

He gave me a look over his shoulder that mimicked my regret. "You too." Dammit.

I made my way back to Nick, who was staring intently at the curtain through which I'd disappeared. He breathed a huge sigh of relief as I came back into view. But there was something else in his eyes ... pain, maybe. The pilot came over the loudspeaker, talking about the plane being damaged by the storm and an emergency landing. The passengers set up a subdued cheer at that. I wondered how many would be brave enough to continue on to their final destinations.

I dropped into the seat next to Nick, and he looked like he couldn't decide whether to hug me or throttle me. I made the decision for him, launching myself at him and holding him as tightly as I could. After a moment, he held me back and stroked my hair. I put Apollo behind me in the reality of Nick's strong arms and feelings I knew to be all mine with nothing ever done "for my own good" without my consent. I breathed Nick in—his spicy, woodsy scent, as if he'd just been for a run in the woods instead of a near-death experience. His body was radiating heat, and for a second, I wanted to drag him back to the bathroom, tear off all his clothes and celebrate our survival ... only I'd been in there earlier and was fairly certain it wasn't remotely possible. Not unless I was some kind of contortionist and his shoulders were a lot less broad. But since I wasn't and they weren't, I just held him and held him and held him.

"Don't you dare *ever* do that again," he said finally, his breath warm, almost hot, on my ear.

I almost asked, "Do what?" but really I knew. Regardless of

why I'd done it, I'd run out on Nick in the face of almost certain death. I'd chosen to spend what could have been our final moments with another man. But it hadn't been like that. I hadn't picked Apollo over Nick. I'd chosen to DO something rather than huddle up when the storm struck. The fact that I hadn't made a bit of difference shouldn't matter. I'd had the best of intentions. Still, I'd have felt a helluva lot less guilty if I'd had anything to show for leaving him alone. The fact that we were all still alive was nothing short of miraculous. I should have been there for him.

"I'm sorry," I said, looking away. "I thought … I thought maybe I could do something."

"And did you?" The hand stroking my hair had stilled.

"No," I admitted. "It was all the pilot's skill and maybe the gods running out of steam."

Nick let out a heated breath. "So then we have no way to fight them if they come at us again?"

"They'd have finished us off if they could," I answered. It wasn't nearly as comforting as I'd meant it to be.

"Great."

When Nick would have pulled back, I held his hand and refused to let it go. He didn't fight me, but it was an awkward silence that fell between us, full of a million and one things we didn't know how to express.

The emergency landing was a rough one. *Really* rough. But the passengers cheered again, with more fervor this time, as we touched down and slowed to a stop. Some even kissed the tarmac when the ground crew brought stairs to get us all out rather than taxi us to a gate. Others held up the line by picking a fight with the flight crew and threatening lawsuits. I felt terrible for them, especially since I knew there was nothing they could have done.

We waited for Jesus on the tarmac, since he was even farther back on the plane than we were. The lights of the runway lit his face quite clearly. All the color had fled, and the usual swing had gone straight out of his step.

"I think I found God," he said as he approached us, eyes as big as peanut butter cups, which sounded incredibly good right then. Or, just pure chocolate, hold any pollutants like nuts or caramel.

"Which one?" I asked.

CHAPTER FOUR

"But why *is he sitting in la, la waiting for his yiayia?"*
—Yiayia, misconstruing Lee Dorsey's "Ya Ya" song

J esus didn't turn back for home, though he complained loudly that he would talk to Apollo about hazard pay. We didn't turn back either. It wasn't so much bravery as stubbornness—on my part, at least. Zeus and Poseidon were *not* going to ruin the first reunion I'd had with my family since the Rialto Brothers Circus had given me the heave ho. They weren't going to ruin my cousin Tina's wedding with a funeral. I felt pretty strongly about that, since the funeral would likely be mine.

I could be flippant or I could be afraid. I'd found it was pretty difficult to be both at once.

The airline whisked us all off to a private lounge as soon as we hit the terminal, presumably so we couldn't frighten other flyers with the horror story of our ordeal. Jesus helped himself to a good bit of the complimentary booze they supplied to help us drown out the horror and blunt our memory.

Finally, though, we were rebooked on a flight from our emergency landing airport to New York, where we'd catch the next leg of our flight. Jesus grabbed some of the free booze in their tiny travel sized bottles and brought them along for fortification. Nick and I didn't risk it, both determined to stay sharp for no good reason I could tell. It wasn't like we'd be any better in the face of a new attack than the last, but still, I wanted my wits about me, such as they were. Plus, I wasn't so sure how ambrosia and booze would mix. Would the whole super-healing thing allow me to get drunk or would the ambrosia treat booze as some kind of poison to be fought? I didn't really need my body becoming a battleground.

That thought lasted until takeoff. At the first bump on the runway, I shrieked and grabbed at the bottle of vodka Jesus had tucked into the seatback pocket in front of him. I downed it like a shot as Jesus eyed me sourly. "By all means, *chica*, help yourself."

"Got more?" I asked.

He toed open the shoulder bag at his feet to reveal enough booze to open a fairy bar.

Not that fairies existed … that I knew of.

I reached for two more bottles but was stopped by my seatbelt. Then we were lifting off, being bounced around by stray air currents, and my heart nearly stopped in panic. I grabbed Nick's hand and he grabbed mine right back. Jesus gripped my other hand, and we sat there like a ring-around-the-rosie of fear.

Nick smiled at me, and those incredible midnight blue eyes crinkled at the corners. "It's going to be okay," he lied.

"How can you be so calm?" I asked.

He brought my hand to his chest, and I could feel that his heart had picked up all the beats mine had dropped. It was going double time.

"I'm not calm. I'm confident. The way your luck runs, you

will *not* die before I get to see you in a puke green bridesmaid's gown. And take pictures. And hang them up around the precinct."

That surprised a laugh out of me, and I felt the vice grip around my heart begin to ease.

"You're right," I answered.

His smile got even bigger. "Can I get that in writing?"

"Now that really would be the end of the world."

This kind of moment, this banter, was exactly why I'd fallen for him to begin with. "You still want that vodka?" Jesus asked, watching Nick and I have our moment.

"No, I'm good," I heard myself answer.

"More for me."

Nick and I smiled like fond parents half an hour later when Jesus fell fast asleep like a child who'd tuckered himself out. He snored softly, and his head lolled onto my shoulder. If there was drool, I'd never let him live it down.

I didn't sleep. By the fifth hour, it was glaringly apparent that wouldn't change any time soon. I didn't know if it was the ambrosia heightening all my senses or my new oversensitivity that made every single air current feel like a death sentence. I'd become the princess and the pea, only with the outside air my mattress and the deceptively fluffy clouds pillows waiting to smother me. Paranoia was a symptom of ambrosia *withdrawal*. It wasn't supposed to happen when I was dosed, which I'd made sure of before leaving the apartment. Maybe all that fear-fueled adrenaline had rushed it through my body faster than normal. If so, it was a terrifying thought. I'd need to find a new supply when we landed in Greece. I only had one contact there who could get me what I needed … and I hadn't seen him since our crash landing when he and Serena had been whisked away, I presumed, to some kind of VIP lounge where they were pampered and placated. I had his number, but he'd pointed out recently and rightly that I only used it when I needed something —when it was convenient for me—and then I pushed him away again. I'd never been a user … before ambrosia. I didn't want to become one now. I needed to quit it, regardless of the possibility of deadly withdrawal, but there was always a reason it was a bad time. I was in the middle of a case; my uncle had been taken by a killer cult; my cousin was getting married …

I didn't want to go through the shakes, distraction, sweats, cramps and fainting spells I knew would come in front of my family. I was already the black sheep. I didn't want to become the pariah.

After, I swore to myself. After Zeus and Poseidon were safely recaptured and Tina married off. Then …

In the meantime, I did have another god on speed dial if I got desperate. Desperate enough to become further indebted to the trickster god? Willingly? The conviction that I wasn't an addict was getting harder and harder to maintain. I had to be going through withdrawal to even consider such idiocy.

"Go 'sleep," Nick murmured when I'd shifted for the one zillionth time since takeoff. Fidgety, unfocused, barely able to sit in my seat … yeah, I recognized the symptoms. Maybe I hadn't taken enough ambrosia to hold me over. Maybe I was building up a tolerance.

"Sorry," I whispered back, endeavoring to be still.

If I wasn't careful, this ambrosia addiction might kill me and save the greater gods the trouble.

We had a *three-hour* layover in New York. I was dead tired by the time we got there and yet wired, as though if anyone touched me, I'd flare up and short out. It was a fragile feeling that I didn't like one bit.

After an internal slugfest between my id and my ego, I decided on an over-the-counter sleep aid for the nine-hour flight from New York to Athens. I'd already been up for almost twenty-four hours at that point, and I knew that if I didn't get some sleep soon, I'd be insufferable … assuming *that* ship hadn't already sailed. Plus, Nick deserved me passed out on his chest so that he could sleep himself. Jesus was on his own. Yes, he'd left drool on my shirt. I showed him the pic I'd snapped with my cell phone on airplane mode. All I'd had to say was "company website" for all the lost color from earlier to flood back into his face in a furious blush.

I grinned evilly.

"You're a wicked, wicked woman," he said.

"Don't I know it."

The sleep aid didn't kick in until well after takeoff on the next leg of the trip, but once it did, I slept like a baby until the wheels touched down in Athens, jarring me awake. I cried out, and Nick's arm tightened around me. I was crushed up against his chest, seatbelt buckle digging into my hip and no armrest between us. When I lifted my head, I saw that Jesus wasn't the only one to drool. I wiped my mouth, trying to look like I *wasn't* swiping away spittle, and patted Nick's shirt as if I could blot it dry with my bare hands.

"Don't worry about it," Nick said. "I'm not."

That was the other great thing about him. As a police detective, he'd been faced with all manner of bodily fluids. A little spittle was nothing.

There was no coffee between us and customs. None. There *was* a terrifically long line of people. But it moved surprisingly swiftly. I understood why when we got to the front. After looking over our paperwork and asking a perfunctory question about the nature of our visit, the customs agent rubber stamped us and sent us through. I didn't really know what it was supposed to accomplish. Did they really expect someone to give "terrorism" or "smuggling" as the reason for their visit? Was it just to be able to say, "Ah ha, caught you in a lie!" when people were nabbed later?

Anyway, we were through and on to the baggage claim area when I spotted a placard with my name on it—last name at least —in the oversized hands of a suited-up chauffer who looked like the right-hand man of some Bond villain.

Of course, we *were* in Greece, where the name Karacis wasn't exactly the oddity it was in America, so I wasn't necessarily the target audience.

"Here!" Jesus said before I could think it through. He waved a hand so there could be no mistake where "here" was. "We're Karacis."

"Vittoria?" the chauffer asked, turning toward me.

"Tori," I answered. "And you are?"

"I am Viggo. Your Uncle Hector has sent a car."

My shoulders dropped about half a foot in relief. We weren't about to be spirited off to some evil lair. ("No, Mr. Bond, I expect you to die.")

But my *Uncle Hector*. He was nearly a myth, a barely remembered figure tossing me in the air and giving me pony rides until my sides hurt from laughing. But then there'd been some scandal with some princess or contessa or something, and he'd dropped off the face of the earth. I'd been too young to remember the details, and no one was going to share such secrets with me then. By the time I was old enough to ask the right questions, I was busy getting into trouble of my own. But rumor had it that he was richer than Midas and at least twenty thousand times cooler. I felt a childish glee about seeing him again … even if he *was* the one financing Apollo's return to the big screen and, at least temporarily, my life.

"He's here?" I asked stupidly.

"He sent a car and waits for you at the hotel, where he's throwing a special reception."

"A reception?"

I hadn't gotten the memo. In fact, my plan had been to rent a car, drive to the hotel and fall facedown onto a bed to sleep the night away before making the two hour trek up to Mount Parnassus the next day for some sightseeing before the wedding festivities got under way. At the moment, I was most excited about the facedown, quickly unconscious part of that whole equation. I was hot, I was tired, and I probably still had slobber tracks on my face. I was not ready to face the family in my current condition.

Nick took in my shell-shocked look. "Yes on the car, pass on the reception," he said for me.

"I'm afraid it's a package deal," he said with a smile.

"Now wait—" I was jet-lagged, and the heavy-handed tactics were making me cranky on top of it. Jesus held a restraining hand to my arm to keep me from unleashing a can of verbal whoop-ass.

"Did I mention that your uncle is picking up all accommodations and has arranged a limo to take you all to your destination on the morrow?" Viggo asked, sweetening the pot.

On the morrow … Who talked like that?

Before I could speak, Jesus jumped in to accept on our behalf. I gave him a completely ineffective death glare. "What?" he asked. "We go, we sip champagne, we vanish into the night. *Quelle horreur.*" He was Spanish … speaking French … in Greece. Well, why not.

I sighed. "Fine, I'm too tired to argue."

"I didn't even know that was possible," Nick said. "But I'm noting it for future reference."

I smiled tiredly at him and led the way to our baggage carousel, where for once I let someone else wrestle my baggage from the belt. Viggo was built for it, after all. In fact, in his huge hands, my big, hard-sided bag looked like a mere briefcase.

The car, when we got to it, was a sleek white thing with what looked like a boomerang mounted on the front. I knew that meant something about the make or model, but I was too fuzzy headed to think what. But the long and short of it was that it was fancy-schmancy, and where it swooped inward at the sides it was accented with silver-gray paint. It almost looked like one of the clouds that had practically smothered us on the trip over. I shivered.

"Cold?" Nick asked, already shrugging out of his shirt.

I shook my head, but I didn't explain. I should be thankful

about Uncle Hector's generosity. I didn't have any rational reason to distrust it, except that in Greece we knew the expression wasn't, "*Never* look a gift horse in the mouth," but *always*. After all, we'd taken Troy that way.

Just to be on the safe side, I called Yiayia as soon as we got into the car. "*Egona*, you are here!" she said in lieu of "hello."

"I am," I admitted. "I'm, uh, on my way to the reception."

"Wonderful! I should be up momentarily as well. We're just putting the finishing touches on our couture." *We?* "I understand that your friends have put in an appearance. You didn't tell me—"

The phone seemed to move away from her mouth, and I heard a bit of a scuffle in the background. Or maybe not a scuffle, because ... was that giggling? At her age?

"Yiayia," I shouted, "What friends? What are you talking about?"

But then there was a *thwump*, as if the phone fell to the floor, and then ... nothing.

Stunned, I hung up and tried again, but the phone just rang and rang and went to voicemail.

"Step on it," I told Viggo. "Please hurry."

My internal alarms weren't blaring, but I still didn't know the rules. Did they only go off when *I* was in danger? Was there some kind of range? Even without them, I had a bad feeling about things.

What friends could Yiayia be talking about? *Zeus? Poseidon?* Both were known to be able to change their forms ... or at least had done so frequently when they were at full power to seduce a woman in the guise of her husband or by trickling in as a golden mist through a locked door. Could they be crashing the party? But how would they have gotten out of the States so quickly given their fugitive status? And why pose as friends at all?

"Something's wrong," I told Nick.

"What?"

"I don't know, but Yiayia sounded … strange. And her phone went dead."

"Maybe she lost reception?"

"Maybe. I'll just feel a lot better when we're there. How far are we?" I asked Viggo.

"Ten minutes," he answered, holding up all ten fingers to show, leaving none on the wheel.

I gulped as another car barreled past, nearly smashing us against a white washed concrete wall that was too close for comfort. I nodded quickly to show that I got it, the better to return his hands to the wheel as quickly as possible. He recovered his mastery of the road, and overtook the car that had overtaken us, as though they were in some kind of street race he was bent on winning. Just as he pulled past, he swung quickly right, off onto an exit that took us onto a much quieter street that led to another, and then past Hadrian's Gate and the Temple of Olympian Zeus. Oh, I'd missed Athens, where antiquity and the everyday sat side by side and there was beauty everywhere you looked.

"Is that—?" Nick started to ask, pointing up a hill overlooking the city that was capped by stunning near-ruins.

"The Parthenon," I answered with a smile, suddenly feeling a lot less weary. "Yeah." His look of awe made me so proud of my country … well, my *other* country. I'd been born in America, but this was the culture I'd been born to and *this* was what ran in my blood. This. Beauty. Antiquity. Home.

But I was still worried as hell about Yiayia.

Viggo pulled into the miniscule drive before a big, white pillared hotel that overlooked the Temple and Hadrian's Gate. I jumped out before he even had the engine turned off, trusting that the guys could handle the luggage. I ran to the front desk, but was too jet-lagged to remember to speak Greek until I'd already started in English. "The Karacis/Galanos reception? Where is it?" I knew they'd never give me Yiayia's room number, but even if she hadn't made it up to the party, someone there would know where to find her, and these *friends* of mine....

"Garden Terrace, top floor," the woman behind the counter answered back, also in English.

I thanked her and hit the button for the elevator, but lost patience with it when it didn't arrive instantly and instead dashed for the staircase just beside it. I reached the top sweatier than I'd intended, but there'd been very little air in the staircase, and even less in my lungs by the time I reached my goal. The stairwell let out on a small alcove, and I followed the noise—and the signs—through a beautiful restaurant enclosed on three sides by glass to take advantage of the views, and out onto a devastatingly beautiful terrace. The outer door was on the Parthenon side of the city, and the view ... stunning didn't even begin to cover it.

But I wasn't there for the view. In fact, I'd have been just as happy to turn tail and run.

The party was in full swing and none of it safely *inside* the restaurant. All of the partygoers were packed together on the terrace balcony enjoying the beautiful evening and the city's most amazing sights. I took a deep breath, then another, trying to get my panicked reaction under control. Just the thought of stepping out onto that balcony—so high, a dead drop below, teeming with people who might accidentally jostle me over the edge ... I knew it was irrational, that the hotel would have built the balcony walls high enough to prevent that, but fears weren't rational, and heights ... that was a phobia pure and simple. I barely glanced out the windows in airplanes. I'd never climb to the top of the Empire State Building, and I didn't want any part of that balcony.

Still, *Yiayia and answers.* It was a toss-up which would be stronger, my fear or my curiosity.

I made myself take a step, then another. And another. Toward the balcony. Toward the press of people, looking for familiar faces to latch on to. I didn't recognize a good half of the people, and avoided everyone's gaze, familiar or not, in my search for Yiayia. I didn't see her. I ignored the waiter who stepped in front of me offering cocktails and stopped dead when I heard a tinkling little laugh. *I knew that laugh.* My head whipped around searching for the source, and I found her up against the terrace rail—my best friend Christie, and right beside her, hand resting on the small of her back, was Hermes.

Apparently, I'd found the friends Yiayia was talking about. Some of the tension eased out of my shoulders, as my most immediate sense of impending doom started to ebb. I should have known from the lack of internal alarms that Yiayia couldn't have been talking about Zeus and Poseidon, but how could I ever have guessed it would be Hermes and Christie?

"Christie?" I said, raising my voice to carry.

She turned from the rail and spotted me even from across the terrace. A smile burst over her face. "You're here!"

The party seemed to part for her, and then she was kissing me on both cheeks in the European way.

"I'm here," I answered. No debating that. "But why are you? Not that I'm not happy to see you, but what about your big shoot over in the Riviera?"

"I'll get there! But it's days away. Usually I get in a few days early to acclimate, but Greece ... France ... close enough! When your friend called and offered up his private jet—well, that beats a commercial flight any old time."

I eyed Hermes. "Private jet?" I asked.

"Being the CEO of a worldwide messenger service has its perks."

"What I don't get is why *you* didn't take advantage," Christie said.

I wondered what story he'd given her, but all I got from the look on his face was a challenge. Was I going to blow his cover or maintain his secret identity? There was no fear of the outcome, only interest.

"Yeah," he said prodding. "You know you can take advantage of me any time."

Christie swatted at him. "Oh, you!" Like she'd already grown used to his flirting.

Like it was old hat. Like it was *cute*. I gave Hermes the hairy eyeball.

"My tickets were nonrefundable," I lied … or not. Who knew with airline travel these days?

"Oh, well—"

"Can I get you girls a drink?" Hermes asked, sliding a hand down Christie's back in a way that made me want to slap him. Setting them up … worst idea ever. "Tori, you look like you could use one."

"Sure, whatever."

Probably two of the more dangerous words ever spoken. I could just imagine him making it a double, but he was off like a shot before I could take it back.

"Oh. My. God. Why didn't you tell me about him sooner?" Christie gushed the second he was out of earshot. "You've been holding out on me! I mean, sure I'd met him in the middle of all the insanity in San Francisco, but not *met* him, met him." I was sure that made sense in her head, if not so much when it came out of her mouth. "And he's so *charming!*"

"He is?"

"You don't see it? How do you not see it?" she gasped.

"Well, of course, I mean, I just think of him more like a brother—"

And speak of the devil. "There you are!" A bearlike arm wrapped around my shoulders. "The prodigal sister returns!" Spiro slurred. He squeezed me too tightly and breathed his beery breath into my ear. "Who *is* this gorgeous creature you're chatting up?"

Spiro *would* see it that way. Last I'd seen him, he'd been hopping mad about me exposing his little love nest with Lenny Rialto's new wife. I hadn't *meant* to reveal it, but that didn't change the pyrotechnics that resulted and nearly got my family expelled from the circus. It had only been smoothed over with a lot of ouzo, guy talk and, I suspected but couldn't prove, my brother subsequently seducing Lenny himself when they were in their cups. Oh, and the decision to let me go. Me and only me, for kicking over the whole hornet's nest.

Rumor had it that our family line had started with the god Pan beer-goggling one of the immortal gorgons. If I'd taken after Medusa's half of the family with my gorgon glare, Spiro had definitely taken after Pan's with his libido. If it was pretty and over the age of consent, it was fair game.

"She's off limits," I stage whispered back so that Christie would overhear.

Hermes reappeared at her side as if on cue. "Ouzo," he said, handing me a glass. "And a white wine spritzer for you," he continued, bowing to present it to Christie. *A spritzer.* Probably the girliest of all girlie drinks.

"Where's Yiayia?" I asked Spiro, trying to distract him from Christie, especially with the god of chaos taking it all in. The last thing any of us needed was him having fun at my brother's expense. "I tried to call her, but—"

The look of I-know-something-you-don't-know that flashed across Spiro's face was not comforting.

"Let me guess, it went to voicemail? She's probably off with her new—*cough*—paramour."

He actually *said* cough. But that wasn't the startling part. *Yiayia. Dating again.* It was ... Pappous was barely in his grave ... barely *two years* in his grave, anyway, and I'd thought ... Well, I guess I thought that all of her crazy obsessions had taken his place. I couldn't imagine another person filling it.

"Her what?" As if I'd misheard.

"Egona!" Yiayia's voice rang out behind me, cutting through the babble of the party all around the terrace.

I turned and ... and ... *stared.* Every bit as paralyzed as if she'd hit me with the gorgon glare. Yiayia and a young man. Young for her, anyway, by at least twenty years, and with a beard fully as long as her own, starting from some truly impressive mutton chops, flowing down over his chest and out to the sides in a thick handlebar mustache. All of it flaming red. He wasn't wearing a kilt and a tam, but he might as well have been. He looked like he'd stepped straight away from the Scottish Highlands.

Yiayia embraced me, her beard tickling my ear as I hugged her back. She took after the gorgon side of the family for sure, which was how she'd gotten the bearded lady gig with Rialto Bros. When I stepped out of her arms, I noticed that her eyes were glowing. Not literally, like Serena's, but with happiness.

"*Egona*, let me introduce you to Fergus. Fergus, my favorite granddaughter, Tori."

Fergus smiled, or so I assumed by the twitching of his facial hair. I couldn't actually glimpse lips or teeth. I held out a hand and he used it to pull me in for a bear hug, thumping me gently on the back.

"Any relation of Lorelei's ..." I'd known they must be on a first name basis, but still hearing her given name on his lips sounded odd.

Plus, my brain stuck on the question of how on earth they found each other's lips to kiss. While I tried to steer quickly away from that thought (*avert! avert! avert!* I insisted, scrambling all my brain cells to turn that ship around), I couldn't help but wonder about the Velcro effect. Did it take real effort to disengage? Ack!

At least I was no longer thinking about my fear of heights.

"We met at an extreme beard and mustache competition," Yiayia continued, heedless of the mound of mental floss I was adding to my shopping list. "Fergus beat me. The first time I've faced a worthy opponent since puberty."

"*Yiayia!*"

"What? I can say puberty. There, I said it again. *Puberty, puberty, puberty.* Speaking of which, where's *your* young man?"

I didn't even want to think how those two things—Armani and puberty—connected up in her brain.

"He went to freshen up. I'd, ah, better check on him," I said, retreating like the hounds of Hades were nipping at my heels.

I hurried back through the restaurant and to the elevator, using the time it took to arrive to collect myself.

Yiayia dating.

Hermes and Christie dating. Apollo and Serena … dating? My brother on the prowl.

What *was* it about weddings?

As I stepped into the elevator and contemplated which number to press, I realized I had no idea what room I was going to and no way to call Nick. Yes, finally, *finally*, it was Nick. With my whole family gone crazy … er than usual, he was the most familiar and least insane thing in my world. Unfortunately, we'd only arranged for one of our phones to work in Greece, figuring we'd be together the whole time and didn't need the extra expense. I rode the elevator to the lobby, calling Jesus on the way down, knowing *he* had an international calling plan already.

"Hey, where's Nick?" I asked, burning to get to him and a semblance of normalcy.

"In your room, I'd guess," he answered.

"Right, which would be?"

"Oh, number 501."

"Thanks."

I disconnected, rode the elevator *back* up to floor five and knocked on the first door to the left—501. Right next to the elevators. Oh joy. I hoped they were quieter on the outside than on the inside. Nick opened the door at my knock and stood in the entrance in a white dress shirt open down the front, exposing an incredibly nice chest with equally nice abs. I stepped right up to that chest and wrapped my arms around him. Nick eased back into the room, pulling me with him and closing the door behind us.

"You okay?" he asked. He stroked my hair and held me to him, resting his chin on the top of my head, because while I was *not* diminutive, Nick was tall enough to make me look semi-petite. Or maybe it was being overwhelmed that made me feel small. I listened to his heartbeat and let his breath stir my hair, so content for a moment that I forgot he'd asked a question that required an answer.

"I am now," I said.

I felt him smile against the top of my head. It made me smile back. "But—" he said for me.

"But … you know that part in a story summary where it pretty much boils down to *and wackiness ensues?*"

"Yeah."

"It's ensuing."

He pushed me back from him gently and smoothed the hair away from my face—pushed it aside, anyway. Actually smoothing or taming my vipers' nest of hair would probably take years of training, not to mention a bullwhip. If Nick could truly accomplish that, he'd fit right in with my family of circus folk. Thank gods he didn't.

He looked straight into my eyes, his own deep blue lit with amusement and, possibly, a four-letter word I wasn't yet ready to contemplate. It began with an "l" and ended with commitment.

"Let me just button up, and I'll help you face the insanity. I'm looking forward to it, actually."

I smiled back at him, all gorgeous and refreshed as he was, and realized that as little as I usually cared about appearances, I was going to have to step up my game. "Give me a minute to regroup," I told him.

I dragged my suitcase into the bathroom and did the best I could to make myself presentable, including the world's fastest shower. At least Christie's spa day had given me a head start. Even my eyebrows were more or less under control.

When I stepped out twenty minutes later, I was wearing a dress the color of a tawny port that made my amber eyes seem almost gold, low wedge sandals Christie had made me buy, and some smoky eye shadow. I looked as good as I was going to get, which, even I had to admit, wasn't half bad. I was no Serena Banks, but I would do.

Nick whistled, and I forced myself not to look around for the cause. "Thank you," I said, flushing. *Not* blushing. "Shall we go?"

Nick got to the door of the room before me and reached for it. "Anything I should know?" he asked.

"I think I'm going to let it be a surprise," I said mischievously. "Jesus coming with us?"

"He's right across the hall. He says to knock when we're ready."

We knocked and, for a wonder, Jesus was ready. He wore a shirt the color of which I didn't know how to describe—as if lavender had a pinker twin sister—and a diagonally striped tie the same shade, but deeper and darker, together with bands of deep blue and white. He looked like an Easter egg, but then, what did I know? No doubt it was all designer. Certainly, it fit him like a glove, the shirt like it was tailored for him, showing off the many hours he spent in the gym doing Zumba or hot yoga or whatever the cool kids were doing this week.

"Oh wait, my cuff links!" he said when he was halfway to the door. He was back a second later with a pair of silver and blue cufflinks that …

"Is that lapis?" I asked him. Because the swirl in the Greek key pattern of the cuffs was the exact blue of the stripe in his tie, the color of Armani's eyes, and the gorgeous lapis lazuli Greece was famous for. "Did you buy those just for the trip?"

Jesus looked away, and I had a sudden suspicion. "It was a bribe, wasn't it? To work for Apollo."

He wouldn't meet my gaze. "Maybe."

I rolled my eyes, since staring him down wasn't doing any good.

"Jesus."

"Bosslady," he said with the same amount of exasperation. "You don't pay me enough to afford nice things. And anyway, he didn't have to bribe me. Who could resist a free trip to Greece? I just didn't want him to think I was easy."

Nick snorted, and I shot him a look. "You're not helping."

He held up his hands as if to say that I should leave him out of it, but his amusement didn't ebb.

I threw my own hands up into the air, an expression that always made me think about having to catch them on the way back down.

Then I grabbed each man by the crook of the arm and escorted them to the terrace—until the narrowness of the stairs forced me to let them go. When we got to the top I regained Nick's arm and let Jesus fend for himself.

Nick didn't slow as we hit the terrace and saw Yiayia with her young man, but he did mumble an, "Oh Jesus, Mary and Joseph," under his breath.

I smiled. As I'd known it would, having him there, even more disconcerted than I was, relaxed me. I could enjoy his reactions instead of focusing on my own. Meeting my family was definitely a spectator sport.

"You're enjoying this," he accused me.

"Yup."

"Madre de Dios," Jesus said behind us, and I turned, already anticipating the reaction I'd see on his face.

And … it wasn't what I'd expected.

He looked gobsmacked, all right, but he wasn't looking in the right place. I followed his gaze across the terrace, tracking the source of his distraction. As far as I could tell, he was looking across at Christie, Hermes and Spiro, who were chatting away in a corner. Spiro was laughing at something one of them had said, the hearty sound carrying easily across the other conversations, just as Christie's laugh had earlier.

Jesus had met Christie and Hermes before, but Spiro? Was he ... oh *hell* to the no. I snapped my fingers in Jesus's face.

"Jesus. *Jesus*, snap out of it!"

He shook it off and turned on me with irritation. "What?" he asked. "I can look. You're not the boss of me."

"Technically, I am. Anyway, trust me, you don't want him. Spiro's a heartbreaker."

His irritation ebbed away in the face of pure, unadulterated lust. "You must introduce us. Wait, you're not speaking from experience, are you?"

I nodded very gravely. "Sadly, yes. He's my brother."

Jesus's mouth opened and closed, and I grinned at the sight of him speechless for the second time in two days. It had to be some kind of record.

"Come on, let's get a drink," I said, turning for the bar, but keeping toward the inner wall, well away from the view and the drop off.

But when Nick and I reached it and turned to find out what Jesus wanted to drink we discovered he was no longer with us. Instead, he was back across the terrace staring into my brother's eyes as they shook hands.

Worse yet, my brother didn't immediately surrender the hand he'd been given.

CHAPTER FIVE

"My family's never met a stranger … or, at least, anyone stranger than them."
—Tori Karacis

Yiayia and her—friend? boyfriend? passing acquaintance?—Fergus joined us at the bar, mercifully cutting off my line of sight to Jesus and my brother and the moment they seemed to be having. At least there wasn't any sappy music playing. Or a dance floor, though the sun was cooperatively starting to set … the mood. It wasn't the fact that they were both men that bothered me. I didn't give a damn about that. It was the fact that either one by himself was a handful. Together, it would be like kerosene poured on a chemical fire.

Maybe I was upset because they were both mine in totally different ways, so they couldn't possibly become each other's, but I was pretty sure my concern was more noble than that. Spiro was the king of hookups and heartbreaks. Not only didn't I want to see Jesus hurt, I didn't want to live through the diva-sized meltdown should Spiro stomp all over his heart. And he would, unless he'd changed a helluva lot since I'd last seen him.

"Fair warning, Lenny Rialto is on his way up," Yiayia said next to my ear. "I'm sure you will both be on your best behavior, yes?"

"I will if he will," I answered her, not looking forward to the meeting, despite my casual response. Really, none of the problems had been my fault. If Spiro had just kept it in his pants ... or not lied to me about where he was going and who he was meeting so that I hadn't been so all-fired curious to find out. Or if he'd been *any* good at discretion. Yet, as good as Spiro was at causing trouble, he was equally good at smoothing it over and staying on good terms with his former lovers, hence the fact that he was still in and *I* was out.

"If he will what?" Nick asked.

"And *this* must be your young man!" Yiayia gushed before I could answer him. She grabbed Nick by both shoulders and leaned in for a kiss on each cheek.

Nick looked slightly stunned as she pulled back. I could tell only because I was watching for it. His policeman poker face shuttered his expression almost instantly.

"And this must be yours," he said to Yiayia, holding a hand out to Fergus.

Fergus gripped his offered hand in a meaty fist and used it to pull Nick in for a chest bump sort of man hug, thumping him on the back before releasing him.

"Nick, eh?" he said, voice gruff. "I've heard a lot about you." Although it came out, *I've 'eard a lot aboot ewe.*

"If you're ordering, I'll have an Oban, straight up."

"Make that two," Yiayia said, smiling up at Fergus, an odd twinkle in her eye. I didn't like it one bit.

"Lorelei," a voice boomed from off to the side.

We all turned, except Nick, who stepped up to place our

order. I thought I might recognize the voice calling out for Yiayia, but it had been so long …

Sure enough, Uncle Hector steered toward Yiayia like a ferry to a dock, their meeting inevitable. He was smaller than I remembered him. Or maybe I'd grown. The last time I'd seen him I'd been just a child. But he was no less powerfully present. He looked, in fact, like the Dos Equis "Most Interesting Man Alive"—incredibly tan, his silver hair and dark eyes contrasting nicely, and his teeth whiter than white, showing in a smile that invited everyone in range to smile with him. Or better yet, laugh, even though he hadn't yet told the joke that sparked in his eyes.

He held his hands out to Yiayia and froze for a moment as she took them. Suddenly I felt extraneous, just like with Jesus and Spiro. Fergus cleared his throat, and Uncle Hector swept us all with his overpowering attention, as if the pause had never taken place.

"And my favorite niece!" he said to me, drawing his hands back from Yiayia to hug me and kiss both of my cheeks before putting me back from him at arms' length. "Stunning!" he proclaimed me. The old liar. "Why, you are every bit as beautiful as I knew you would be."

He treated Nick and Fergus to handshakes—no cheek kissing or chest bumping—and turned back to Yiayia. "And you, Lorelei, you haven't changed a bit."

She fixed him with a dubious look. "In what? Twenty years? Fifteen? When was it you last saw me?"

"It seems like yesterday, and yet it's been far too long."

Nick rescued us then, turning from the bar with our drinks in hand and passing them around. He asked what Uncle Hector would have, but he held up a flask all his own and wrapped an arm around Nick to move him away from the bar as he would have tried to pay.

"The whole thing's on me," he said proudly. "Have to impress the investors, you know."

"Investors?" I asked, pings of curiosity driving away the jet lag that was starting to tug at me.

"You know about the film, yes? A romance, and it opens at a wedding! We have a wedding, the film has a budget, and *voilà*! We kill two birds with one stone." Before I could ask any of my million questions, he exclaimed, "Ah, here's one of our investors now!"

We turned to follow his gaze—straight into the smiling face of Hermes. *Of course.* I'd been wondering what he was up to at the party. Apparently, he'd been up to helping bring Apollo to Greece and partially financing his new film. But what motivated him—mischief or patriotism? It was hard to believe that he'd invest for completely unselfish reasons. Setting a blockbuster film among Greece's impressive sites would certainly stimulate tourism and help the floundering economy, but I doubted he was free of ulterior motives. There had to be something in this for Hermes. Were the financial rewards enough? Or did he have something more mischievous in mind, perhaps tapping Christie for a role in the movie, to cozy up to her or to make her indebted to him. Gods thought like that—sacrifice, tribute, tithes. Debts.

"Surprised?" Hermes asked, seeing the look on my face. Before I could respond, he turned to glad-hand my uncle. "Hector, it's good to see you."

They did the whole hail-fellow-well-met greeting, shaking hands, pulling in for a chest bump, kissing on both cheeks. And yes, it was a lot of physical contact for a country where the forecast generally called for hot and sweaty with a better than even chance of deodorant fail. But the nice breeze blowing across the terrace made the heat bearable. Truthfully, it was a gorgeous night and, unlike in LA, you could actually see some of the stars that had appeared in the sky as the sun went down.

"Where are the man and woman of the hour?" I asked, realizing I hadn't seen hide nor hair of Tina and her fiancé.

"Apollo and Serena?" Hermes asked. "Probably still"—*cough*—"freshening up."

"I meant the bride and groom," I said wryly, refusing to let him tweak me.

"Oh," Uncle Hector answered, "they've gone on ahead to Delphi to meet with the set designers and dressers. It all has to be perfect for the big day, you know."

Apparently, that was Serena's cue to stumble into the party and collapse into Uncle Hector's arms, her face drained of color, eyes rolling like a spooked horse.

CHAPTER SIX

"Two things a man will always catch—a cold and a swooning woman."
—Yiayia's words of wisdom

U ncle Hector was trying to revive her when my phone rang. I pulled it out of my cleavage—there'd been no place else to put it in this dress, and I'd forgotten a cute little evening bag—and answered it.

Apollo.

"Tori, I need you. Not like it sounds. I need you down here. Now. Room 527."

"Does this have anything to do with Serena in a dead faint?"

"Just get here. You'll see."

"Okay, we're on the way."

"No!" he said, an edge of ... panic? ... to his voice. "Just you." I looked at Armani, who was listening in.

"Go. I'll try and get the full story here," he said, looking toward Apollo's leading lady.

I quirked an eyebrow. "Okay, but if you have to do mouth to mouth on her, you're not allowed to enjoy it."

His lips twitched. "Deal."

I went. The number of times Apollo had come when I'd called, the least I could do was return the favor. Plus, the curiosity was killing me.

I raced to the stairs and down them, nearly flattening a man on his way up, who pressed himself against the wall to avoid a collision. I hit the fifth floor at a dead run. Of course, 527 was all the way at the end. And *of course* I didn't have a single weapon on me. I kicked off the strappy sandals that would only twist my ankle in a fight and held one like a bludgeon, wedge heel out, ready to brain anyone who jumped at me.

The door was open, and I threw my other heel at it to knock it farther inward and see if it prompted any attack. The shoe hit with a thump, bouncing the door back into the inner wall and revealing an empty room. The clothes Apollo had worn earlier were thrown across the desk, which meant either he'd changed or—

"Tori?" he called.

The voice came from the bathroom, the one place I couldn't see into from the doorway, because *that* door was firmly shut.

"Yeah," I called back. "You decent?"

"Funny you should ask ..." He didn't sound like it was funny ha ha. "Would you close the door to the hallway and come in here a second. There's something I need to show you."

I stared at the bathroom door in disbelief. "Uh huh, I've heard that one before."

"This is serious."

I hadn't really thought it wasn't. Apollo wasn't a practical joker, and if he wanted a woman in his bed ... or bath ... he certainly didn't have to resort to trickery. It was just that the thought of what I might find ... what would make a god call for my help ... maybe I wasn't *that* curious.

"Okay." I closed the outer door and put my hand to the bathroom door handle. "Ready or not, here I come."

I twisted the handle and the door swung inward. No inner alarms blared. My heart didn't race, and my palms didn't sweat. At least, not until I stepped in and saw Apollo, only half dry from the shower, holding a towel around his hips. *Holding it there*. Not snugging it shut.

Not only did my heart race then, but my mouth went dry. Not so my panties ... no, I wasn't going there. Suffice it to say there was a reason there were so many statues of Apollo and why he'd left such a string of tragic loves behind him.

"That what you want to show me?" I asked, nodding at the towel.

"It's not what you think," he said.

"Really," I asked dryly.

He opened the towel.

He was right. It wasn't what I thought. Or rather, it was *exactly* what I thought, just in a brand new, never-before-seen form.

I stared.

"If only you'd shown so much interest before I, uh, got wood. Literally."

Because yes, it looked more like the limb of a tree than, well, a certain body part integral to his adult film career. And at the moment, it appeared petrified.

With effort, I made myself look away, up to his face. "Okay, two questions to start. No, three. When did this happen, how did this happen and what does this have to do with Serena looking like she'd seen a ... *you?*"

"Serena snuck up on me in the shower. As you know, we'd agreed to a pretend relationship to take the heat off you and help promote the new film. I guess she decided some method acting was in order."

Well, you couldn't really blame a girl for trying. "And the when?"

57

"Right about the time she appeared. When I spotted her, she had this ... *look* on her face and something didn't feel right. When I looked down to kind of check on things—" He swept his hand down over his petrified parts.

"Okay, I get it. You can put that thing away now." His eyes sparkled just for a second, like the literal woody was almost worth my discomfort, and I couldn't resist adding, "Though before we see about changing you back, maybe you want to sprinkle a little Miracle Grow down there."

He froze with the towel only halfway around his hips. "I don't really think I need the help, do you?"

Unwillingly, my gaze was drawn back to the part in question. "No, that might be too much of a good thing," I choked out.

"I could demonstrate," he said, waggling his brows at me.

"Down boy. I'd be worried about splinters. Anyway, how can you be so calm about this and how on Earth do you think I can help?"

"Remember how you told me you'd save me back someday? Well, I'm calling it in."

"So you want me to find out who's doing this to you and get them to reverse it?"

"That's the idea."

"What about Serena?"

"What about her?" he asked.

I gave him a *get real* look. "Well, this all started with her walking in on you. Do you think that's a coincidence?"

"Well, I *did*. I mean, as far as I know, she's human. She doesn't have the power to pull off something like this. And why would she?"

"You tell me, loverboy. Did you do anything to piss her off? And while we're at it, I'm not sure she's entirely human. I saw her eyes glow on the plane."

"Glow, seriously?"

"Seriously. Gah, I can't talk to you when you're ... like that. Get some clothes on and we'll figure this out."

He grinned, but moved toward the door, and I backed out to let him pass. The sooner his petrified parts were covered up, the sooner I could think straight. Theoretically.

He grabbed a pair of pants that had been folded over a chair. His towel slipped as he started to step into them and I quickly averted my eyes, even as curious as I was to see how in the world he was going to tuck that thing away.

"So, Serena," I said, pretending interest in the artwork on the walls. "How much do you know about her?"

"Just the official bio, but those are usually more fiction than not. She's a California girl, born and bred. Discovered at a cattle call for Myron Landau's last film. Instant celebrity. Nothing mysterious about her."

"Uh huh."

"Not to sound arrogant, but why would she want to hurt me when that would derail the film? This is a big role for her."

"Could you be replaced?"

"No, don't worry about my ego. I'm just fine," he said, buttoning a shirt over his massive chest ... not that I was looking. "Yes, in theory I could be replaced. In practice, no one worth their salt is available on such short notice. She'd be shooting her own career in the foot."

I thought about that. I didn't know what I'd seen in her eyes. With the gods begetting here, there and everywhere, it was likely that half the people on Earth had some kind of ancient blood running through their veins. I myself had the gorgon glare, but I couldn't turn men to stone ... or wood. Still, I could hardly condemn Serena for her ancestry. And I suspected the fact that I hadn't trusted her on sight was more about jealousy than precognition. Jealousy I had no right to feel.

"Okay then, maybe not Serena. Then who?"

"Anyone with transformation power. All the major players have it—Zeus, Poseidon, Hades, Hera. Plus, it's a particular talent of the water divinities, given that water has no fixed form."

"So the list of suspects reads like the Olympian family tree?"

"More or less."

I crossed my arms over my chest. He wasn't going to like this next part one bit. "I'm going to have to bring Armani in on this. I can't leave him in the dark on the investigation. This is too big for one person, even if that one person is me."

"Well, that ought to make his day."

Oddly enough, it didn't. I was going to wait to tell Nick about Apollo's, uh, condition, until after maybe a few beers and some mellowing. Introducing him to my crazy family *and* the thought of another man's priapic state on top of our harrowing travels seemed like cruel and unusual punishment to me.

But Nick hardly needed his cop skills to realize that there was a story behind a traumatized Serena collapsing in front of him. He pulled me aside the second I reappeared on the terrace.

"*What* is going on?" he demanded.

Hesitating wouldn't make the news any more palatable. "Apollo's turning into a tree," I said, as no-nonsense as I could make it.

"Say what?"

"She didn't tell you?"

"She hasn't said anything. Her eyelids have fluttered and she's moaned once or twice. I'm fairly certain she's milking the attention for all it's worth."

I felt girlfriendly relief at the disgust in his voice.

"Nick," I said, voice dead serious so that he'd know I wasn't joking. "Apollo's being transformed … into a tree."

Nick let his head hit the wall behind him. "You mean we take our first romantic trip together—to a wedding, no less, and not only does my competition come along, but you've taken his case?"

"Um—"

"Let me guess, the suspect list consists of everyone he's pissed off in the last several centuries? You might want to add me to that list."

Well, that had gone better than I'd expected. "Um." I wasn't normally at a loss for words, but here I had absolutely no idea what to say.

Nick rolled his eyes. "You're *sure* that 'tree' won't be a good look for him? It might be the role he was born to play."

"Nick—"

"Never mind." He turned on a dime and took off toward the doors back into the hotel.

"Where are you going?" I asked.

"To the room. I haven't slept in, like, twenty-four hours. I can't even process this right now. If I don't hit the sheets, I might hit something else." I had to trust that he didn't mean me.

I stood frozen in place, afraid that if I didn't go after him, it would seem like I'd chosen Apollo's needs over his. Afraid that if I did, Apollo, who was already hardheaded enough, might continue to petrify until there was no getting through to him at all. My stomach ate itself up with the fear that I was about to lose one or the other somehow. But only one would be lost to a fate worse than death. That decided me. Tomorrow or the day after or the day after that I could make things up to Nick. But I didn't know how much time Apollo had or how long it would take me to track down the culprit.

As the evening wore on and jet lag dragged at my heels, it was evident that I was a failure. I'd spent the evening ignoring the fact that I was several stories up, shaking hands with Uncle Hector's investors, chatting up nearly forgotten cousins, and avoiding Lenny Rialto. I recruited Christie, with her actor's eye for body language, and Jesus, with his critical eye for everything else, into helping me look for anyone suspicious. Of course, I had the ulterior motive of trying to distract both from their dates from hell. But by the end of the night, I had to admit defeat on all counts. We hadn't noticed anything strange—at least, no stranger than normal when it came to my family, who set a pretty high bar—and both Christie and Jesus had gravitated back to their fatal attractions.

Tomorrow I'd find a way to talk to Serena and to quietly quiz my fellow guests on the trek to Mount Parnassus. For now, I was done in. My heels felt like medieval torture devices, my dress had grown itchy, and all I really wanted were sweats, a tank top and blissful oblivion.

I got two out of three.

CHAPTER SEVEN

"Love is a serious mental disease."
—Plato

W hen I got back to the room, Nick was already asleep. Passed out was more like it—a rumbling snore going as he sprawled over more than his fair share of the bed. On *top* of the sheets, of course, so that it was impossible for me to slide underneath. On top of all that, he was wearing boxers, by which I knew how upset he was. If I'd been forgiven, he'd be pleasantly naked. On some level, I'd known that wouldn't be the case or I wouldn't have been thinking about a tank and sweats, my comfort clothes.

I sighed and gathered up my stuff so I could change in the bathroom for minimal disturbance. Then I did my best to contort myself around him. When it was clear that wasn't going to work, I lay down and shimmied back against him, lifting the arm that was hugging my pillow to place it over my waist instead. But even in sleep, Nick turned from me, rolling over to face the wall and leave me my entire side of the bed, cold and lonely.

I lay there for a long time, listening to him snore, willing him to wake. But my powers didn't run that way. Eventually, his snore quieted to a dull roar, and I dropped off to sleep lulled by the sound.

There was no telling how long it lasted before something woke me up. Nick's body was blocking my view of the alarm clock. He hadn't moved one iota, so he hadn't been the trigger for my sudden wakeup.

I let my eyes adjust to the darkness of the room. Nothing seemed changed. No grim reaper stood over me, slashing down with the bladed weapon of doom as had happened once before. I still had nightmares about *that*.

Slowly, quietly, I got up, leaving Nick sleeping as I canvassed the room. It didn't take me long to see what was out of place—a piece of paper slipped under the door.

That's weird, I thought. There shouldn't be a bill. My understanding was that Uncle Hector was taking care of all this. I could always straighten it out with the front desk in the morning. But when I picked it up, I saw it wasn't a bill at all. It was a warning.

You're next.

I unlatched the safety bar on our door, turned the lock and eased the door open to check the hallway, even knowing the messenger would be long gone. As expected, the hallway was deserted. Quiet. Dark but for some low night lighting recessed along the ceiling.

But there was enough illumination to spot a door opening halfway down the hall and Jesus emerging—wearing the clothes he'd had on earlier, minus the tie that dangled from his hand rather than his neck. His shirt collar was open two whole buttons and there was only one conclusion. I ducked back into the room before he could see me see *him* do the walk of shame. I could guess whose room he'd been coming from; I knew for a fact it wasn't his. I also knew I didn't want to know even this much. I wanted mental floss for the sudden vision I had of Spiro and Jesus together. A new manifestation of my psychic abilities? I sure hoped not. On second thought, mental floss was too mild. I was thinking maybe frontal lobotomy. Sadly, I lacked the proper tools.

I crumpled the warning note in my hand and curled back up to Nick, wishing for a big old goblet of oblivion from the River Lethe, the river of forgetfulness. Unfortunately, Hades had a monopoly on that, and he wasn't exactly my biggest fan. At least he was no longer trying to kill or control me.

Unless *he* was behind the threat. Somehow I doubted it though. It was more his style to maim first, gloat later. Which meant I was back to my original enemies: Zeus and Poseidon. If they (or an agent for them, since I hadn't yet been struck by lightning or another freak storm) were behind the note, what was the purpose? To keep us unsettled until they could deliver their coup de grâce? Was their agent behind Apollo's petrification as well?

I laid there wide-eyed for most of the night, pondering this and other mysteries of the universe. Not so easy with Nick beside me, snoring like he'd swallowed an active buzzsaw.

I'd been sure I wouldn't sleep at all, so I was doubly surprised the next morning when Nick woke me getting out of bed. He disappeared into the bathroom without so much as looking my way.

A wakeup call came five seconds later, while I was still debating what to do about Nick and about to settle on the cheap ploy of getting naked and striking a provocative pose to ensnare him when he emerged from the bathroom.

A woman's voice told me in unaccented English that Uncle Hector had arranged for a complimentary breakfast buffet to run from nine until eleven, after which our transportation would be leaving for Delphi. A quick glance at the clock showed that it was eight thirty. Plenty of time to eat and get ready.

In the bathroom, I heard the shower start up and gave up on the idea of a provocative pose. I hesitated to sneak up on Nick in the shower after what Serena had walked in on with Apollo, but I figured no guts, no glory. So I dropped my tank and sweats into a heap on the bed and headed naked for the bathroom, only to find the door locked.

I steamed.

What if I'd desperately needed the facilities? Not that we were yet at that point in our relationship where I'd do anything with him in the same room, even behind a curtain with water running to drown out the noise. Still, I liked to have my options open.

I studied the closed door. It was meant for privacy, not security. I could jimmy it with a credit card. But should I?

Yeah, as if self-control was really an option.

I got my wallet, grabbed a credit card to some store I'd shopped in maybe once or twice and went at it.

The door popped open quicker than it took me to lick my lips, and I dropped the card on the counter, took a step toward the shower and flicked aside the curtain.

Nick whirled like I'd goosed him. His eyes went wide, and there was a razor in his hand, held like a weapon, which would have been a lot more effective if it hadn't been the plastic traveling kind.

"Tori, you scared the hell out of me!" he said, not happily. I ignored his tone.

"You have room in there for me?"

"The door was locked," he pointed out.

"So it was."

And *that* was when he realized I was naked. I could see it when the cranky started to ebb from his face and something else took its place. He looked over as much of me as the curtain didn't conceal and suddenly there was more of him to lather.

"Well, I suppose it would be nice to have someone to wash

my back," he said. The blue of his eyes deepened and he stepped back to make room for me.

"*Just* your back?" I asked, raking my gaze over him. Nick was unbelievably gorgeous at the best of times—thick dark hair falling over his brow, amazing jawline, broad shoulders, narrow waist, washboard abs—the stuff of romance covers. But wet and naked, his hair slicked back so that I could really see those expressive blue eyes ...

"We can start there and see where it takes us," he answered.

I didn't ask if that meant I was forgiven for fear he'd say "no." I stepped into the water and just went with the flow, so to speak.

We made it down to breakfast with twenty minutes to spare before the end. The fresh fruit plate had been picked nearly clean but for a few grapes, but there was still coffee and croissants, and I was all for carb-loading after that shower. Honestly, I was shaky, and I didn't think it was for lack of food or caffeine withdrawal. I was going to have to find a source for ambrosia, stat. I probably should have asked Apollo about it last night, but, well, seeing him au naturel like that played havoc with my mind.

The terrace restaurant was deserted when we arrived, except for Hermes and Christie, who still lingered over coffee. She'd gotten hers iced and was drinking through a straw, her trick, I knew, to avoid staining her teeth.

She jumped up when she saw me and gave me a huge hug. "I was just waiting to say goodbye," she said in a rush. "I've got to get to my shoot, but if there are no delays, I'll be back for the wedding. Hermes invited me to be his guest ... if that's okay with you."

"Of course!" I said, putting mock enthusiasm into my voice, not because I didn't want her there, but because I'd rather have her safely away. I didn't want her becoming collateral damage if ... when ... Zeus and Poseidon came at me again, which made me wonder whether I should be here at all, drawing potential fire down on my friends and family.

"Good, I'll see you in two days then," Christie said, oblivious to my turmoil. She was happier than I'd seen her in a good, long time. Since Jack(ass) had broken her heart. "Tell Apollo I hope he feels better."

"What did you hear?" I asked, maybe a little too sharply.

Enough so that Christie picked up on it instantly. "Why, what do you *know*?"

"Nothing," I lied.

"Uh huh. You *will* tell me. But later. We have to get going."

She kissed me on both cheeks to say goodbye. Hermes rose from their table and did the same, saying into my ear as he hit my second cheek, "You *are* okay? You look a trifle ... piqued."

"I'm fine, which is more than I can say for you if you pull one wrong move with my friend, *capisce*?" I was about to say *you break her, you bought her*, but that might just give him ideas.

"Of course, *agape*. She is safe as houses."

Yeah, I knew what Vesuvius had done to *them* and Hermes was just as much a force of nature.

"Safer," I insisted.

He winked and was gone, making no promises.

Nick stood holding his plate, looking between me and their retreating backs. "Why didn't you warn her off if you didn't approve?" he asked.

"Tried that. Didn't work."

"She has a thing for bad boys, huh?"

I nodded, biting the head off a croissant that had never done a thing to me but dare to be light and flaky.

"Seen a lot of that," Nick said. "Rarely ends well."

I swallowed the bite of croissant that had turned to ashes in my mouth and glared. "That your idea of comfort?"

"You want comfort, you don't come to a cop. Hey," he added, grabbing my hand before I could decapitate a second pastry, "does Christie seem the typical type to you?"

I eyed him. "No," I admitted.

"Then there's a good chance her results will vary."

It was exactly the right thing to say, and he must have read that on my face. "I made it all better?" he asked.

"Mostly."

"Good." Then he mumbled, "If only Apollo's petrification was as easily solved."

I went a lot easier on my second croissant and gulped coffee to wash it down. "We'd better get going before our transportation leaves without us," I said once I'd consumed enough caffeine to care.

We retrieved our bags from the room and met up with the others in the lobby.

In front of the hotel, two gleaming white stretch limos waited and Odd Job … er, Viggo … stood, directing people toward one or the other based on the list he held. It turned out the film people were going in the first limo, family in the second. There'd be no chance for me to interview any of the suspects, Serena top of the list, regardless of what Apollo thought. But the two-hour ride *was* the perfect opportunity for me to catch up on my missed sleep.

For the second time in as many days, I drooled on Nick's shoulder … until we hit the switchbacks and I was catapulted upright and knocked awake by my head hitting the window. From there on up the mountain it was an unending thrill ride. And by thrill ride, I mean sheer heart-stopping terror as each time it looked like there was no possible way the limo could make the turn in the space provided and we'd go shooting off a cliff, cinematically falling end over end down the mountain, ending in a fiery wreck at the bottom.

By the time we reached the top and pulled into the almost forty-five-degree angle of the parking lot of our mountain view hotel I had nearly shredded the leather interior with my fingernails and was seriously in need of a drink. Or ambrosia. Or all of the above. And then a way *down* off this deathtrap. Times like this, I doubted my ancestry. We Greeks had a habit of building on the very tippy top of impossible places. They were the holiest, the most strategic ... at least, that was supposed to be the reasoning. Heights were certainly religious experiences for me. Nothing made me pray so much—*ohgods, ohgods, ohgods*—as being perilously close to cliffs, summits, high wires and other insanity.

I felt a prayer coming on now.

No one was happier than I was to come to a complete stop, but Nick had to be a close second. I noticed as he helped me out of the limo that his hand had gone nearly white from my squeezing of it and that he was flexing and tightening his fist in the hope of getting blood to circulate back through.

"Sorry," I said sheepishly.

"You going to be okay?" he asked.

I sampled the air outside the limo, trying to breathe deeply and failing. It felt thin, frail, too cool, as if it could barely sustain itself, let alone actual life. I remembered Apollo speaking to the West Wind back in San Francisco. I wondered which wind spirit might rule the roost on Mount Parnassus and whether it might be prevailed upon to pump up the volume. I'd have to ask Apollo when he wasn't too busy turning into a tree.

The thought was like a slap in the face. I had to get it together. People were counting on me—my cousin to fill out her wedding party, Apollo to solve a mystery. *Apollo*—now *there* was someone with problems.

Breathing ... yeah, I had this. No problem.

I tried again and managed to breathe a little deeper this time, taking in maybe enough oxygen to get to my next breath.

"Totally," I lied to Nick.

Fake it 'til you make it, Pappous had always said.

I grabbed my luggage from the back of the limo like the others, and Viggo held us back until the important people in the other limo were swept in ahead of us.

We were met inside by two women in hot pink suits and even brighter smiles. Their skirts stopped right above the knees. Their smiles stretched from ear to ear. Tina's friend Junessa, and her other boss, besides Lenny Rialto, Althea Fielding. The three had become thick as thieves after Junie had recruited Tina to sell Eterné, sort of like Avon or Mary Kay but focused on eternal youth and beauty, just like the name implied. Both women were wearing Eterné's signature color—fuchsia—and were bedecked with sample bags they handed out to the wedding guests as we arrived.

Junie squealed when she saw me and swallowed me up in a backbreaking Amazonian hug. Actual Amazons were mythical, so far as I knew. So, no, the female warriors hadn't had breasts removed to better aim their bows. But if they *had* existed, Junie would have fit right in. She was wearing ballet flats right now, but even so she was nearly six feet tall, all of it lean muscle. Her gorgeous cherrywood skin glowed with health and her dark hair shone under the overhead lobby lights. I thwapped her on the back and coughed to signal my surrender, and she let me go.

"Sorry. I forget you're not a hugger. You look fantastic!" she said, pulling back to study me more critically. "Except—" She wet her finger and scrubbed at the drool stains at the corner of my mouth. I jerked away, and Armani laughed.

"I've been wanting to do that myself."

"Why didn't you?" Junie asked.

"I didn't want to lose a hand."

Junie grinned at him. "Oh, she's more bark than bite."

"Really?" Althea cut in, handing her last bag to Yiayia as she sailed by. "Don't you remember the time in that bar where the good ol' boy wouldn't take no for an answer and Tori almost made him eat his arm?"

"You brute," Nick said, proudly.

"Oh, we have some stories to tell," Althea promised mischievously. "Catch us later."

"It's a date," he said.

"No, it isn't," I said sourly, waving goodbye to them as I pushed Nick toward check-in.

"Jealous?" he teased.

I snorted, only because I couldn't honestly tell him he was wrong. Junie and Althea got more than their share of attention —not the least of which from my brother, who'd tried to score with them ever since Tina had brought them around. As far as I knew, it was still girls two, Spiro zip.

Where Junie was tall and muscular, Althea was smaller and coltish with one of those natural size zero bodies ... maybe size two, tops. She could wear spaghetti straps without worrying about completely unnecessary bra straps. In other words, she was sleek like a model. She had big brown doe eyes, wheat-gold hair pulled back into a complicated braid and perfect sun-bronzed skin. No freckles, no wrinkles. It was enough to make me an eensy bit interested in what was in the little pink sample bags they'd handed out.

"So, what's the story there?" Nick asked as we waited our turn, jerking his head to indicate our fuchsia-wrapped friends.

"Beauty cult."

"Huh?"

"You know, like the Back to Earth movement, only not. Less digging in the dirt and more miracle makeovers."

"Okay," he said, smiling.

I huffed. "You know those sell-from-home cosmetic companies? They're like legal pyramid schemes. You recruit ten people, and they recruit ten people ... The cultish part comes in with the rules on how you should appear in public, because you're always representing the brand. It's not just a product, it's a way of life ... that sort of thing. Tina got drawn in a few years ago."

Nick rummaged in his bag and came up with a catalogue featuring a smiling woman in a faux fur wrap. "Oh, I see, very ominous," he said.

"Go ahead, laugh. But don't come crying to me when you get suckered in by their manscaping gel or anti-aging aftershave."

"Seriously?"

"Oh yeah. Spiro has a whole duffle bag full of product. At one point, I think he was going for customer of the year."

"How'd that work out for him?"

"Well, he does have some pretty smooth skin. I think Jesus can attest to that."

Speaking of whom …

"*Chica*, have you *seen* the stuff in here? Do you know what these samples are worth?"

"No, why don't you tell me in extreme detail."

"Sarcasm does not wear well on you," he answered with a sniff.

"Really? Do they have a cream for that?"

"Don't make me separate you two," Nick cut in.

Then it was our turn at the reception desk, where we were very efficiently set up with adjoining rooms.

"Like I'm your child or something," Jesus complained.

"Heaven forefend," Nick answered.

The reception guy, thank goodness not another model of perfection but a *maître d'* sort of man with a mustache that looked anemic next to Yiayia and Fergus's facial hair, gave us a map and a schedule along with our keycards. I glanced down at the schedule—production meeting, rehearsal, rehearsal dinner … *Production meeting?* Were they kidding? All told, it looked like they'd left us maybe an hour and a half to ourselves over the next few days.

"Oh, and you're expected to dress for dinner," the reception guy said. "I'm sure they'll explain everything in the meeting."

Dress … as opposed to *undress?* I was about to ask when Nick elbowed me as if he could read my mind. I stuck my tongue out at him, and Jesus looked mildly disgusted at my immaturity. I could live with that. I was on vacation and, anyway, Christos was the head of the PI firm again now that we'd sprung him from the crazy Back to Earth cult, so I didn't have to be the big boss.

And while I was reminded … "Has Christos Karacis checked in yet?" I asked the reception guy.

He typed a few keystrokes into his computer and said, "Yes, would you like me to connect you to his room?"

I told him I would and ended up leaving a message. He owed Apollo as much as I did … almost. He'd want to repay the debt, and considering that I had no idea exactly where to start my investigation, I could use all the help I could get. Normally, I'd start digging into the victim's past, but when that comprised centuries and many of the tales had been lost or mutated by time and retellings … it was a tall order. I couldn't begin with his routines and regular encounters, because he was away from all that here in Greece. He'd traveled from his present back into the land of his past.

So, the past it was. I had at least two primary sources onsite —Hermes and Apollo himself. Yiayia could fill me in on everyone's more modern escapades. And meanwhile, maybe I could get lists from Uncle Hector and from Tina on anyone involved with the productions, wedding, or film. Because with my family, it was *always* a production.

Fingers snapped before my face, and somebody grabbed my arm to steer me away from the reception desk.

"Earth to Tori," Nick said, as if maybe it wasn't the first time. "Lunch?"

"What? Oh, yeah." Because now that he'd mentioned it, the croissants and grapes I'd had for breakfast hours ago were not cutting it.

"And shopping?" Jesus asked hopefully.

"Have you forgotten that we have a mystery to solve?" I asked him.

"Never fear. I'll keep my eyes open for anything suspicious. Like a girl who doesn't like to shop," he added under his breath.

"I heard that."

"Heard what?" he asked, all innocence.

"Never mind. We'll meet back down here in twenty," I told him. Shopping might not be a priority, but food and caffeination were other matters entirely.

"But—"

"*Twenty* or we leave without you."

He gave a long suffering sigh and a tight nod and led the way to the elevators. Our room was small but nice—photos of the nearby Temple of Apollo at sunset, some of the fallen columns and pedestals peeking out of a springtime profusion of flowers. Any other adornments were unnecessary. Nick headed straight for the window and twitched back the sheer curtain obscuring the view. He whistled, and I took a step back. The view looked out over … nothing. Or, more accurately, nothing but sky. We were above even the clouds, which seemed totally unnatural. Panic started to flutter against my breastbone like a frightened baby bird.

"Could you …?" I nodded at the curtains as Nick's head whipped around in response to the tension in my voice. Instantly, he let the curtain fall back into place.

"Sorry. Are you sure you're going to be all right to go out and eat? I could bring you back something."

"I am *not* going to let this defeat me. Let's go."

He smiled. "That's my girl. Just let me use the facilities."

He disappeared into the bathroom. I fought down the baby bird and forced myself closer to the window a step. Then two, then I stopped, told myself it was just stupid and that *I could handle this*, but I knew I was lying. I made myself take the last few steps without pause. My inner alarms started blaring, my heart started racing, sweat broke out all over. What if this was my precog kicking in, telling me I was right to be afraid?

There was only one way to know. I reached out for the curtain like it was a live snake and twitched it back, flinching as I did, feeling stupid the whole time. Nothing happened. I didn't get sucked into a vortex or whatever I subconsciously thought would happen. It didn't lessen the fear.

I looked out. It was a beautiful day. The sun was shining, and, now that I really looked, I could see that the view outside wasn't an *instant* drop off. There was a lip of land where the groundskeepers had laid out a little garden with a bench to sit on and enjoy the view (ha) and a fountain gurgling away with a central figure shaped like one of the Korae pouring water out of an amphora.

But the Korae wasn't alone. I *felt* something else down there. Someone else. Malevolent, glaring. I couldn't see him ... her ... it, but that expression "if looks could kill" suddenly meant something deep down in the pit of my stomach. I momentarily forgot about the height, my need to know stronger than my fear. I stepped forward one more baby step and stared down. Nothing. Paranoia? Ambrosia withdrawal? Reality? I didn't know. And the not knowing was worse than the growing ball of acid burning its way through my stomach.

"Ready?"

I jumped and spun around, that baby bird all riled up again.

Nick stood between me and the exit, hands up as though I might strike him. *That* was when I realized I'd ended up in a battle stance, ready to kick his ass from here to Athens and back again.

"You scared me," I accused.

"Sorry, I wasn't trying to."

He had on khaki shorts and a deep blue V-neck tee that picked up the midnight blue of his eyes. Next to him, I was a rumpled mess. "Five minutes," I promised him, looking at the room clock and knowing I'd never hear the end of it if Jesus made it to the lobby before I did.

"But while I change"—paranoia or precognition ... I had to know—"would you look out the window and tell me if you see ... anything at all?"

Nick glanced from me to the window. "What am I looking for?"

"Anything," I said, slipping away before he could ask any more questions. I didn't want to lie and pretend I'd seen something I hadn't, adding hallucinations on top of paranoia.

"Nothing," Nick called to me as I hit the bathroom and

squeezed toothpaste onto my brush. It was completely tasteless, by which I knew: ambrosia withdrawal.

First taste, then color would leach out of the world. All of my senses, so sharp on the food of the gods, would deaden and dull. My mind would lose focus, my muscles their competency. Things were about to get ugly.

I was going to *have* to pin down an ambrosia supply. Just until we put this wedding behind us, saved Apollo, recaptured Zeus and Poseidon ... Would it never end? I'd never know. As long as I continued on the ambrosia, I'd never be able to trust myself. Were the shakes hyper-caffeination or withdrawal? Was my concern paranoia or prudence? It was no way to live. I knew this. *Knew* it. I knew too that prolonged withdrawal could mean my death. But, if I was being perfectly honest, I didn't believe in my own mortality. It was just an excuse.

I was an addict.

I pushed the thought forcibly aside and got ready as quickly as I could, given that I'd lost all enthusiasm for the outing. I owed it to Nick *not* to keep him cooped up in a hotel for his first visit to Greece, to show him something even I hadn't seen of my native country. I owed it to Apollo to investigate. My own issues were going to have to take a number. Probably that of the beast.

We hit the lobby one minute behind schedule and still had to wait five more for Jesus.

The single road into town wound down the mountain without side streets so much as alleys here and there crowded with yet more houses. Shops took up the first floor of almost all, selling jewelry, souvenirs, local arts and everything else from postcards to purses.

"Oh my!" Jesus said, stopping short before one of the shops, awe in his voice. We halted to keep from crashing into him and followed his gaze up and up to a shelf above our heads in the doorway of the souvenir stand where a bottle of ouzo stood in a satyr-shaped bottle. The reaction was brought on by the fact that the satyr was, in typical satyr fashion ... all revved up and ready to go. More than just erect, his equipment curled upward almost to his chin. The bottles were mainstays of every tourist trap in about every shop in Greece, but whenever I saw the proportions, all I could think of was, "ouch!"

"I've got to get one of these to take back with me," Jesus announced, disappearing into the interior of the shop.

"What about you?" Nick asked, eyes crinkled in deep amusement.

"Who needs the bottle when you've got the real thing?"

He snorted, though the smile on his face said I'd scored points. But it vanished almost instantly, as something in the shop window caught his attention.

"Did you notice anyone following us?" he asked quietly. I forced myself not to look around.

"Where?" I asked.

"Two storefronts back on the other side of the street."

I pulled a hair band out of my pocket and whipped my head to the side, the better to gather my hair into a ponytail, and spotted a man in a black robe, hair crazier than mine, unkempt, facial hair spread over his chest like a bib. He was pretending to study a display of jewelry with the kind of attention Spiro might give a pretty girl … or boy.

"I see him," I said, finishing up with the hairband, lashing my unruly hair into place in case a chase was in the offing.

"You note the way he's staring at the jewelry?" Nick asked.

"Yeah."

"He was staring at *us* like that a second ago. Well, *you* specifically."

You're next. I felt oddly relieved rather than alarmed at the thought. That meant that I wasn't crazy *or* paranoid. I'd felt someone watching back at the hotel. The man in black had to be the culprit, maybe even the one who'd left the note back in Athens. There couldn't be *two* people stalking me. I wasn't that popular.

So, he wasn't a hallucination, but a real threat … potentially. Only one way to find out.

"You're looking a little maniacal," Nick said. "I'm almost afraid to ask what kind of plan is running through your head."

"How about whammying him with the gorgon glare and dragging him off somewhere for questioning?"

Nick looked at me like I'd grown a second head. Okay, so maybe crazy wasn't completely out of the question. "You want to kidnap a man off the street for looking at you funny?"

"Well, when you put it that way … What do you suggest?"

"We keep an eye on him and stop him if he makes a move."

Oh sure, without a badge to flash or any kind of official standing, it was the most sensible course of action. I was just so much better at the direct approach.

"I was afraid you'd say something like that."

Jesus came out then, looking ridiculously pleased with his purchase.

Nick glanced at his watch. "We don't have much time left. Should we grab lunch, like we talked about?"

There was a lovely taverna on the other side of the road, but it was cantilevered out over the edge of the mountain, and there was *no way* that was happening. I said so.

"Gah, I'll get us lunch to go," Jesus said. He handed his precious bottle to Nick. "Here, hold this."

The shape was apparent right through the clear plastic bag. Nick didn't look like he was secure enough in his masculinity to be left holding it. I took pity on the poor man and relieved him of the package.

Jesus came back shortly, juggling three Mythos beers and three gyros. We looked around for a place to eat them. The streets were narrow, with no margin at all between the cars cruising by and the walkway, so that we couldn't sit on a curb without risking our feet, and with sidewalk and storefront space at such a premium, there were no benches.

"*Chica*, I hate to be the one to break this to you, but you are a pain in the ass," Jesus said helpfully.

I looked at Nick. "A good boyfriend would disagree," I told him.

"I'd have aimed higher," he said to Jesus. "Pain in the neck, maybe." I stuck my tongue out in their general direction.

In the end, we risked our toes and ate on the curb, pulling our feet in whenever a vehicle came by. It wasn't dignified, and I expected trouble at any moment over our location with the open containers and all, but as the taste of slow-cooked lamb, onions, tomatoes and tzatziki sauce burst over my taste buds, I forgot to care. In America, every Greek restaurant served gyros. In Greece, Jesus had been lucky to find them. They weren't restaurant, but street food here, like hot dogs and soft pretzels in New York City. But here or there, they were just about perfection. Unfortunately, that first burst of flavor quickly faded away, leaving me unsatisfied. Bereft, even. And no matter how many bites I took, I still felt empty. Hunger gnawed at me like a junkyard dog at a bone.

I glanced up and down the street, looking for our tail, and found him across the way, staring into yet another storefront, not so subtly watching us via the reflection in the window. In that same window I caught sight of a second black robed figure. I pretended to stretch so that I could casually look around. Behind us, half in and half out of a shop, pretending interest in a rack of postcards, was another man in black, more priestly than secret-agency. When he felt me looking, he grabbed up a few of the postcards and disappeared into the shop. I hoped the proprietor got at least a little business out of our creepy surveillance.

"Yeah, I see them," Nick said without me asking.

"The one who just went into the shop ... I think I'd like to talk with him if you'll keep an eye on his friend."

There were no testosterone-fueled protestations that he should be the one to confront the creep, which was one of the many reasons I adored him.

"But no trouble," he warned. "I shudder to think what your *yiayia* would do to me if you were arrested on my watch."

I smiled at the very thought, almost tempted to find out. But not quite.

"I'll be good," I promised, giving him a quick kiss as I jumped off the curb.

I sauntered into the shop the man in black had disappeared into. I didn't bother pretending interest in anything. I'd seen it all before—the embroidered linens, the baubles, the bangles, bottle openers in the shape of satyrs or nymphs, pottery, soaps and oils. I was shopping for a man in a black robe. The shop, as jam packed with touristy trinkets as it was, wasn't very big. I could almost see the whole place at a glance, and the only person in it was the proprietress, who bustled up to me, her reproduction coin earrings jingling, and asked what she could help me with.

Short of tearing apart her shop, all I could do was ask, "A man just came in here. I was hoping to talk with him."

She glanced around the small shop and back at me. "There's no one else here." She looked me right in the eyes as she said it, a little too purposefully, and I knew she was lying. I couldn't blame the man on my ambrosia withdrawal, not if Nick had seen him and this woman was covering for him. I wished, not for the first time, that my powers ran to compelling the truth out of people, but all I could do was stop her in her tracks.

"Freeze," I said, putting everything I had into it.

She froze, mouth half open, as if it had been on the tip of her tongue to say more. But she was going to have to hold that thought.

I stalked to the checkout counter, where three postcards lay abandoned, and peered over it. There was no black robed man crouching behind it. Just to be doubly sure, I rounded the counter for a closer look. Nothing. It took no time at all to survey the rest of the shop. There weren't any other places to hide. There *was* a door at the back, covered over by a tapestry. I might have missed it if the pots in front of it hadn't been slid away to allow access, disturbing the dirt on the shop floor. I dashed to the tapestry, pulled it aside to reveal the hidden door. I yanked on the handle, but it wouldn't budge. Locked. And me without my lock picks. I thought about kicking it in, but given the disturbance in the dirt, the door opened toward and not away from me, and regardless of the way they made it look in movies, I'd break my leg before I'd break most doors. Oh yeah, and there was that whole not-getting-arrested thing. I'd promised.

Regretfully, I admitted temporary defeat and slunk back outside. "Gone," I said to Nick and Jesus as I approached.

"His friend too," Nick said, nodding to where the other man in black had been.

"*Skata.* I've had enough of this cloak and dagger crap already. Why can't we just have a nice, straightforward wedding?"

"Speaking of which, we'd probably better get back. Production meeting in T minus twenty."

"What're you, an astronaut?" I asked, suddenly irritable. Another thing, maybe, to blame on ambrosia withdrawal.

"Am I the only one excited about this?" Jesus asked. "Come." He linked an arm through each of ours, and I grabbed up his ouzo bottle from the curb so it wouldn't be left behind.

We let Jesus drag us off. I continued to look into storefront windows to see if I could spot our sneaky surveillance, but there was no further sign of them.

We met Mom, Dad, Uncle Christos and his girlfriend—which seemed so weird to say at their age, since she was hardly a girl—coming through the door of the hotel, just back from a sightseeing trip of their own.

"Tori!" Mom gasped, throwing her arms around me and waving Dad in for a group hug. He grumbled, as always, but complied. I didn't take it personally. Dad was the least touchy-feely guy I knew. Pretty ironic for someone whose livelihood and welfare depended on making contact—catching and being caught during the family acrobatic act. Maybe that was it. With life and death on the line there, maybe all other contact felt gratuitous. But Mom sure didn't feel that way. She more than made up for him. And gods knew Spiro was touchy-feely enough for them both.

I hugged her back hard. It was so good seeing her again. It'd been hard when circumstances forced me to leave the Rialto Bros. Circus behind. I could have fought for my place, but … I think we'd all known I never really belonged.

When Dad dropped out of the hug and Mom finally let me go, I found I had tears in my eyes. I wiped them quickly away and introduced Nick, who was treated to a handshake from my father—two pumps and done—and a warm embrace from my mother.

"We were so glad when Tori found someone to keep her out of trouble," Mom said, looking earnestly into Nick's eyes. Mom was a petite woman, weighing in at maybe a hundred pounds— less after sweating some off in a performance. She had mounds of dark hair, brown eyes, long lashes and a heart-shaped face. People wanted to protect her. Me, that was a whole 'nother matter.

I shot Nick an amused glance, which he mirrored back to me. "Well, I try, ma'am, but it isn't easy."

"And who is this?" Dad barked, jutting a chin at Jesus, who smiled, bowed deeply and introduced himself.

"I'm Jesus, Christos and Tori's executive assistant at the agency. When trouble calls, I'm the one who takes the message."

I didn't think that came out quite the way he'd intended, since it didn't puff up his importance the way he liked. I blamed jet lag.

"Shall we?" he asked.

Christos made an "after you" gesture, and Jesus led the way to the meeting room—where I was jumped immediately upon entering.

"*There* you are!" Tina said, mugging me. I'd have called it a hug, but her arms were like steel bands propelling me forward, leaving the others in the dust. "Come on, they want to meet my bridesmaids."

"*They?*"

She paused in her manhandling to give me a quick once over. "You look good, except for some puffiness around the eyes. Flying always makes me water-retentive too. Don't worry, we've got a cream for that. Remind me to give you a sample."

I bucked out of her embrace. "Good to see you too. Congratulations, by the way." Just like that, the disapproval left her face, and she beamed like a prison searchlight.

"Sorry. I'm just ... nervous. I want everything to be perfect, and I know the film stuff is paying for my dream wedding, but ... OMG, the stress!"

A young blond man with a pompadour, a shiny vest and a clipboard bustled up to us. "This the last bridesmaid?" he asked, giving me the same critical stare I'd gotten from Tina. "Let's get her with the others."

It was his turn to hustle me about the room ... or try to, anyway. When I growled, he drew back his arm and instead crowded me toward Althea and Junessa.

He eyed the three of us—the Amazon, the wispy wood nymph and *me*, the wild woman, probably still smelling of onions and tzatziki sauce. His face scrunched when he looked at me, but all he said was, "I can work with this."

This.

"*Hello.* Living, breathing person right in front of you," I snapped.

"As if I could miss you breathing," he sniped back.

Damned onions.

"Okay," he said, clapping to get our attention as if we were wayward children. "Tomorrow you're due at 11:00 AM *sharp* for hair and makeup," he said to Althea and Junessa. He pointed to

Tina and then to me. "You and you, 10:00 AM. You're getting the works."

I started to protest that I'd just gotten "the works," courtesy of Christie, and I still wasn't over it, but Tina looked so happy that I bit it back. *Not my day, not my day,* I chanted over and over to myself.

"Also, tomorrow—no alcohol. No caffeine, if you can manage it. Makes you bloaty and adds to those dark circles under your eyes." Why was he looking at me? "Now, off with you. The meeting will start momentarily, and that should tell you everything else you need to know." He made shooing motions, and I stood my ground until Tina bumped my shoulder.

"Thanks for this," she said to me. "I know it's not your thing."

I looked down, feeling like a behemoth next to her, just like I had my mother. Tina, too, was a tiny little thing, small and wiry, the better to fold herself into impossible spaces as the contortionist for the Rialto Bros. sideshow, where Yiayia performed as the bearded lady and where Pappous, rest his soul, had once been the strong man.

Something was different about Tina. I struggled to put my finger on it.

"Your overbite!" I exclaimed. So tactful. And oh-so-obser-vant. How had I not noticed right away?

But she didn't slap me down as I deserved. "You like it? Jason is amazing! Did I tell you how we met?" Of course she had. She'd told anyone who would listen … twice … but I let her go on. "I had my jaw reset. Jason did the work on my face and then fell in love with it. That's what he said. Have you met him yet? He's unbelievable. Tori, I'm so in love!"

The wedding had pretty much tipped me off to that, but once again I bit my lip. Tina and I hadn't always been close—the dainty flower and the tomboy—but we had always been family, and it was good to see her happy. Good to see *everybody* all together again after I'd been away for so long. For a second I was able to forget death threats and mysterious priestly stalker guys and think familial thoughts.

Tina's gaze shifted suddenly to something—someone?—behind me, and I whirled, ready for a fight, only to see an unassuming man with his hands up in the universal "don't hit me" sign.

I hadn't realized I'd swung around into a ready stance. Twitchy. Hair trigger. I was going to have to get better control. I glanced back at Tina for assurance that she knew the stranger before me, and from the look on her face, figured that I'd just met Jason. Good thing he wouldn't have a mark from the impression I'd just left on him.

"Whoa," he said. "Down girl. I'm just here for my beautiful bride." I quickly got out of the way of the lovers as Tina leapt into his arms.

I studied them as they clung to each other. Jason was a head taller than Tina, with light brown hair. He was handsome in a baby-faced kind of way men often grew facial hair to disguise. No piercings or prison tats that I could see. No psycho, serial killer vibe that I could pick up, and my internal alarms didn't buzz, which might not mean anything at all. They tended to be pretty danger-focused, and at the moment he looked like a lover, not a fighter.

Prissy blond boy with clipboard called the production meeting to order before I could be formally introduced, and I refound Nick and Jesus and sat with them to listen to an hour about how we shouldn't look right at the camera, interact with the stars, mug for shots, wear patterns that would strobe on film, drink too much, yada yada, etcetera so forth.

Even so, the room was buzzing with excitement when it was all over. The coffee, tea, fruit and cookies on the food service table at the back of the room gave people an excuse to linger and compare notes on what they'd wear and who might be willing to do who else's hair or lend a hand on makeup.

Althea and Junessa were quick to offer miracle makeovers, though I had no idea when they'd find time to provide them between the rehearsal, dinner and 11:00 AM makeup call. I wondered if they could write off the wedding as an Eterné business expense. I'd bet they'd make a small fortune among the guests.

"I'll catch up with you," I told Nick as we left.

"Where are you going?"

"I have to check in on Apollo and see if he's got a list for me yet of potential enemies. Plus, I want to see what he might know about the men in black."

"I'll go with you," he said, putting a hand to my lower back to escort me.

I panicked. "No," I said, and then thought furiously about what excuse to offer, since I couldn't tell Nick about needing my ambrosia fix.

"I mean, *yes*, that would be great. But I have a better use for you."

"Oh yeah?" he asked suggestively.

"Interviewing Serena."

"Oh."

"Don't say 'oh' like it's some hardship. I'm sure she's recovered from her dead faint by now. But no seducing her secrets out of her."

"What if she starts it?" he teased. I hoped he was teasing, anyway.

"I'll leave that up to you. Just know that while I'm currently unarmed, I'm still dangerous."

"Aw, jealousy, the sincerest form of flattery. I'll try not to be too irresistible."

"Too late," I told him. I stood on the balls of my feet to give him a kiss. Then I called Apollo to find out where he was and if he could tell us where Serena might be, but as soon as the call connected, I felt a zing of forewarning streak through my body and instead of "Hello," I heard, "—answer that!" in a sharp female voice. I was pretty sure what had come before was the command, "Don't."

"I sent it to voicemail," Apollo said on the other end of the phone line.

"Liar. Hand it over."

I didn't know the other voice, but she didn't sound friendly, and my sixth sense sent me running for the stairs, once again ignoring the perfectly good elevator. Just recently, my precognition had developed its own GPS, and when I hit the top floor of the hotel, I looked left and right, and raced in the direction that made my heart pound. Nick pounded along behind me.

Just as we hit the door to Apollo's room, we heard, "Well then, I'll scream." It was the same voice I'd heard on the phone. I had no idea what was going on, but I was going to find out.

"Hotel Security," I called through the door. "Open up."

"Your choice," the woman inside said, too quietly to be intended for my ears, which meant whatever happened next would be up to Apollo.

"Mr. Demas, are you all right in there?" I called.

I reached for the door handle, even though I knew that it wouldn't budge. I hated always being right.

"Help me!" the girl inside suddenly screamed. "He's a beast!"

I planted one foot on the floor and lashed out with my other, like I'd learned in kickboxing class. The door didn't give, but my leg did, pain arcing up like a lightning strike from my heel to my hip. I staggered back, into the far wall, using it to hold me up. Nick checked to see if I was okay and then took a running start at the door himself. As he struck, it seemed to buck on its hinges, splintering around them. He bounced back from the blow and took another shot at the door. This time it gave way, and Nick burst into the room. I pushed myself off the wall and staggered through behind him.

In the center of it, between a bed and a desk the size of an old mainframe computer stood a nearly naked girl, her dress torn and fire in her eyes. I thought she was aiming for fear, but what I saw there was triumph. She launched herself into Nick's arms, sobbing and ranting about how Apollo had attacked her, while I looked from the girl to Nick to Apollo with shock written all over my face.

"Dare I ask what happened?" I said to Apollo, who watched the girl like she was a viper who might suddenly strike.

"Nothing, I swear to you! She did that to herself. Well, first she tried to seduce me for a part in the movie. When that didn't work, she tore her dress and said she'd cry rape if I didn't go along with her."

The sobbing had quieted significantly, I noticed, while the girl listened for what Apollo would say.

"Liar," she yelled, turning on him, but staying within the protection of Nick's arms. She raised tearful eyes to me, squeezing out a drop of moisture. "He saw me in the hotel and said I'd be just perfect for a part in his film. I didn't know I'd be auditioning in his bed. When I refused, he went crazy. He tore my dress and he ... he ... he would have ... if you hadn't come along ..."

Disgust made me want to backhand her, but that would only give her a mark that might help with her story. With all the actual abuse that went on in the world, the thought of someone using a false accusation to get ahead made me more than sick. It made me mad. And I knew it was false. Apollo might not have the best reputation in the world, but if his condition didn't make assault highly unlikely, what I'd overheard of their conversation certainly did.

"Get out," I said to her.

She looked utterly dumbfounded. I was a woman. I should believe her. She turned watery eyes to Nick. I had to admit, she was quite the actress. "Please, you have to believe me. You have to help. What if he does it again and you're not here to stop him?"

Nick took this one. "I don't know the penalty *here* for filing a false police report, but in the States, there's jail time."

Her eyes got really wide. "But, I'm telling the truth."

"Uh huh."

"Tell them," she said, appealing to, of all people, Apollo himself. "I'll drop the whole thing, if you'll just—"

"No," he said.

"Freeze," I said, not prepared to take any more. She froze, her mouth open mid-protest.

I looked from the girl in her ripped dress—sleek chestnut hair straightened to within an inch of its life falling in a shining curtain down to her waist, not at all mussed as if there'd been a struggle over her virtue—to Apollo—looking a lot less spooked now.

"I swear, I never touched her," he said again.

I believed him. But still, she could cause trouble if she really wanted to. "I'm not sure the press will care. It'd be juicy enough to hurt you and the film Uncle Hector's so invested in."

Nick shook his head at me. "You can't just go around freezing people."

"What would you suggest?" I asked.

Because freezing her had been the *most* civil of my thoughts. The ease with which we could hide her body being the least. Not that I'd been serious about that idea.

"Sadly," said Apollo, "this isn't the first time something like this has happened. But last time was back in the States, and I was, uh, with someone already when the girl broke in."

I rolled my eyes.

"We're calling hotel security," Nick cut in, offering that suggestion I'd asked for. "Or the police."

Apollo and I exchanged a glance. That would be the by-the-book way to play it. It was also a likely path to accusations and tabloid headlines. We'd both been there and done that.

"Or I could switch clothes with the girl and we could put her out into the hallway," I suggested.

Nick's eyes narrowed at me, and I didn't think it was just

because of the disparity in our sizes. My clothes would likely swim on the girl. "If you strip her down, *that's* assault."

I sighed. I could see his point, even if I didn't like it.

"Serena could cover for you," I told Apollo. "You're trying to bulk up your 'romance' to promote your film, right? Would she say she was with you when crazy-girl broke in?"

Nick threw his hands into the air and paced to the phone over on the desk. "You will *not* suborn perjury," he said, reaching for the receiver.

I turned on him. "Oh, like you told Internal Affairs that Detective Lau flew off on the back of a dragon? Or that Zeus and Poseidon were ancient Greek gods?"

His tension didn't ease. "I left things out. I didn't lie," he said. "And *you*," he accused Apollo, "are awfully blasé about this whole thing."

Apollo looked as though he tried to grimace and couldn't. "I feel like I've had Botox all over my body. I can barely move. My heart is struggling to beat. Look for me tomorrow and you may find me a grave man."

My heart sank. It was a bad thing when an actor began quoting Shakespearean soliloquies. This one hadn't turned out so well for Mercutio.

Crazy girl twitched, and I demanded again that she freeze. One problem at a time. "So what do we do?" I repeated.

"*I'll* go have a talk with hotel security," Nick announced, brooking no argument. "They need to know they have a breach in any case. I'll tell them what we overheard and what we saw, and we'll get this all worked out. *You two* ..." He glared at each of us in turn. I felt like I was back in LA, facing him across an interrogation table, back when we were more adversaries than anything. It hurt. "Try not to conspire while I'm gone."

He about faced and left, sucking much of the air out of the room with him.

Apollo and I looked at each other. He was ... less than he

had been without his typical glint and smirk to draw you in. His eyes had lost their sparkle. His mouth was set.

"I wish there was something I could do for you," I said, meaning it wholeheartedly.

"I wish you could too. I guess this would be the time to mention you might have a point about Serena. Apparently, she's already campaigning to have me replaced."

"But you said—"

"I know what I said, but if this petrification keeps up, I don't see that they'll have any choice but to find somebody new. It makes me wonder if she knows something we don't about my chances of recovery."

"So she knows your paralysis isn't limited to ..." My gaze dropped somewhere south of the border.

"It's starting to become obvious."

I hadn't liked Serena from the start. It was probably terribly unprofessional of me to feel a little leap of joy at the idea of collaring *her* for the crimes against Apollo.

"I was planning to have Nick interview her. In the meantime—"

"Ambrosia?" he asked.

"How can you tell?"

"You're shaking."

I looked down at my hands. I hadn't even noticed. Not good. *Seriously* not good. I wondered if Nick ... of *course* he had. He was a detective. He noticed everything. Crud cakes.

"Do you have any with you, and would it help *your* situation?" I asked.

"No and no. Gods don't need ambrosia to heal—not from anything natural. As for the unnatural, we can't undo what another power has done ... not unless it's in our wheelhouse. In other words, Zeus could dispel a storm someone else raised, but he couldn't return to water what Dionysus had made into wine. Make sense?"

"Sure, clear as mud. I think I need some kind of course in

remedial mythology. You say 'another power.' So it wouldn't take a god to do this then?"

"Circe could have done it. Or some other enchantress. A few others. No, it wouldn't take a god."

"Gah, this just keeps getting better and better. Anything else I need to know? Any other potential players in this drama? Nymphs … banshees … Big Foot?"

"Nymphs, maybe. I've, uh, had run-ins with a few of them." And by that, he meant liaisons, not all of which would have ended well. "Sirens are water divinities, so they'd be loyal to Poseidon. Can't rule them out. Banshees are second cousins to the sirens, but they only predict the deaths others cause. As for Big Foot, you've got me. Maybe one of the giants still roaming the Earth?"

"Really?" I asked, momentarily sidetracked. "*Whatever.* I'll talk to Serena, but in case we're barking up the wrong tree"— Apollo gave me a dirty look—"I need a list of every divinity you've pissed off in the last millennium. I can run them past Yiayia for last known whereabouts and find out who's in the area."

"Done," he said.

"And the ambrosia—"

"Ask Hermes."

"Hermes?"

He stared. "You haven't figured it out? Tori, Hermes runs a *worldwide messenger service.* The only one as far as the ancients are concerned. Anything imported or exported he's got a piece of the action."

"So the Back to Earth movement—you think he *knew* about their secret ingredient?" We'd busted the Back to Earth cult just months ago. It had been run by Dionysus … *the* Dionysus. He'd not only resurrected his fertility cult, but was lacing the food of his adherents with a special additive, trying to turn his own followers into super-humans, essentially his own Latter-Day Olympians. The problem was, not all survived the transformation. He'd been getting ready to distribute Back to Earth produce on a national level.

"I can't say what he knew about their end game, but their supplies ... yeah, he'd have been involved."

I seethed. I could feel the steam building in my gut, getting ready to burst forth and sear everything in its path. *Hermes.* That dirty, rotten, sleazy, conniving bastard.

"How much can she hear?" Apollo asked suddenly, nodding toward the frozen floozy in our midst.

"Huh?" It was so far off my train of thought that it took me a second to process.

Then I knew fear.

"I've—uh—never tested it." I knew there was disorientation after the freezing, but how much would she have heard and understood? "It's not like anyone would believe what she had to say," I told him, in a whisper now. "I mean, raving about gods and banshees."

"They might. Some do believe that sort of thing. Otherwise we'd all have long since faded away."

There was a knock at the broken door, which seemed to startle the girl out of her paralysis, which was a good thing, because hotel security didn't wait to be invited before sauntering in.

The girl reeled and looked about frantically. She spotted the man in the suit coming through the doorway and launched herself at him. "These people are crazy!" She started. "Please, you have to listen!"

The whites shone all around her eyes, and she looked like a deer in headlights. The security man grabbed her hands as they reached for his shoulders, or maybe his neck, to cling to him. He took them gently but firmly in his hands and looked her in the eyes. "Why don't you come to my office and tell me all about it?"

I sensed the steel under the suggestion, but she seemed to feel that she was getting somewhere and sagged with relief.

Security guy looked over her head at the rest of us. "I'll want your statements as well. Later."

We all nodded back solemnly. The girl didn't have a leg to stand on, but the sick feeling inside my gut said that wouldn't stop her. "You need a keeper," I told Apollo when they left. Only as the words came out of my mouth did I realize I was echoing Jesus.

"Are you volunteering?" Apollo asked. Nick growled.

"There's not enough money in the world," I told him. Ambrosia? Apparently that was another story.

"Nick, why don't you talk to Serena, like we planned. Also ask her about trying to get Apollo replaced on the film. Apollo, you get working on that list. I have to see a man about a"—*drug habit*—"suspect." And so it began ... the lies, the slipping out on my own. No, I didn't have a problem. But apparently it had me.

"Who died and made you boss?" Nick asked.

"No one, yet. I'd like to keep it that way," I answered.

"Oh the drama. I think you might have missed your calling," Apollo said helpfully.

I gave him the stink-eye. "Hey, this is *your* drama. I'm just along for the ride. Everyone has their assignments. We'll reconvene later."

"It'll have to be a lot later," Apollo said. "Sounds like I'll have to talk with security, and then I have to get into makeup. We're doing some of the sunset shots tonight. The conditions are supposed to be perfect. With any luck, the half lighting will hide my ... condition."

"You get gorgeous," Nick said. "Don't worry, we'll do all the heavy lifting." I rolled my eyes. The testosterone levels were starting to get cloying.

I pushed Nick out ahead of me, but thought of something just as we were leaving and turned back.

"Have you noticed any priestly types hanging around, all dressed in black, none-too-subtle?"

Apollo looked surprised. "You mean like Greek Orthodox priests?" Because they too wore the black cassocks.

"Not exactly. Kind of hermit-y looking, really, like they might only come to civilization now and then for supplies?"

He had his thinking face on, eyes up and to the left, as if he were visibly reviewing his mental files. "I don't know about the various sects anymore. Back when our sanctuaries were held sacred, each god and goddess had their acolytes. Now ... the men in black could be anybody."

"Well, keep an eye out. Nick and I were followed today."

"I will. And, Tori, *thank you.*"

I blinked. "Just evening the score."

"Still."

"You're welcome," Nick called from the doorway, a reminder that *he* hadn't been thanked—for his help or the sidelining of his girlfriend.

"Thank you too," Apollo called. "I owe you a boon."

"Just stay away from my girl," Nick said.

My girl—like there was some ownership involved.

"I keep trying," Apollo said, "but apparently our weaves are intertwined."

Before I'd "met" the Fates—Clotho, Atropos and Lachesis, that would have seemed like poetic drivel. But the three sisters wove our destinies. I'd seen my thread nearly cut from the great weave, the pattern more complex than I could ever follow. I knew that what Apollo said was true. If our destinies were interwoven, it was beyond even his power to untangle them. And it was clear to me that Clotho, Atropos and Lachesis had watched *way* too many soap operas in their time. They enjoyed the drama.

I didn't want to think about that. I finished pushing Nick out the door, followed him through and shut it behind me as best I could.

"Seriously," Nick asked, once we were alone, "what do you see in that guy?"

"I don't see anything in him. I'm with you."

"Uh huh. Try telling him that. Anyway, I guess I'm off to interview a gorgeous, green-eyed starlet. But not to worry, I'm with you."

Jealousy kicked me in the gut even though the interview was my idea. "Fine. Point taken. I'll try not to be an ass about it if you aren't."

Nick smiled, and it lit up those midnight blue eyes of his. "Deal." Serena would never know what hit her.

I pulled out my phone and dialed Hermes. "Where are you?" I demanded.

"The hotel bar," he answered, amusement thick in his voice. "Where are *you*? And while we're on this path, what are you wearing?"

"I'm on my way."

"And to the second question?" he asked.

"My butt kicking boots."

"Nothing else?" he asked hopefully.

"No, I'm prowling the hotel au naturel." A cleaning lady I passed looked at me, startled. "You'll see for yourself in a moment. Stay where you are."

"Sir, yes, sir," he said and hung up.

He wouldn't believe me, as well he shouldn't, but maybe I'd intrigued him enough to stay put. We needed to have words.

Thank gods *this* hotel bar was on the ground floor rather than the rooftop with a grand view out over the clouds. I still hadn't managed to catch a full breath, and felt on the verge of hyperventilating or blowing up into a full-on panic attack at any second. If Tina had picked some mountaintop chapel for her ceremony—and, really, what other options were there here at the top of the world?—I was going to lose it. Maybe it wasn't ambrosia I needed. Maybe it was Xanax. Or a cybercafé where they could just Skype me in for the ceremony.

I found Hermes drinking alone at the bar, two tall glasses in front of him full of clear liquid. Water? Surely not.

He slid one toward me as I sat down on the stool next to him, and I gave him the hairy eyeball. "What is it?" I asked.

"Try it and see."

I looked around for the bartender, hoping for a straighter answer, but no one was in evidence. I held the glass up to my nose and sniffed. My eyes nearly rolled back into my head at the scent. When I tried to chase down a comparison, the smell seemed to shift on me—jasmine and honeysuckle one minute, then vanilla and sandalwood, cinnamon and cloves ... In short, heaven.

"What is it?" I asked again, unable to wait for his answer before tipping the glass back to let just a drop touch my lips.

The taste exploded on my tongue, starting small and then overpowering my taste buds like one of those kids' toys that expanded exponentially in water. It was—

"Nectar," he said, the glint in his eyes jollier than Old Saint Nick's and at least a hundred times more mischievous.

My heart kicked, and I would have spat it back, but it had disappeared, seemingly straight into my being, skipping mundane things like my stomach.

"Nectar as in ... *nectar*. Of the Gods?"

"Is there any other kind?"

"But—"

"Oh, the bartender won't mind. I slipped him a *very* nice tip to assure he wouldn't notice me pouring from my own flask."

"But I'm not—"

"A god? Well on your way, I'd say. You've survived the ambrosia. And you know what they say—what doesn't kill you makes you stronger."

My hands trembled as I pushed the glass away. It took all my willpower to actually let it go. I knew, *knew* nothing would ever taste the same again, and considering that everything had already gone to ashes ...

I glared at Hermes. "What's happening to me?" I asked him.

He always seemed to know more than he should. Maybe he had answers he shouldn't.

"You tell me."

"Why are you trying to suck me deeper in?" I asked.

"Why are you trying to get *out*?" he countered.

"None of your business," I said. This wasn't going at all the way I intended. I had to retake control, if I'd ever had it. "Look, I do want to get out, but not until after this whole wedding thing and—" I couldn't say it. Bad enough going to Apollo, but he was the one who'd hooked me, and I felt that in some twisted way he owed me, even though the ambrosia had saved my life. But this—this was like meeting my dealer. I'd lied to Nick ... or anyway left out a critical part of the truth ... and I felt like I was about to make a deal with the devil.

"And what?" he asked.

"Nothing. Forget I mentioned it." I started to stand, and Hermes grabbed my arm, stopping me. I was afraid he'd feel me shaking and tried to pull back.

"Wait," he insisted. "You came here for a reason. Here, I'll buy you a drink more to your liking." He snapped his fingers, and the bartender appeared like magic from a narrow doorway in the back wall, practically hidden behind a wood-latticed area with wine bottles filling every slot.

"What'll you have?" Hermes asked. I was surprised he'd bothered to solicit my opinion, he'd been so high-handed so far.

"Diet Coke," I ordered.

"Come," he said, "you can do better than that."

"You asked. I answered," I said, waiting to see if it took before retaking my seat.

The bartender waited, looking for Hermes's approval before making a move. Either he was a male chauvinist by nature or that'd been a helluva tip Hermes had given him. Hermes gave the bartender a wink and a nod, and I watched carefully to make sure there were no special additives. Even then, I took only a small sip before committing. Seemed fine. Tasted like swamp water. I sighed and looked longingly at the nectar.

"So, you came for more than my scintillating company?" Hermes asked.

"What did you know about the Back to Earth movement, and when did you know it?" I snapped.

"Is that the question you really want to ask?" he said, downing the last of the nectar in his glass and pushing it aside, just like my question. "What's done is done. No longer relevant."

"It's relevant to *me*."

"What's relevant to *me* is that you sit here in a bar discussing a case that is closed instead of looking into what ails my friend Apollo."

"Fine, what do you know about that?"

"Nothing. If I'd wished him harm, I would have taken a backseat when Dionysus and his bacchae were out for his blood. Or when Hades and his brood …"

"You didn't exactly help."

"No, but I warned. As far as the fight, what would have been in it for me?"

I wanted to hit something. Him, by preference. But I had the feeling that wouldn't go well. Not in my current, shaky, under-oxygenated state.

Hermes was playing some kind of game. He was always in the thick of things—warning, needling, riddling. Never quite helping or hindering. But he'd just given something away I don't think he'd intended. Whatever he *had* done, there'd been something in it for him. I just had to figure out what.

"You tell me," I said, echoing his earlier words. "What's in it for you now?"

"No," he said simply. Cheerfully. "That's for me to know and for you to figure out. So much more fun that way. Here, we'll play twenty questions. By my count, you've already used, hmm, let's say ten, so choose the rest wisely, Grasshopper. And for every question I answer, I get to ask another."

Gah! More games.

"Fine. First question: did Dionysus get his ambrosia supply from you?"

"Yes. My turn."

"Wait, yes? Just like that? Did you know what he was planning to *do* with all that ambrosia?"

"Tsk, tsk, tsk, you're really not very good at this, are you? That was two more questions already. You are down to seven and I haven't even asked my first."

I was afraid my teeth would crack from me grinding them. *"Fine,"* I said again. "Shoot."

"How many gifts has Apollo given you?"

It took me a minute to process. I'd expected Hermes to go for something crazy personal, like my bra size, or grill me about Christie and how best to get into her bikini briefs. I'd never expected a serious question. It was on the tip of my tongue to ask why he wanted to know, but thank goodness I wasn't oxygen deprived enough to let it out and waste yet another of my questions. Which meant the strategy of answering a question with a question was right out. No playing dumb for me. And I didn't know Hermes well, but it didn't take a genius to realize that if I didn't answer his query, he'd be finished answering mine.

"Just the one," I said. He hadn't asked me *what* the gifts were. Just how many. Two could play at his game of minimalist responses.

"Very good," he said, eyes glittering.

"Now, about that ambrosia," I prompted.

"I never asked Dionysus what he intended with it," Hermes said.

Ah ha. "That wasn't my question," I told him, pinning him with my no-nonsense gaze. "I asked what you *knew*, not what you inquired, or what you were told."

The glittering in his eyes took on a more sinister glint, like snake venom.

"I knew that it was too much ambrosia for personal use. Beyond that, I could only speculate."

Damn, and double damn. Hypothesizing didn't count as *knowing*. I was going to have to start thinking like a lawyer. Or a snake-in-the-grass trickster god.

"Now," he said, "what exactly has Apollo given you and what have you given in return?"

He cupped his hands together under his chin and stared steadily at me, awaiting my response.

"That's two questions," I said, "linked together by an 'and.'"

He gave me a crocodile smile. "Why, so it is. Which brings us neck and neck at seven questions remaining."

"Fine. He's given me precognition and I haven't given him a thing." Except grief, but I was pretty sure that didn't count.

I had to think carefully about my next questions. "So let me be really clear," I said after a moment. "The Back to Earth plans to addict people to ambrosia are no more." I made it a statement. "Do you have plans to pick up where they left off?"

"You're getting better at this," he commented. "There is far too much regulation in the food industry. No, I have no intention of picking up their mantle. Now, back to Apollo. You haven't yet given him anything in return. But what do you owe?"

The question chilled me, because the answer was more complicated than it should have been. Overtly, I didn't owe anything. I hadn't asked for my precognition, and Apollo had never mentioned any strings attached, but I knew the story of Cassandra, the prophetess of Troy. Apollo had given her the power to see the future, only to curse her never to be believed when she spurned his advances. Hermes had centuries more knowledge of Apollo than I had. Could it be that my bill had not yet come due? Or could Apollo have learned from his mistakes and outlived his past? I knew what I *wanted* to believe. But wanting didn't make it so.

"I don't know," I answered.

"Ah," he said, unhelpfully. "Ah."

Now I was torn. As much as I wanted to ask him about the consequences of doing the little dance Apollo and I were doing, I only had six questions left. I suspected that Hermes was *trying* to sidetrack me, which meant I couldn't let it happen. Plus, the wedding rehearsal beckoned and I still had to change. I needed to start asking essay questions. Yes and no answers were getting me nowhere.

"What's your present scheme?" I asked him.

"Scheme? Singular? Oh ho, girl, I'm hurt. You underestimate me."

"You haven't answered the question."

"I'm trying to play fair. Do I tell you about my very explicit plans for your charming friend or do I share with you ... no, no, I think I'll keep that one to myself. Let's just say that Back to Earth, in addition to showing poor judgment, thought too small. Health food, bah. Some will want it, yes, but not enough. Ask yourself, what is it that everyone wants? Where's the real money?"

My heart clenched. People were dead because of the Back to Earth cult. If Hermes was thinking even bigger we were in trouble. Was he still trafficking in ambrosia? Nectar? Either one was more addictive than crack and twice as deadly to kick, at least for mere mortals. Even granted that the gods weren't known for keeping it in their pants, so traces of their bloodline would be flowing through a whole lot of veins, it still left tons of people in danger. Even those with a smidgen of divine blood weren't guaranteed to survive the kind of changes ambrosia would make to their system. And should access to the drug suddenly stop for any reason, death was the likely end game.

"You can't," I gasped.

"My dear, I don't know who you think you're talking to, but I surely can. Also, you still have no idea what exactly we're talking about."

"So enlighten me."

Hermes clicked a finger against his teeth thoughtfully, annoyingly. "Have you not heard all the doomsday prophecies?" he asked. "They're not really about the end of the world. They're about the end of *this* incarnation. Out with the old, in with the new. The system's broken. Rapture or zombie apocalypse, either way things aren't intended to stay the same. I'm just planning to"—he pretended to pluck the right phrase out of midair —"guide the course of future events."

He was a maniac. Unconsciously, I'd distanced myself, leaning away. "You're insane," I told him.

He looked me dead in the eyes. "Am I? If you saw a train wreck coming, wouldn't you wrest control of the train to avert the crisis? I know you. You'd do it in a heartbeat. We're the same."

"We're not."

"I assure you, we are. And you don't want to be a thorn in my side on this. Thorns get removed. With prejudice."

I stared, stunned, unable to form a response. Suddenly everything—Apollo's petrification problem, my ambrosia withdrawal and overcomplicated love life—seemed petty. What was Hermes up to? What was his end game? Was there—

My brain stuttered to a stop, and it took everything I had to force it to go on.

Was there a chance that I'd somehow been a pawn in Hermes's game, whatever it was? Had he helped me before so that I would remove the greater gods from the playing field— Zeus, Poseidon, Dionysus, Hephaestus, even Hades to the extent that he was still sulking? Who was left to stop him? Little old me? My gorgon glare didn't work on the older gods. What else did I have? My precognition was no good without the *power* to stop my visions.

"Are *you* responsible for what's happening to Apollo?" I asked suddenly.

"You're getting colder. As I've said, I don't have anything

against Apollo. Even if I did, I'd hardly need to waste my time on him with Zeus and Poseidon on the loose and happy to run him down."

Hermes reached in front of me and grabbed my glass of nectar, tossing back the remainder. Then he returned the glass to the bar and rose from his stool.

"By my count, there are still questions to be asked and answered. However, I believe you have a rehearsal to get to, and I have a … thing. So, we'll have to pick up again another time."

He threw money down on to the bar to cover my soda—too much—and strode out as if he didn't have a care in the world. Meanwhile, he'd just rocked mine, and not in the good way. I tossed back my soda like it was something a helluva lot stronger and sat there stunned as it bubbled its way down.

But not for long. I didn't have the luxury of time to process what I'd just heard. I had notes to compare with Nick and a wedding rehearsal to get to. If Hermes was in business with Uncle Hector, maybe I could even manage to squeeze some information out of him between learning where to stand and how to adjust the bride's train just so for pictures.

I pulled out my phone to call the room, to see if Nick had escaped Serena's clutches so I'd know where to meet him—changing seemed a no-go given how much time the interview with Hermes had set me back. But the phone just rang until the hotel voicemail picked up. I left a message telling him I was on my way, in case he got back to the room before I did, then hung up and dialed Christie. I was going to have to warn her off Hermes and find a way to make sure the warning took. I didn't know what he was up to besides "no good," but I didn't want her stuck in the middle of it.

I decided to take the stairs rather than the elevator up to my room, afraid I'd lose cell service. I took the steps two at a time while I waited for Christie to answer … and waited. She was probably off at her shoot. I hit my floor and stepped out of the stairwell, about to leave Christie a message, when something lashed out from nowhere to knock the phone from my hand. It was so close to my ear that the blow caught that too, and my head whipped around with the force of the impact. I caught a glimpse of black robes, and then that black seemed to fly at my head and was suddenly smothering me. Fabric choked off my vision and my air as something was yanked over my head. Frenzied, I lashed out every which way. I made impact with something that *oofed*, but then I got lightheaded. The hood over my head smelled sickly sweet and ...

My body fell like a disarticulated skeleton. I lost consciousness before I ever hit the floor.

CHAPTER EIGHT

"The world is a construct of our observation and experiences. Still, it's disconcerting when it winks out."
—Tori Karacis

My eyes snapped open as my body rocked roughly into something that grunted in pain. But opening them didn't help; something was blocking my view. I couldn't see, couldn't breathe. I remembered then being grabbed and reflexively jerked my hands toward my face to remove whatever kept me in the dark, but they wouldn't move, lashed as they were to the sides of my body by some sort of restraint.

"Tori?" a voice came from beside me, the same direction as the grunt. It was muffled, but still identifiable.

"Apollo?"

He let out a breath. "Thank gods it's you and you're okay," he said softly.

With every breath I took, I felt more lightheaded rather than less, and I knew the hood over my head must have been treated with something like chloroform. I didn't think I was meant to wake, at least not so soon. Ambrosia gave me almost godlike powers of healing, but with so much time passed since my last fix, I didn't know how long that would last.

I had to focus on keeping awake.

An engine coughed and then roared to life, and I could feel the rumble of the machine all around us. Wherever we were, we'd soon be on the move with no one knowing where to find us or even that we were missing yet. And the only person who could sense my alarm, through our unwanted mind link, forged when he granted my precognition, was right here with me.

"Can you move?" I asked in a whisper.

"No, you?"

"No."

"See?" he asked.

"Not a thing."

We were both silent then. What was there to say? Apollo was the god of many things—the sun, music, poetry, prophecy ... none of them action hero oriented. Oh, he was wicked with a bow and arrow, but partial petrification and the lack of an actual weapon didn't bode well for fighting our way out. Ditto for me. I could stop men in their tracks, but only if I could look them in the eyes. Whoever these men in black were, they'd come prepared. But for what? Who were they? Why were they after us? Where were they going?

All good questions. I wanted to demand the answers, but I didn't see a reason for anyone to respond to me, even if I could make myself heard over the engine.

I squirmed as best I could, trying to determine, at least, whether we were in the trunk of a car or somewhere a bit more spacious. I hadn't gotten the sense of a cramped space when I'd been struggling to bring my hands to my face, and sure enough, I could wiggle around freely, except backward, where I pressed up against Apollo's hard body. And not just gym-hard, either. It was clear the petrification had spread.

"I don't suppose that's something useful you're sporting, is it? Like the handle of some kind of sword?" I asked him.

He snorted. "It's called a haft, and no, that's not what you're feeling. Although, as far as usefulness, that would depend on the situation."

I supposed that was true. If rescue depended on writing an SOS in the snow, he'd certainly be packing the right equipment. The mental picture somehow made breathing a little easier. My panic started to recede.

"Thank you," I whispered.

"Don't mention it."

I wondered with that strange empathy between us whether he was breathing a little easier as well. I was glad he only sensed my emotions and not my mental pictures.

"So, how are we getting out of here?" I asked.

A sudden hard turn rocked me away and then back into him. Damned switchbacks. Were we climbing *higher* on Mount Parnassus? I was instantly back to hyperventilation and light-headedness.

"Wait and see?" Apollo suggested. I could barely remember what we were talking about, gripped in the steel bands of fear.

Apollo squirmed closer to me, putting a chin over my shoulder to hold me in place as the vehicle rocked and twisted us farther away from help. "Hey, hey," he murmured near my ear, "it's going to be all right. I'm a god, remember. I didn't get to be this insufferably arrogant without cause."

He was trying to make me laugh, and I appreciated the attempt, but this time ... I blacked out for a second as the scent of the sack over my head overwhelmed me and came back to him urgently whispering my name. "Tori! Stay with me, Tori. We're going to need our wits about us."

I couldn't feel engine vibration anymore. "Have we stopped?" I asked, still groggy.

"Yes," he whispered.

"Where?"

"Delphi," he said.

Well, duh … But wait, did he mean the sanctuary and not the town? Given his connection to the place, maybe he could sense it like he could me … things bound to him. I pushed the thought down into a deep dark place along with my fear of the heights. Or I tried to.

"Your place of power?" I asked to be sure. "Can you—?"

"Trying," he said. "There've been a few reenactments here over the years, some things that have kept the faith, but mostly lots and lots of tourists. I have to dig deep."

The vehicle rocked on its wheels and a door slammed, then a second. Another one opened and in rushed cold air. Suddenly, Apollo's comforting form was ripped away from me, and I heard him *ooph* as he hit the ground. I felt the impact myself as a sharp pain shooting up my back, a disturbing new feature of our connection. Was it the power of the place or the strengthening of my sixth sense with the elimination of my sight?

Someone grabbed me by the ankle, and before I could react, I was sliding backward myself, bumping over indeterminate things that clanked and bruised. Metal tools, maybe.

I braced for the impact with the ground, but as I started to drop, I was grabbed around the waist and hoisted up onto someone's back, a shoulder creasing my gut. I hung there like a sack of potatoes, my nose smashed up against knobby vertebrae.

I let out an "ouch" and started to squirm. My captor stumbled with the ferocity of my fight, and a second later pain burst through my skull as I was knocked over the head.

My awareness fled like shadows from Zeus's lightning.

Fear woke me again. Pounding fear, and someone nudging my shoulder. "Tori. Tori, wake up, please."

"Huh?" I asked brilliantly.

The pounding fear receded, and I realized it hadn't been my own. I realized something else as well—I could see. Not much. Just enough to know that my view was unobstructed, but wherever we were wasn't bright enough for much detail.

"I pulled it off with my teeth," Apollo said, "as soon as I managed to get rid of mine."

I squirmed around until I was facing him, ignoring the protests of my bruised body ... and froze when I saw that the slight glow which allowed me to see anything at all was coming from him.

"Sun god," he explained without me asking. "They don't realize it, but the guys who captured us are fueling my power with their belief. Whoever they are, they know *exactly* who they've taken hostage."

"They?"

"Your men in black. Skinny, unshaven, look like they haven't bathed in a while. Smell like earth, patchouli and incense." Right, I remembered.

"What do they want with us?"

"They're waiting for dark," he said, looking away.

"Apollo—"

Reluctantly, he met my gaze again. "What do they want?" I repeated.

Apollo threw himself forward, and a wave of feeling swept me, crashing over me, submerging me just as his lips hit mine. Hot and still soft. The petrification hadn't made it that far yet. I was so stunned, so overwhelmed, I just lay there. Lust and love and want and fear and regret and resentment, right and wrong and even more right ... they were all jumbled, all powerful, and all poured into the kiss.

My arms strained against my bonds, desperate to get around Apollo even while I tried to find enough of myself left to push him away, but there wasn't enough of me that wanted to, not enough to pull together into action.

The impact felt … cataclysmic.

I thought I'd drown in him with the tsunami of emotion crashing over me. I made a sound, like a whimper. Too much. It was all too much. He drew back.

I found his gaze easily enough, and he looked concussed.

"No," I said, now that *he'd* found the power to stop. It was too little, too late, and I wasn't even sure whether I was telling him no, don't stop or finally drawing the line.

"I had to," he said softly. "If we're going to die, I had to do that at least one more time. But it … it wasn't like the first time. It was …"

I latched onto the one part that I could deal with, as twisted as that was. "Die?" I asked.

My voice didn't even quiver. No, that was for the rest of me, still shaking from the emotional storm or from ambrosia withdrawal or just from the cold.

"Have you ever heard of the Selli?" he said.

Holy non-sequitur, Batman. "The who?"

"Zeus's priests, from back in the old days. Based on their talk, that's who we're dealing with here, a surviving sect, still doing his bidding."

"Lovely, and the dying part?"

"They seem to be planning a blood sacrifice."

When I'd joined my uncle's PI business, I knew there'd be times when things might get a little hairy, but I was thinking hand-to-hand combat, maybe, or a shootout or two in the entire course of my career. Blood sacrifice had never even popped up on my radar.

"I'm sorry, my hearing must not be working. *Blood sacrifice?*"

Apollo was silent for a second, and I could sense him listening, making sure no one was on their way back for us before he asked gravely, "How much do you know about Delphi?"

"Dedicated to you, site of the famed Oracles … um, that'd be about it." I'd intended to read up before we came, but there'd never been time.

"This was a sacred site well before I came along, dedicated to the Titan Rhea, the mother of Zeus, etc. I sort of … took it over."

"By wrestling the Pythian Serpent," I remembered. It was a pretty famous story.

Ranked right up there with Hercules strangling the hydra in his crib.

"I was young and stupid. And, in my defense, the time of the Titans had passed. Rhea had seen her husband Kronos devour their children. It seemed to be a popular thing to do back then. Then she saw him deposed by Zeus, whom she'd saved from being eaten by feeding Kronos a stone instead. She'd watched Zeus battle her fellow Titans for supremacy. Her heart just wasn't in the whole goddess thing anymore. Anyway, I didn't defeat her so much as repurpose her place of power. She'd already more or less withdrawn with the other Titans."

"And the point of the history lesson?" I asked, my back shrieking at me as I nearly dislocated my shoulders in the attempt to get loose of my bonds.

"The point is that Delphi has always been strategically important. The story goes that when Zeus let free two doves from either side of the world, they met in Delphi. The ancients called it the 'naval of the world.' There's a great deal of power here."

"Where does the sacrifice come in?"

"From what I've overheard, they want to awaken the power of the place, I suspect to somehow restore Zeus to his former glory."

"Does it have to be *our* blood?" I asked. Not that spilling anyone else's was okay in my book. What I wanted to know was whether, if we got free, they'd go after softer targets. How deadly were these guys? Priests, that didn't sound so scary … until I thought about augury and reading entrails and the ritual sacrifices of various religions in bygone days.

"It has to be my blood, at the least. My ties here are strong.

They'll need to be broken before others can be established, just as I had to spill the blood of the Pythian Serpent, Rhea's avatar, to make Delphi my own." We were both silent for a second at that. "On the upside, there may be a window of opportunity after my blood reawakens the sanctuary and before I grow too weak when we might be able to seize the moment."

It wasn't much, but it was hope, and I latched onto it. As much as I didn't want to walk that aisle tomorrow in a puke-green gown, going out this way seemed even worse. I might die of something other than embarrassment.

"Are you fading?" I asked suddenly.

"Sun's going down," Apollo said, meeting my gaze. "I can't hold the light much longer."

Skata. I looked quickly around, hoping to see more than I'd seen before, squinting, trying to extend my senses. If only I'd asked Hermes about that ambrosia after all. Funny how he now seemed the lesser of two evils. But as far as I could see, which wasn't far, there was nothing that could be used as a weapon. Earth and stone, all well-fitted together. No loose stones or jagged edges.

"Where *are* we?" I asked.

"At a guess, the Athenian Treasury. It's the only intact structure on site."

"Great." Nothing better than a prison meant to hold valuables in and intruders out. "Do you have anything we can use to get free?" I asked. "Pocket knife, unclipped toenail. *Anything?*"

"Just my teeth," he answered.

Phantasmagorical. The way his light was starting to dim, there was no way we had time for him to chew through my bonds or for me to untie him.

Especially not when the sound of stone sliding against stone signaled that our time was up. Apollo let his glow go out, but it was replaced by the blaze of flashlights striking our faces.

"Don't look in her eyes!" a male voice called out in Greek. "Get the cover back over her face," he further demanded.

The lights flicked away from our faces and over the ground, as no doubt they searched for the hoods that had cut off our sight.

My precognition kicked into high gear, but it didn't take a psychic to know that my hood couldn't be hard to find and that I'd soon be blind again, in addition to helpless. I tried desperately in the dark to search out the eyes of our kidnappers, to catch them with the gorgon glare, but they were too wary, and in no time, I was grabbed from behind, the hood once again yanked over my head.

Then I was hoisted up off the ground and against someone's chest, being force-marched out of wherever we were. I already knew flailing around only made my bonds cut into my flesh and didn't do a damned bit of good, so I changed my strategy. This time I tried to make myself smaller, cringing in on myself, trying to loosen the bonds now that I'd hopefully strained and stretched them in my earlier struggle. I felt them ease up, but they were still a long way from falling to the ground, and as soon as I expanded my chest for a breath, they'd tighten back up again.

I wasn't the damsel in distress sort, counting on rescue, though under the circumstances I couldn't help but wish that Nick or Uncle Christos or *someone* would come looking for us. But who would know to search for us *here*?

I could feel when we stepped from wherever they'd been keeping us into the fresh air. For one, whoever held me pressed down hard on my head to get me to duck through an exit clearly smaller than I was. For another, the night air was cooler. There was very little breeze, but at this altitude—

A lethal injection of fear shot through me at the thought. Here we were at the top of Mount Parnassus *and I couldn't see a thing*. The kidnappers could walk me straight off a cliff, and I'd never know it until I was banging tits over tail down the side of the mountain, my body crashing against every cliff and outcropping, screaming in terror all the way, at least until the pain or the fatal blow knocked me out.

I froze in fear, unable to take another step into the unknown. My kidnapper tripped at my sudden stop, knocking me forward. I panicked, twisted, trying frantically to clutch at him, to take him with me as I fell, but he was faster.

"Tori!" Apollo called out, feeling my fear and probably thinking the worst.

I was shocked as hell when I hit the ground hard instead of dead falling into nothingness. As I hit, I heard a sharp blow and a cry of pain, which I felt against my temple. Phantom pain ... Apollo's. I knew then that he'd been struck for calling out. I listened for what was happening, but I heard nothing, felt nothing. Had he blacked out? Surely just that.

"Let's get them into place," the man giving orders said as my captor wrestled me back upright.

"Gi, help him."

Or, it sounded like *Gi* anyway. It might have been a name or a letter. But if I didn't live, it would hardly matter. Unless I could somehow follow up from beyond the grave.

I concentrated on the link between me and Apollo. Unwanted as it was, I'd spent the time since learning of it in denial and had done my best to keep my emotions from leaking out. So I didn't know what it could do. Could I goose him back to consciousness? Feed him some of my strength? Did I have enough to spare?

Apollo had told me that it was strong emotion that leaked through our connection. I used that now. I let all of my fear pour out, all of the gratitude I'd never been able to show him for fear that he'd take advantage of the debt I owed. But I was still holding back, and I knew it. If I admitted to the knowledge that I'd always been able to count on Apollo, that no matter how I pushed him away, he'd always been there for me, then I'd have to acknowledge that I'd been unfairly holding his past against him. Who wouldn't make *some* really heinous mistakes over the course of a few millennia? If I admitted all that … then Nick was the only thing really keeping us apart. Not that he wasn't enough.

Nick. What would he think when he discovered me gone?

Apollo's eyes snapped open. I knew it, because the world suddenly came into view, and I knew I wasn't seeing it through my own eyes. It was strange, though, like an out-of-body experience. I was disoriented by the difference between where my body knew itself to be and where I felt … and saw … that I was. So the men in black hadn't replaced Apollo's hood as they had mine. Okay, that I got, but seeing through his eyes? This was new.

All around were quiet columns and silent structures lit only by a nearly full moon that seemed far closer here than at home, as if we could reach up and lasso it like in the old Pecos Bill tall tales.

Then suddenly Apollo's vision canted in a stomach turning twist, and I felt a cold blunt pain to my back, as if he was slapped down onto something. A broad column base? Some kind of altar?

The vision tweaked out as I was slammed down as well and a more immediate pain rose up in my back.

"She weighs more than she looks," my captor complained gruffly, and I thought *damn, he'd better kill me now or I'll make him pay for that.*

Not that I cared so much, really, but the anger kept the fear at bay. "Blades," his compatriot ordered.

Someone else came forward. I heard it in the swish of his robes. So there were at least three … against the two of us, all trussed up. But conscious. At least we had that.

Then the chanting began. One voice started—one strong voice that I almost, *almost* understood. Not quite Greek, but not quite anything else. Like the difference between modern and old English. I felt like if he'd pause between each word or if I could see it written out, I *might* grasp the meaning, but none of that was about to happen. Then the other voices joined in, and there was no chance to decipher. It wasn't musical, but it was intense. Something seemed to rise up from the ground and shiver through me. My skin pricked with power, suddenly too tight for my body. My hair wanted to stand on end, but couldn't, held down almost painfully by my hood and clothes, which, like my skin, felt too constricting. I wanted to be naked, and I didn't, because then I'd have no protection. But also no restrictions. Against what, I had no idea, but it felt like everything surrounding me was leashing something in and at the same time felt too fragile to hold for long. Like a water balloon filled to bursting.

The chanting hit a crescendo, and I could feel movement I couldn't see off to my side, something crashing down, disturbing the swirls of power pricking me within and without. Apollo cried out, and pain exploded in my chest, as if I'd been the one pierced. An immense rush of power—too much, too intense, like raw nerves being cauterized—rushed into me where I felt the phantom blade ... like an electroshock to my heart. It spread throughout my body, wakening my limbs and blasting through any barriers I still had in my brain. Light flashed through my head as the power spread like ball lightning across every single synapse. I arced up off the altar they'd placed me on. I was an overloaded conduit, bursting with the power and pain. I was going to go up in flames.

Then suddenly, I wasn't just arcing off, but rising up off the altar ... floating. The power took me over, within and without. Hands grabbed for me, but I barely felt them. They were insignificant in the face of what I felt myself becoming.

Knowledge and insight bombarded me. Not in any way I could grasp and hang onto, build into a picture, but with snippets and snapshots and feeling and *knowing*. I could see the past and the present and the *future*. Was this what Apollo's oracles had felt in this place? Was this what had driven them mad? Caused them to speak in riddles?

Somehow, my hood was gone, and I could see outside my

head as well as within.

Three men stood below me, as I floated up like a saint ascending, my hands down to my sides, still tied, though I knew I could end that at any time. The men looked panicked. This hadn't been any part of their plan. I knew it, and I laughed. What came out ... there was something alien to it. I had my own reverb. I was *more* than me.

Apollo lay on a slab of stone, staring at me, somehow still alive, even though his chest lay cracked open like a walnut. Like Prometheus, who'd had his heart pecked out each day by eagles ... or his liver, depending on the source. *Liver*, I knew suddenly. I knew everything.

One of the priests rushed to Apollo's head and put the blade to his throat as if he would slit it if I made a move.

"*No!*" I roared. I felt the power reverberate out of me like sound waves. The priest with the knife was knocked to the ground and sat stunned.

Apollo moaned in pain. The other two men in black backed away from the scene.

"*I am Rhea,*" I said, shocking myself. My eyes widened, I knew, but it was the only thing I seemed capable of controlling. If they were windows to the soul, then I wasn't the only one looking through them. *I wasn't alone.* The power I felt flowing through me wasn't mine. *Rhea?* The *Rhea?*

"If there is any more blood to be spilled here, *I* will spill it," the voice issuing from me continued. "I" looked at Apollo. "You will not reclaim this place of power. I have found a new avatar, and it is mine now."

The priest on the ground didn't rise. He didn't dare. But he did recover himself enough to say, "Mother Rhea, we've come to kill Apollo, your usurper, so that he will never bother you again."

"*Liar!*"

It thundered out of me with a force that shook the earth and cowered the men in black. I felt her satisfaction throughout my body, a rush like the high of ambrosia hitting my system. But then I saw Apollo's chest cavity quiver, the knife still embedded within, and I tried to fight back the euphoria. I didn't know if the knife was enough to kill him, if even now he lay dying. I was afraid I might find out. I struggled to rise up and retake my own body, to help him. But Rhea seemed to thrash in my mind, throwing me against the walls of my own skull. "Do you think I don't know all? See all? What else have I to do these many millennia but watch and wait?" I realized that she wasn't even talking to me. She could squash me like a fly with barely a thought. No, the priests held her focus. "You have not come to drive out the usurper but to install a new one in his place. Zeus might have taken my kingdom, but he couldn't hold it, could he?"

The priests didn't answer, but two of them looked to the leader, as if he might have a response that would appease her … or a plan. He looked lost, terrified, and trying not to show it. He glanced around frantically for inspiration to fuel any kind of plan. I saw it … or *she* saw it, which right now was the same thing but with more potential for trouble.

But we—*she*—waited, interested to see which path he'd choose, because I could feel all the promise in the air. My brain —*hers*—unfocused, clicked through a dozen potential actions and series of branching outcomes. The second he reached for the knife in Apollo's chest, the *Now* snapped into clarity and actuality. Instantly, the goddess controlling me lunged and the knife plunged into Apollo's chest was in my hand instead. The priest was lunging too, but an infinity too late. I was slashing for his throat before he could even close on the spot the knife used to be.

The blade sliced. His skin ripped open like a busted seam. Blood spurted. Already I was whirling on the other two priests, who'd risen to come to his aid. One rushed in from the left and the other from the right. I continued on my slashing arc and buried the blade in the chest of the priest on the right. It sank deeply and stuck when I tried to yank it out. I had to use a foot to kick off his body, and the knife caught on bone before sucking free. The other priest reached me. Hands or something equally ineffective crashed down on my back, and the anger that he would DARE touch me rose up like someone had just tossed accelerant on the fires of Hell.

I swung around with my newly liberated knife, noticing distantly that the tip had been left behind in the last priest's chest. It didn't stop me—*her*—from slashing the rough edge across any part of him that happened to be in my way. His cheek opened, and blood geysered once more. I could *feel* the power of the place further awaken all around me, fueled by blood and belief. Difficult for the men in black not to believe in the goddess tearing them to shreds, even when she was wearing another body. Pain tended to be *very* convincing.

It wouldn't help them now, or me, watching a horror movie play out from inside my own head. I fought, but like trying to fly with broken wings, it did no good. I was fairly sure it didn't even register with Rhea.

The priest took another run at her, and she let him come. He'd grabbed another knife they must have brought with them for backup. But it wouldn't matter. She could see all—what would come and how it would end.

She moved my hand in a lightning strike, grabbing his knife and breaking bones. More powerful than I'd ever been, even after an ambrosia infusion. The power of the place was still flooding me. Overloading my system, which was not meant to hold it or the goddess. I felt the crackle of the electrifying energy singeing my synapses, frying my senses. For now, though, I was a live wire, electrocuting on contact. The priest cried out, but was cut off when the broken knife in my hand slammed into his stomach. And not just the knife. I was knuckle deep in his internal organs. The rush of it, the life force flowing straight out of the priest and into me, chased what was left of my consciousness straight out, and—

Gone.

CHAPTER NINE

"Gods and Monsters? Isn't that a little redundant?"
—Tori Karacis

A chill swept over me, and I reached for the comforter, cursing Nick as a cover hog ... tried *to reach for the cover, but couldn't move.* My body wouldn't respond. It felt frozen, though it wasn't cold enough for that. Could I have been petrified somehow? Like Apollo ...

Something stirred in my memory. Us getting kidnapped, being laid out for sacrifice and then ... nothing.

I started to panic. What if this was it? What if the chill was of the grave? What if I couldn't move because I was all but dead already? Not enough blood left to keep my limbs alive and motivate them to move.

I couldn't hear my own heartbeat, but beneath me ... warmth. I could feel that much. It was the only warmth in my world. And it came with a heartbeat, pounding loudly, as if it was pressed right against my chest. Apollo then? Alive?

The heartbeat and the warmth argued for it, but the fact that the warmth seemed liquid, like spilled blood … His or mine? I couldn't remember.

My brain felt sandblasted, as if the infrastructure to catch racing thoughts had been blown away. Thoughts, fears, and hopes whipped around, but like the rest of my body, my mind seemed too paralyzed to catch any of them.

All I knew was that something had happened here. Something big. The jury was still out on whether I'd live to tell about it.

The chest beneath mine rose and fell, focusing me on the moment. A sound came with it. "Tori."

I wanted to answer and couldn't. My lips wouldn't move.

The body beneath mine shifted, and I felt my body start to slide. *Felt*. It was the first physical sensation beyond warmth. With it rushed pain, everywhere. It overrode even the attempt to gather my thoughts.

Nausea rushed in, but had nowhere to go. Even my gag reflex was dead, immobile, and the bile sank back into my stomach to lie in wait.

Outside myself there was swearing in a language I almost thought I understood.

Older than me. So old—

"My gods, Tori. We've got to get out of here."

My head rocked from a blow I felt only when the pain suddenly concentrated in one spot, my cheek. "Tori, snap out of it. We have to get out of here before someone discovers … all this."

He slapped me again, and I heard myself moan.

Then a sound of frustration, and I was grabbed, not gently, and hoisted up. The world rocked and Apollo held me in his arms. That bile reared its ugly head again and threatened to return with a vengeance. My stomach roiled like a storm tossed sea. But was, as I'd been, unable to rebel.

Rebel? But why? I couldn't catch the thought, as hard as I tried.

My body lurched again, suddenly, and my feet hit something hard, like the ground. All at once the acid that had been burning its way up erupted. I doubled over, coughing and spewing it, causing a yell and a sudden movement outside myself. Someone —Apollo—braced me from behind and patted my back. I wanted to tell him it was torment, but my throat had been burnt out and I couldn't speak.

I blinked away tears from my violent purging and only then realized I *could* blink again. I was as weak as a kitten, completely dependent on Apollo holding me upright, worried about keeping my feet under me.

Until my newly opened eyes lit on the carnage all around us, and I learned we had much, much bigger things to worry about.

I blinked up at Apollo, every muscle in my body protesting the simple turn of my head. "Did you do that?" I asked.

His eyes were a bottomless pit of pain. I fell back away from him—or would have fallen if I hadn't caught myself on a still-standing column. "What?" I asked, filled with dread. There was no way that pain was caused by killing in self-defense. There was more to it, and the way he was looking at me …

I looked down at *myself* and saw my chest, matted in blood that was tacky and thick. It wasn't just the "blood spatter" pattern on all the CSI shows with the blowback from a bullet wound or the cast off from a blunt force weapon. It was up close and personal lifeblood spilling out as I—

I hit a mental wall, and my knees buckled. My back scraped against the stone as I slid down it to the ground.

Had *I*—

The wall hit *me*. With a vengeance. My vision, my world blinked out and swam back again, but when it did I was lying in a puddle of bile and blood with Apollo crouched over me, smoothing hair away from my face.

"You saved my life," he said softly, as if that would make it all better. "Or, anyway, Rhea killing them kept them from killing me. This wasn't really *you*, you know. None of this was your fault."

They were just words. My hand had wielded the blade, had buried itself in some guy's flesh. I knew that now. I *remembered*. I was the one covered in their blood. I searched inside myself for any sign of Rhea, to cast her out or rail at her or assure myself that yes, truly, this had happened and there was nothing I could have done to stop it. But if Rhea was still in possession, she was playing it cool.

"Come on," Apollo continued, reaching for my arm when he saw that I was coming back to myself. "We have to get out of here before anyone finds the bodies."

I couldn't process. "*Find?* Shouldn't we report them?"

Apollo looked at me pityingly and continued trying to pull me to my feet. I wasn't being any help. Escape felt … pointless. Three men were dead. *I'd* killed them. Sure, they were trying to kill us, but … it hadn't been self-defense. Not for me—or Rhea. I remembered it all now. There'd been anger, hunger, righteousness, but no fear. I hadn't—*she* hadn't felt threatened. She'd felt vengeful.

I started to shake. Hard. So hard my teeth clacked together and I almost shook loose of Apollo's hand.

"You're in shock," he said. "And no wonder, but you can break down later. For now, I have to get you out of here. No arguments. We can't report this when you're the one covered in their blood."

It seemed pointless—to protest, escape, report, breathe. All equally hopeless. What could the authorities do, after all? Arresting me wouldn't stop a disembodied mother goddess. I wasn't even sure she wouldn't take possession again to prevent that from happening, and I was afraid of what that would mean for any authorities.

My shaking grew more violent, but Apollo held on and dragged me from the site.

It was dark. There was no constant glare of city lights and pollution like in LA. Just darkness barely lightened by the moon and stars, even with no clouds to blot them out. I focused on putting one foot in front of the other and not thinking about the dead priests. Someone's sons, certainly. Brothers? Lovers? Who was left behind to mourn and how could they without knowing ...

I stumbled, and Apollo kept me upright.

"No guard?" I asked, surprised, looking around the ruins.

"No money for them. There's only one way in, and it would have been closed hours ago."

So the bodies wouldn't be found until morning. Were there predators up this high? Scavengers who would ... The bile rose up again, but not with enough force to spill over.

Right, not thinking about them. Not my fault. But I couldn't bring myself to believe it. My body, my rules. My parents had taught me that before we'd even had the first sex talk. It was like a mantra, and it had been totally blown to smithereens. If I wasn't safe inside my own mind and body, where was I safe? And who was safe from me?

Right, fleeing the scene of a crime now, complete mental break later. After my murder indictment. Maybe I could claim insanity. I already had the family history.

Apollo was moving slower than normal, I noticed after a minute. "Are you okay?" I asked.

He didn't answer right away. "Healing," he said finally, "and talking to the winds. Getting help."

I craned my aching neck to stare at him. "You couldn't have done that *earlier*?"

"No winds where they had us locked away, and then I was distracted taking a knife to the chest."

"Oh, that. And between times?"

He looked away. Between incarceration and attempted sacrifice, I'd been knocked out. Had all his focus been on me?

"I tried. He wasn't taking calls," Apollo said.

"Who wasn't? Hermes?"

Apollo snorted. "I wouldn't trust Hermes to help me cross the street."

"Who then?"

"Pan."

I stopped short, and Apollo, still holding my arm, propelling me along, nearly fell on his face with the sudden loss of momentum.

"Pan," I said, confirming. "As in my possible progenitor Pan?"

"You don't know?" he asked.

"Know what?" I snapped back. I'd *killed* tonight. I really wasn't in the mood for guessing games.

"Your Uncle Hector."

My brain refused even to process that thought, still fried from earlier or just unable to accept any more impossible things before breakfast ... or rehearsal dinner. Oh gods, that rehearsal dinner. Tina was going to kill me. And right now I could only think that it would solve all my problems.

"Uncle Hector," I repeated stupidly.

"Ask your *yiayia*. She knows. Or ask him yourself. He's on his way."

My brain had truly blown a fuse. Suddenly, my divine heritage had gone from theoretical to actual. Oh sure, I'd come to terms with the gorgon glare; there was no denying *that*. But divinity ... Although, actual relation to the god Pan, the earthy divinity best known for his sexual appetite, explained so much about Spiro.

Uncle Hector. Now I understood why I'd never known quite where he fit into the family tree. It seemed to be kind of an emeritus title. I wondered ... did everybody know? Or was everyone but Yiayia as ignorant as I was?

"Tori, stay with me. We have to get past the road block so that Hector can pick us up."

"I haven't gone anywhere," I snapped.

"Not physically. But mentally you're so far away your feet have stopped moving."

I cursed, colorfully and bilingually. It didn't help anything, but it felt good. I had so much pent up … stuff—horror, shock, panic, horror, stunned disbelief, horror—that it was a release valve of sorts, letting off just enough steam to get my feet moving again.

We made it past the gated-off portion of road and down a little ways from the bloodshed and ruins, when a car, running dark with no lights, pulled up to us. The passenger side window rolled down, and Uncle Hector ordered, "Get in."

Apollo opened the back door for me and gently lowered me in, then he took shotgun. "That your blood?" Uncle Hector asked as he got in.

"Mostly."

Uncle Hector only nodded, like he picked up bloody men on dark mountain roads on a regular basis. He was completely unfazed. "Tori-girl, how are you?"

There was no way to answer that. "In shock," Apollo said for me.

Hector nodded, popped the car into gear and somehow managed a three-point turn on the narrow road. We drove for a mile or so before he felt it safe to turn on the headlights.

"I didn't make any excuses," Uncle Hector said as he drove. "Would lead to too many questions, and I wanted to get out of there in a hurry. Plus, I didn't know what kind of injuries we were gonna have to account for. But you two disappearing together, that's caused quite a stir." He took his gaze off the road to look back over his shoulder at me. "Your young man is fit to be tied. Caused quite a ruckus saying you'd gone missing. Nearly derailed the rehearsal. Stayed behind to search for you. Had hotel security all up in arms."

Nick.

My heart broke. How was I going to tell Nick that I'd killed, even if I hadn't been the one in control of my body? That I'd left the scene. That I could feel Apollo's pain …

Even without a psychic connection, I could sense *Nick's* pain, because I knew what I'd be feeling if situations were reversed and he'd gone missing after threats to his life. I'd fear the worst. He was a Los Angeles police officer, a detective. He'd seen a lot more of the worst than he had of best-case scenarios.

"Cell phone?" I asked.

Uncle Hector reached into the console cup holder and handed me the phone that sat there. "Wait a minute or two though. We want it to ping off the right cell towers." If I'd had my head on straight, I'd have thought of that.

When Uncle Hector—I still couldn't think of him as Pan—gave me the nod, I dialed the hotel. But Nick wasn't in our room. Of course not, he was out looking for me. I hung up before the voicemail came on and then called again. This time I asked the front desk to give him a message, just that I was okay and on my way back.

"We need a cover story," I said the second I hung up.

"Ahead of you there," Uncle Hector said, far too cheerfully, especially under the circumstances. "You went for a walk together and ignored the signs about loose scree and falling rocks. Happens all the time. You got hurt, went bumping down the mountain, got stuck on a ledge. Apollo had to figure out how to get you up safely and didn't dare leave you to go for help. I presume you don't have your phone on you?" he asked Apollo, who shook his head. "So, he couldn't leave you, and he didn't have a phone to call for help."

"You've done this before," I said, not sure whether I was accusing or admiring.

"*Egona*, I've been sneaking into and out of bedrooms and coming up with alibis since long before you were born."

"How do we explain all of this blood?" Apollo asked.

"Change of clothes," Uncle Hector answered, "in the back."

On the floor in front of me was a dark backpack. I tore open the zipper and out fell PowerBars, mini water bottles, a first aid kit and a profusion of clothes. I looked from it to Uncle Hector.

"Just one question, why am *I* the one getting rescued in your scenario?"

I hadn't meant to be funny, but his laughter fell about me as I ripped into a PowerBar, suddenly consumed with the munchies, maybe trying to fill the empty void that was my soul.

But once I'd consumed the calories, all I wanted to do was sleep. Playing host to a psychotic mother goddess after her millennia of slumber apparently took a lot out of a girl. Ambrosia or nectar would probably perk me right up, but now that the supplier was suspect, the cost was far too high. This wedding had already become more about death than a new life, and it wasn't even over. None of it. Apollo's blood and near sacrifice had awoken Rhea, and she didn't seem inclined to slip quietly into that good night.

Sleep. It seemed to be the best thing. Already my body was shutting down. My eyes were closing. My head lolled back against the headrest, and my eyes shut with a satisfying finality. I had a blissful moment of escape, and then, "Tori!"

I was so sick of hearing it. My eyes stayed shut and my mind blank.

A slap rocked my head from one side to the other, and my eyes snapped open. "What?" I asked without the energy for the heat I felt at the rudeness.

"We're almost there. You have to change."

"Let 'em take me." It came out "Et em ake ee," and my eyes shut again.

There was cursing, and then someone was crawling into the backseat with me, and I was half aware that I was being undressed, but not awake enough to actually care. Then my arms were lifted, and I was slumped forward so my shirt could be pulled off of my back. The wet suctiony sound barely penetrated my cloud of exhaustion. I didn't resist, but I didn't help either. If I was caught bloody-handed, so be it, as long as they let me sleep. Deep down, I knew that wouldn't happen. There'd be an interrogation, mugshots, fingerprinting—things for which I'd probably have to stay upright, but ... Yeah, I wished them luck with that.

The car door opened. Presumably, the car had stopped first, but I hadn't been aware of it. I stayed deadweight as I was lifted out of the backseat. I was vaguely aware of a sense of movement, of being taken from one place to another and being laid down on something, but whatever warned me of danger didn't sound an alert, and so I didn't bother to rouse myself. I wasn't even sure it was possible. Not even for the insistent voices all around me. I did manage to shift into a more comfortable position and fall far, far away from it all.

At a certain point, I became aware of a loud argument, followed some time later by warm arms pulling me into a seated position and someone spooning something into my mouth with the command, "Eat this." That same someone rubbed my throat to make sure that I swallowed, like a recalcitrant kitty with a heartworm pill. Then I was out again.

Blood, seeping, absorbing, awakening. Power rising. Me rising, seeking, laughing at the glory of it, then horrified at the degradation. Finding a new avatar. Strong, that one, but so pointless. Hardly aware of her potential. Wasteful. So much to be exploited, taken over, pathways seldom traveled. Unguarded.

I thrashed, trying to wake, trapped in the dream, wanting out.

A new avatar, linked to the blood sacrifice. Blood I knew. Blood relation. Oh, the flavor. The power, the hum and life of it. I'd nearly forgotten life and the immediacy of the sensations. Almost too much after all this time asleep.

And then those bladed men, thinking they could take it all from me. I saw it in their hearts.

All for my eldest son, Zeus, who'd ruined everything. I should never have fed his father that stone in his place.

Zeus. The name burned. He would not rise again to ascendency.

His time had passed, but the Titans. *I could sense it in this new avatar, in the very earth … the old ways had been forgotten. The* Titans themselves *had been forgotten, along with any remembrance of how they might be defeated. And unlike the upstart Olympians,* their *power had never been fueled by belief, but by the sheer primal power of creation.*

I flailed, trying to throw Rhea out of my head, as I'd tried and failed to exorcise her from my body. I lashed out and struck something, but it might have been in the dream, because …

One of Zeus's human dogs made a move, and as quickly as I willed it, the sacrificial blade was in my hand, slashing, cutting deep. More blood, more power. More elation, more bloodshed. Until I was bathed in it, as I'd been when I'd borne my misbegotten son.

I jerked out of the nightmare, terror blind. There was sound and stabbing light and something weighing me down. I tried to shake it, and panicked when I couldn't move, couldn't control my own body. *Again.* My own personal hell. And then the dark clouds across my vision started to clear but for pixilated pain throbbing around the edges. I looked up into Nick's midnight blue eyes, almost black at the moment. "Shh, shh, Tori, it's just a night terror. Tori, it's me. You're safe."

His cheek was swollen, and it was my fault. The lashing out had been real enough, not simply part of the dream, which wasn't a dream in any case.

The fight leaked out of me, and when he felt me relax, Nick eased onto his side next to me, studying me with concern.

"Want to talk about it?" he asked quietly.

"No," I answered. It hurt to talk. I wondered if I'd been screaming, and then whether it was in my own panic or Rhea's triumph.

"You didn't get hurt walking with Apollo, did you?" he asked, and I could hear something like fear beneath the careful gentleness in his tone. "The news—"

So the bodies had been found already.

I rolled over, away from his probing gaze. What did I tell

him? That I'd committed triple homicide, but I hadn't been myself at the time? Did possession qualify someone for the insanity defense or—

"*Tori.*"

"I don't want to talk about it," I said, knowing he wouldn't be satisfied with that.

"Tori!" he said it sharply, and I rolled to face him so suddenly he almost looked afraid … of me.

"What?" I asked.

The pain in my throat and in my head was already receding, and I no longer ached all over like I had after … No, no tangents. The bodies had been found, Nick was asking questions, and I had to face this. If someone *had* spooned ambrosia into me earlier in the evening, it was the least of my worries. So the pain in my head was gone, but the one in my heart … "What do you want me to tell you? That I killed them? That I was possessed at the time? That I passed out in a dead faint afterward and relived it all in my nightmares? It's all true." Nick looked lightning-stuck. "Apollo and I were kidnapped, and we were going to die, and the only reason I'm still alive is that a goddess more powerful than I am used me as her own personal puppet."

I broke down. I could have counted on one hand with fingers left over the number of times I'd cried in my life. I wasn't prepared for the sudden explosion of sobs that seemed to start from somewhere around my gut and wracked my whole body.

Nick didn't touch me. Didn't hold me, and that only made me cry harder, because I knew I was horrifying to him now. Repugnant, but no more than I was to myself. *I'd had my hand buried in some guy's solar plexus.*

Too late, he finally reached for me, as if it was a duty and not one he was sure he should perform. I knew it as if I still had some fragment of Rhea's all-knowing.

Maybe I did.

I pushed him away and ran for the bathroom, locking myself

inside. It wasn't the most mature response in the world, but we'd blown well past any concern about maturity on the way to post-traumatic stress.

I started the shower, just thinking I didn't want him listening to me bawl, and then realized that beneath my borrowed top there was still caked blood from the attack that had seeped through the fabric of my discarded clothes. All I could think of was getting clean.

I didn't even wait for the water to get warm, but stepped into the shower fully clothed. I didn't adjust the temperature when it turned from frigid to scalding, but stood beneath the onslaught shivering. Burning and yet cold, all at the same time.

I grabbed up the bar of soap and scrubbed everywhere—over my clothes, under. And then I ripped the clothes off entirely and let them lay there on the floor of the bathtub as the water swirled all around, washing me clean.

I'd barely gotten a towel wrapped around me when there was a pounding at the outer door to the room.

I yelled out, "Go away," but still I heard Nick open the door and let someone in. A second later, I knew *who*. Small person, big voice.

"Where is she?" Tina demanded.

"Shower," Nick said.

"Oh my god, what happened to your eye?" Tina asked him, but she was already moving on before Nick had the chance to answer. "Tell her to get her butt out here. I need to see if she's still fit for duty and to walk her through what she missed at rehearsal."

"Tell her yourself," I yelled from behind the bathroom door. "She can hear you."

Somehow, talking about myself in the third person was easier. Like I could escape. I didn't even blame Tina for her attitude. After all, we came from circus stock, where you downed the painkillers, put on your flesh tone bandages, smiled to hide the wince and made sure the show would go on.

If there was time later, you could ice it up and call in the medic.

The bathroom doorknob rattled, and I reluctantly reached to unlock it before she could tear it off the hinges. I wouldn't put it past her.

Tina yanked the door open and we faced each other on either side of the doorway. "You look like crap," she said, showing off her sensitive side. "What happened to you? They said a walk, but I couldn't see you scaling the side of the mountain."

No one could blow your cover like family.

I pulled her into the bathroom with me and shut the door.

"Ooh, secrets," Tina said, belligerence giving way to elfin mischief. "Tell me all. But be quick about it."

I rolled my eyes. The normality of Tina's presence was starting to have a strange calming effect on me. I wasn't sure I deserved calm, but my brain must have decided it couldn't sustain a state of perpetual panic.

"Apollo and I had … things to discuss, okay? So we found someplace quiet where no one would be looking for us, and I slipped and hit my head, that was all."

"Uh huh, someplace to *talk*. Important enough to make you *miss my wedding rehearsal?*"

"In my defense, I was *unconscious*."

"Sure, sure, some excuse. Of course, if I'd been on a private walk with Mr. Hollywood hottie, I'd have swooned too … if I weren't a soon-to-be-married woman and all."

"I did *not* swoon," I answered, indignant.

"There, now you look more like yourself." Her eyes glittered. "You look like you want to take a swing at me. Come on, get dressed."

"But—" After everything that had happened, the last thing I wanted to do was walk down the aisle at her side like nothing was wrong. I felt like I'd taint the whole ceremony just by being part of it. A wedding was supposed to be something sacred. *The show must go on* didn't seem to apply. But there was no way I could explain all that to Tina, even if I was sure she'd see things my way. She'd just see that her wedding party was lopsided and that it was all my fault.

"Okay," I said finally. "But can we stop for coffee and calories before whatever fresh hell you're going to put me through?"

"Andre said 'no caffeine,'" she protested. I guessed Andre was the clipboard guy from yesterday's production meeting.

"No caffeine, no Tori," I said, talking about myself in the third person again.

"Fine, fine," she said. "I'll just tell the makeup artist to give you the teabag treatment before she goes to work on you. Now get dressed."

I didn't get it—teabags were good, coffee was bad? There was no justice in the world.

I hoped the lack of justice would work in my favor for the next twenty-four hours at least. Having the police crash the wedding to arrest me would probably ruin Tina's big day and Uncle Hector's production and put me back on the outs with my family … not to mention in prison.

I went to get dressed, avoiding Nick's arms when he reached for me as I passed him on the way to my suitcase and avoiding his gaze when he tried to catch my eye. I'd just gotten myself together. I was afraid that I'd fall apart again at one hesitant touch.

If I were Christie, I'd probably focus on what I was going to wear, just in case I ended up on the morning news. What went well with handcuffs? Did I go with unobtrusive and demure, completely incapable of cutting down three grown men single-handedly? Since I didn't exactly own pearls and Peter Pan collars, I went for the first thing I touched, but Tina took it out of my hands and reached for a plain white button-up with just enough darting for shape. Feminine but not girly. "A wardrobe staple," Christie had called the shirt when she'd made me buy it.

"Button up is better," Tina said. "Then you can change later without messing up your hair and makeup."

Couldn't have that.

I shrugged and took the shirt, added black skinny jeans and went to the bathroom to change. I didn't bother with makeup or anything else, since I knew it would all be redone, and I didn't wear much anyway.

On the way out, Tina dragged me to the hotel's breakfast buffet, flashed her room key, loaded croissants and fruit into a napkin, and looked pointedly from me to the coffee keg. The carafe was keg-sized, anyway, with both ceramic and foam cups sitting beside it. Unfortunately, they only had a one size to-go cup, which was not nearly big enough, but I didn't think the hotel would take kindly to me grabbing the keg like a football and rushing it out of there, so I made myself two cups, doctored them both with cream and sugar, drank one still standing at the coffee bar and refilled the cup before applying lids.

"Okay, let's go," I said.

She looked like she despaired of my behavior. Since I agreed with her, I didn't say a word, but followed her out into the extra crisp morning air. It slapped me awake better than the cup of coffee I'd already downed.

The sun was shining, glistening off the dew that sparkled on every leaf. The world seemed newly made, pristine. Perfect. It was the kind of day that made you glad to be alive and death seem far, far away. I felt like crap about it, the kind that stunk and stuck to your shoes, clinging to the treads. The kind that stayed with you … like the memory of cutting down three men without missing a beat.

Okay, enough self-loathing. The only way I was getting through the day was denial. I couldn't change what was. Couldn't go back. Couldn't confess. I'd have to go forward. Somehow.

"Seriously, you all right?" Tina asked, studying me. "You and your boyfriend get into a fight?"

"You could say that." I took another sip of coffee and avoided looking at her.

"You love him?" she asked.

I glared at her for the question, but she was family. She was entitled to ask. "We may have irreconcilable differences," I said, avoiding a direct answer.

Like, I'm a killer and he's a cop.

Part of me knew that wasn't exactly right. Guns didn't kill people. *People* killed people. And all I'd been in Rhea's hands was a weapon. But that didn't change the fact that the killing was now part of *my* muscle memory.

Gah, *enough* already.

"If so, you can do better for yourself. You deserve more than a constant struggle."

I let that go. I wasn't entirely sure what I deserved, but I was *not* going to wallow in self-pity or self-loathing or whatever. Rhea was not going to defeat me. That meant I had to woman up.

I braced myself as we reached the doors of a beautiful little whitewashed church with vaulted ceilings and small stained glass windows catching the light. On the upside of things, my preoccupation with death had temporarily overwritten my fear of heights. I'd forgotten even to notice the path we'd taken. Tina held open the beautiful oak door for me to enter, and I prepared myself to be struck down as I crossed the threshold, but nothing happened.

The inside of the little church was painted floor to ceiling with Byzantine-styled frescos representing the saints, the holy family and, looking down from the pinnacle of the vestry, Christ Pantokrator, aka God Almighty. I'd grown up with kind of a loose sense of religion—believing in God, just not really clear on exactly what that might mean. One all-powerful god sounded good, focused. One message. One agenda. But the fact that no one, not even within the same religion, could agree on exactly what that was ... well, it made me wonder. Was Christianity about one god who was open to interpretation? Was the trinity really somehow three-in-one or multiple entities who might sometimes get into turf wars?

Then there'd been Yiayia's beliefs—the old gods still running around in modern day. But they hadn't seemed so godlike with their day jobs and petty squabbles. Not for the first time, I wondered what divinity even meant. Did it just mean cool powers and immortality? Was there more to it than that? Spider-Man's Uncle Ben had said, "With great power comes great responsibility," but the gods I knew didn't seem to have gotten the memo. I wondered about the Pantokrator. I'd have to ask when and if we ever met, and hope he'd forgive me for hanging with the competition. Or at least his—her?—would-be competition. The heyday of the Olympians was long gone, which was why most seemed so obsessed with staging a comeback.

"You like?" Tina asked, indicating the church.

"Beautiful," I admitted.

She smiled from ear to ear. "I know, right? There'll be candles and buntings, a whole bower-type arrangement on the altar … perfect. Come on, I'll walk you through it."

"Can you—" I had to clear my throat. "Can you give me just a moment alone?"

"Sure," she said. "I'll, uh, just sit back here for a minute if you want to say a prayer or something."

She took a seat in a back pew and set the fruit and croissants down beside her. I didn't know exactly *what* I wanted to do, but I took her suggestion and went to the back of the church where you could light candles and say prayers for the deceased. I lit a candle, feeling guilty that I didn't have any money tucked away in my pocket for the offering box. But that was the least of my sins.

I stared at the flickering candle. I'd been in church often enough with my mother, who didn't believe a word of Yiayia's obsession, to know what to do next. I crossed myself and said, simply, "Forgive me, Father, for I have sinned."

I hung my head and contemplated that. I didn't have a flowery prayer to add, just a heartfelt plea. *Forgive me.* All of my being went into those two words. I didn't know who I was asking. Everybody. Anybody with the power to lift whatever part of the responsibility I bore for those deaths at Delphi. The candle flame flickered, flaring bright, dwindling nearly to nothing and coming back again. I didn't know what it meant, if it meant anything. I didn't feel any differently. But maybe it was like antibiotics … it took twenty-four to forty-eight hours to take effect. Or maybe I was grasping at straws.

I took a deep breath and turned to face Tina. "Okay, I'm ready. Show me what you've got." For her sake, I pasted on a smile that flickered like the flame.

She showed me what to do, and I did it, all the while waiting for lightning to strike me down. I might have been thinking more Olympian than Old Testament, but I was pretty sure a monotheistic God, capital G, would have lightning in his arsenal. Or any other natural forces to command—the attributes of all the lower-case-g gods all rolled into one. Luckily, our cousin Mateo would be acting as their *koumbaros*—their sponsor—for the ceremony, so the rest of the bridal party was more for show and support than anything else.

Shortly the set designers arrived to shoo us out of the way, and we were on to hair and makeup at the hotel. I ate my croissants and fruit on the way back, suddenly voracious. The munchies had crashed my pity party and were all about the buffet. Someone had definitely given me ambrosia last night. I wondered if Nick had been there for it and if he now saw me as a drug addict as well as a killer. No wonder he couldn't bring himself to touch me.

I had a lot of time to think about that while I was reclining in the suite that had been set aside for all of us to prep in. I had goop all over my face and tea bags over my eyes. The makeup prep person—like the sous-chef of facial artistry—had first insisted on putting drops in my eyes that stung like the dickens and followed with a hot towel to open the pores, some kind of scrub, soothing cream, cold compress to take down the swelling in my face from last night's tears, and *then* had followed with the tea bags and goop. I doubted that any of my original surface skin remained behind.

The others arrived while I was getting prepped, and conversations buzzed all around me. I ignored them, not really concerned with whether Althea preferred apricot scrub over the cucumber crystal cleanser, but at some point Apollo's name popped up, and my ears—about the only part of me still in their original state—perked up.

"Has anyone *seen* Apollo this morning?" Junessa asked the room at large. "Tori, what about you? Did your savior come by to check on you this morning?"

I lifted the tea bag off one of my eyes to look at her and got swatted by the sous-chef. I glared for the split second before I dropped it back down. I needed all the help I could get and knew it. Even if I didn't care, there'd be all those pictures immortalizing Tina's wedding forever after. I didn't want my ugly mug to break any cameras.

But I'd caught a look at Junessa's face before the tea bag fell back in to place, and there was something less than casual about the intensity with which she watched for my answer. Then there was the fact that she'd called him "Apollo" like they were on a first-name basis. I doubted he'd found the time to start making his way through the bridesmaids, especially since Spiro would likely make sure *he* was at the head of the line. (Because I doubted that Jesus had suddenly made him into a monogamist.)

"You know him?" I asked.

No matter *how* much help I needed, I needed my senses more. There was a mystery here, or maybe the clues to solve one. I lifted the tea bag again in time to see Althea and Junessa exchange a look. The former's was a warning, as if Junie should have kept her mouth shut.

"Not well," Junie answered casually, ignoring Althea's look.

"Mostly by reputation. I hear you know him a lot better." Stupid media.

I shrugged. I must have unintentionally made a face too, because the goop protested and threatened to crack. I wondered what *that* would do to my complexion.

"Shhh," the sous-chef hissed at me. "Quiet."

I took her advice, but only because protesting rarely convinced anybody of anything, and anyway, I was more interested in getting than giving out information. I hoped she'd be compelled to fill the silence. I wasn't wrong.

"I just wondered, because Serena said that his performance yesterday was a little ... wooden."

My gaze sharpened on her. That clinched it. She knew something.

I waved my arms around to signal that the makeup person should get the goop off my face, and she sighed heavily and began wiping it away with gentle aggression. When I felt I could talk without tearing, I asked, "You know *Serena* too?"

Oblivious to my undertones, Tina cut in, "You don't recognize her?"

I was totally baffled now. "No, should I?"

Her disbelieving look was framed by the layers of tin foil all over her head. She looked ready to receive phone calls from outer space. Highlights and lowlights, she'd told me, very excited by the concept.

"Tori," she said, "*Serena Banks*. Before she got discovered, she was circus folk. Her mermaid bit was like the most sought after sideshow act ever. Lenny tried to get her for Rialto Bros., but he couldn't meet her fee."

I stared, gears grinding and clicking into place in my mind. Serena Banks ... mermaid show. *Siren-a* Banks ... *siren*?

What had Apollo said—that the sirens were water divinities, devoted to Poseidon. I stupidly hadn't taken my suspicions of her seriously enough, chalking them up to jealousy. I'd sent *Nick* to talk to her instead of interviewing her myself. *Nick*! To talk to a woman who legends had it regularly lured men to their death. The fact that he'd survived didn't mean anything long term. She was still free to wreak her havoc on him or to finish off Apollo …

"I've got to get out of here!" I said, trying to rise from my chair.

"Oh no you don't," Tina said, lunging up from her seat and holding me down with uncanny strength. "You disappeared yesterday and missed my rehearsal. You are *not* going to miss my wedding."

It was a huge struggle not to fight her on that, but it seemed bad form to manhandle the bride before the wedding, and she wasn't letting me go any other way. "Fine, then I need a phone and a moment alone."

"*That* we can do. I don't think anyone's using the back bedroom."

"Thanks."

She let me up. As I bolted for the back of the suite, I heard Junessa ask, "Tina, what do you call the color of our dresses, I just love them. So green, like spring."

And Tina answered, "Sea glass, though it looks to me more like 'fern' or 'moss,' which is just what I was going for. A foresty kind of look, very natural."

So, not "puke" green then. Yeah, that probably wouldn't have made it past marketing.

Then I was in the back bedroom and shutting them out. I went straight to the phone on the bedside table and dialed the room I shared with Nick. He answered on the first ring.

"Nick, it's me. Did you get anything out of your interview with Serena yesterday?"

"Well hello to you too."

"Nick?"

"She doesn't much like you," he said. "In fact, she offered me 'an upgrade.' I told her I already had the top of the line."

I nearly melted at that. "You are so getting lucky later," I told him. The knot in my stomach began to unkink now that we had fallen back into our banter. "Just stay away from her, okay? I'm pretty sure she's like me … but not. A siren instead of gorgon get. You know, the kind of girl who drives men to their death for fun and profit." Because why lure sailors to their doom unless you were after the booty that went down with the ship? And why Apollo, unless she was acting as Poseidon's agent just like the Selli were working for Zeus?

"Way ahead of you on staying out of her path," he answered.

"Good. Because I'm kind of attached to you and I still need a date for the wedding." Flippant had gotten me this far.

"I'm kind of attached to you too," he said, the warmth in his voice telling me that we were going to get through this.

As soon as we hung up, I dialed Apollo.

When he answered, his voice was stiff and brittle, barely recognizable. The petrification had to be progressing at frightening speed.

"Apollo, it's Serena. I'm pretty sure she's the one doing this to you, acting on Poseidon's say so—"

The door burst open, and I spun around to see Althea standing there, "Let me talk to him," she demanded, holding her hand out as if she had no doubt that I'd obey.

"Huh?" I said brilliantly.

With two strides more worthy of her taller compatriot, she was at my side and ripping the phone out of my hand. "Apollo, tell me how it happened and what you need. We've got your back."

I stared, waiting for understanding to dawn. So she and Junie *did* know Apollo. I'd begun to gather that much, but as to her behavior …

I couldn't hear Apollo's side of the conversation, but Althea answered, "Artemis would never forgive us if we let something happen to you. We'll handle."

She handed the phone back to me and started to walk away. "Wait, Althea, what's going on? Who *are* you?"

She looked amused at that. "I'm the same person I was two seconds ago—Tina's bridesmaid, your friend, and one of Artemis's huntresses."

My mind boggled. "Tina and Junessa?" I asked, sounding strangled.

"Junessa is the same. Tina ... well, I think this whole wedding thing puts the kibosh on the idea of her dedicating herself to a virgin goddess, don't you think?"

Not to mention I knew for a fact that *that* ship had sailed at about sixteen.

"Come on," she finished. "You going to stand there gaping or are we going to kick some siren ass?"

"But Tina—"

"Got it covered."

But a knock at the suite door stopped us in our tracks.

"Hotel security," a voice called from behind the door. "We're looking for Tori Karacis."

I prayed quickly and quietly that it was about the girl who'd broken into Apollo's room yesterday rather than the bodies atop Delphi, but I knew better.

"Here," I said, all eyes turning to me. Not one, but *three* official-looking men had come to collect me. One was clearly hotel security, based on the suit and nametag. The other two wore cheaper suits, and one had a badge clipped to his belt. Not just cops ... detectives.

"Miss Karacis," said the one with the badge showing, "if you'll come with us."

Tina, pedicure foam between each toe, rose from her chair to her full five foot height, facing them down. "What's this all about? My wedding is today. Just a few hours away, and Tori's one of my bridesmaids. *I need her.*"

"I'm sure we'll have her back to you in an hour or two, but we have some questions that need to be answered."

"About what? What on Earth is so important that it can't wait?"

"Murder," the badged man said into the dead silence of the room. Everyone heard it. Tina gasped and fell back a step. "Murder? But ... but who?"

"Miss, if you'll come with us," he said, ignoring Tina's questions and pinning me with his gaze. It wasn't a request, and I didn't mistake it for one.

"Of course—"

"Althea?" I asked over my shoulder.

"Got it covered," she answered.

"But how's she ever going to get ready in time?" Tina wailed. "You can't arrest her. The wedding party will be all lopsided, and there's no way I can find someone to fit her dress at the last minute, and there's the filming—" The hotel security man pushed past the police officers to comfort and calm her, mentioning something about complimentary champagne and assuring her that it would all be okay. I looked at the officers to see what they thought, and they didn't seem nearly as certain of that.

"Call Uncle Hector," I told Tina, figuring that if anyone here had access to decent lawyers, it would be him. Then I followed the cops out, trying to ignore the fact that Tina had been more worried about filling my spot than about my fate. I was sure that on any other day she'd have been a lot more sensitive about the whole thing. Well, fairly sure.

"Right, Uncle Hector, he'll know what to do," she said as the door closed behind me. It sounded pretty final, but I didn't know whether it was my precognition or just my own fears.

"This way," badge guy said, leading me with a hand just barely touching my arm.

This way was toward the elevator, and I noticed that while they didn't actually cuff me, hotel security walked in front and the two cops walked behind, ready to grab me should I try to bolt. I had a hard time not trying it. I had a very, very bad feeling about all of this.

"Murder?" I asked, making conversation to avoid making a run for it. I glanced at the cops as I asked.

Both nodded silently.

"You're not going to tell me who? Or when? We could clear this all up right now if I wasn't in town when it happened. I only got in yesterday."

"You were here," badge guy said.

"Then it's only just happened? Wait, it's no one I know, is it? Please tell me it's no one in the family or any of the wedding guests!"

Fear was fear. Hopefully they'd misconstrue the cause of mine. I hated the misdirection, but last night I'd been in no condition to call the deaths in and now that the cover-up had begun it felt like there was no going back. There was nothing I could do to stop Rhea from behind bars. No way I could make any part of this right. It wouldn't be justice, it would be stupidity to assuage my guilt.

The officers exchanged a look, but didn't say a word.

"Tell me," I insisted.

"Down at the station," the other cop insisted.

I worried all the way there about what they might have on me. I'd been *kidnapped*, for gods' sake. If anyone had seen anything it would be that, wouldn't it? But that hardly helped. If the police thought Apollo and I had fought our way free of our captors, then my little performance had just killed any self-defense plea before it even began.

I wasn't prepared to walk into the small bustling station and see the shopkeeper who'd covered for the man in black sitting in a chair talking to yet another plainclothesman. She looked like she'd been watching the entry, because as soon as she saw me, she knocked her chair over in her haste to rise and point an accusing finger at me.

"That's her," she said, loudly enough to carry. "She's the one who was following that man."

Something welled up in me, strong enough to knock me to

my knees, but I locked them and tried to ride it out. This was alien yet familiar—like Freddy Krueger or Michael Myers or any other horror villain … because that's what filled me, horror. That part was all mine. But the rising tide of power and righteousness …

HOW DARE SHE accuse us? How dare they try to question me and hold my avatar?

Those men were NOTHING.

The last thought roared out of me, and the ground beneath all of our feet started to shake. Pencil holders, phones, and folders started to topple from desks. The shopkeeper tried to catch herself on her chair back, but since it had already fallen, she overbalanced herself and ended up going down hard. She cried out, and inside me, Rhea exalted.

"Stop!" I yelled, not realizing that I'd said it out loud until the ground momentarily stilled and everyone, including the goddess within, momentarily focused on me in surprise. "I want a lawyer."

I didn't really. Waiting for a lawyer would only delay things, and I had a wedding to get to. But I knew they'd set me to wait in some kind of holding cell or interrogation room, hopefully away from any temptation Rhea might have to do harm.

A holding cell might be the safest place for me. With a vengeful goddess, newly awakened, cranky after her millennia-long nap doing a ride-along in my body, I wasn't safe to be around.

But Rhea didn't agree. *At all.* Apparently, she had places to be, and as the vehicle she'd chosen from the motor pool, I was going along for the ride. Suddenly, I was under attack from within. Something *wrenched* inside my brain hard, and it felt like an aneurism or a flash migraine or … something monumentally painful and potentially mind-blowing in the permanent sense of the word. My vision went purple-black. My stomach rebelled, my brain shattered. I fought for consciousness.

"What's going on?" one of the cops, detectives, asked, like this might all be part of some scheme.

There was a hand under my arms now, holding me up, gripping too hard. I hadn't noticed its arrival, but from the placement it went with the voice demanding answers.

"Concussion," I managed "Hit ... head ... last night."

"Damn it," said the other cop. "We need to get her looked at. If she really did hit her head last night, that quake might have set something off."

Yes! I thought. Then ...

No! An ambulance ride or whatever would only delay me getting help for my goddess issues or getting to the wedding. My brain was so scrambled, I didn't know what I was thinking.

"No," I said out loud, but not *too* loud, because my head seemed in danger of shattering. I couldn't hold Rhea down much longer. She didn't like the feel of the cop's hand gripping my—our—arm. She was trembling on the verge of doing something about it, even if it meant bringing the station down around us. "No," I said again, more quietly. "I just need to lie down." My words were slurred as my control over my body faltered.

"Fine," said one of the cops. "You can lie down in a holding cell while you wait for a lawyer."

"And a doctor," said the other. "Because there's no way in hell you're going down with an aneurism on my watch. I'm not doing *that* paperwork."

And then ... and then nothing. I lost control, even to the point of awareness.

I woke in a cell. The bars were a dead giveaway.

Those bars seemed to move as I watched them, and my stomach moved with them—warning: contents may have shifted during fight. I fought my guts back down where they belonged just in time to see a familiar face between the bars. Uncle Hector. I'd never been so glad to see anyone in my life. Well, maybe Nick on my doorstep with pizza, but aside from that ... Uncle Hector stared down at me, studying my face.

"Tori, are you okay? They said you'd passed out." I must have looked at him blankly. "Oh, yeah, I'm your lawyer," he said with a wink. "No need to mention my background is in *corporate law*."

I rose up and reached through the bars to hug him tight. He hugged me back, like I was a little girl again. That was when I became aware of all the other eyes on me from the next cell over. Apparently, I'd been put in some kind of isolation and had a cell to myself, but the one beside me held three women—one with a black eye, one looking scratched as though she'd taken *my* supposed tumble down the mountain, and the third smelling of vomit. The other women stood as far as they could from her in the cell. All three stared disconcertingly at me.

I wondered if Rhea had gone out like a light when I had and, if not, what she'd been doing with my body while I wasn't using it to have garnered such attention from next door.

"Um, nothing to see here," I told them forcefully.

None of them even blinked. It was eerie, like they were waiting for some signal they didn't want to miss. If they weren't behind bars, I'd have likened them to the birds from Alfred Hitchcock's classic and controversial film, massing on the wire.

Uncle Hector looked over his shoulder at them and back to me. "You know them?" he asked dubiously.

I shook my head.

"Well then, let's get you out of here."

"But the questioning ... I don't think I'm free to go."

"I've convinced them it can wait. They know they can't use anything they might get out of you in this condition. I'd never allow it. Anyway, they'd rather you be my problem at the moment."

"Oh." Score one for concussion, I thought. Or maybe it was

the mini-quake and the thought of one less prisoner to evacuate if it happened again.

A uniformed officer opened the door for Uncle Hector, and motioned me out.

Moving hurt, my head most of all.

"You okay?" he asked again, and I realized I'd never answered him the first time. "Do you need a doctor?"

I started to shake my head and quickly realized that was a *bad* idea. "No," I said instead, "exorcist."

"We'll talk outside," he promised.

I thought that was a damned good idea. There was still paperwork to sign and the warning that I shouldn't leave town and should keep myself available. Then we were free of the station.

Free. With a goddess possessing me at will, doing gods knew what to attract the unwavering attention of my fellow prisoners. I didn't like it.

As we got into Uncle Hector's limo, the prisoner with the black eye was just leaving the station, apparently having made bail or whatever herself. Her head turned a third of the way around, almost like an owl's, to stare at me through the tinted windows she couldn't possibly see through. When her gaze locked on to mine, she gave me a very definite nod, as though I should know what she was agreeing to. Uncle Hector's driver pulled away.

"Wait," I said, brain racing and getting nowhere. "Maybe we should stop and question her."

Uncle Hector turned around to see what I was seeing. "Right here in the police station parking lot?" he asked. "Better not. I know that look. She won't tell you anything. She thinks you already know."

"Know what?"

"Whatever it is. She's been mesmerized. It's all over her face. Apollo said that Rhea rose last night, using you as her vessel?"

"Yeah."

"Rhea has many powers, not the least of which is mesmerism. How do you think she convinced Kronos that the stone she fed him was the child Zeus? I don't know what she's planning, but she's had millennia to think on her revenge. I'd say she's just tagged her first recruits."

"How do we stop her? Stop me? I'm not safe to be around people."

"For now, we ward you as best we can. We get through the wedding. Rhea should still be getting her feet under her. She shouldn't be strong enough yet to summon power in someone else's sacred space. The church should be safe enough."

"Should be?"

"It's not exactly a science."

"Can you do wardings? Lay down protections?"

"I don't know that I'm strong enough alone, but I'm sure that if we explain the situation, we may be able to find some recruits of our own."

We had a little over an hour to go before the wedding. Our appearance back at the staging suite caused quite the kerfuffle. Althea opened the door to Uncle Hector's knock. She looked like a Greek goddess—hair half up and half spilling down in ringlets over her neck and shoulders. The green gown draped over one shoulder and hung almost like a chiton. Her eyes got manga-huge at the sight of me, and she yelled back over her shoulder at top volume, "You can stop panicking, she's back!"

"I don't know that I'd call off the panic just yet," Uncle Hector said helpfully. "We need to talk. Get Junie."

Her eyes went from soup bowls to slits. "I don't answer to you."

"What about Rhea?" he asked. "Because she's back and she's *pissed*. Look, I know you don't like me." Because Pan the promiscuous and Artemis's adherents were pretty much diametrically opposed. "But I think it's time for us to come together lest we come apart."

From the look of fury on her face, she was not unaware of the double entendre. "Rhea?" she gasped. "But how—"

"Call your compatriot. I promise to fill you both in."

"Junessa," Althea called over her shoulder.

She appeared, looking like a Nubian goddess, her hair done in the same style as Althea's. Runway fierce.

As Uncle Hector opened his mouth to speak a third person pushed them out of the way and grabbed my arm, yanking me into the suite. I expected Tina, but it turned out to be one of the makeup militia.

"Come on," she said, "there's no time to waste."

I dug my feet in and held my ground. "One minute," I told her. "Give me that and I promise I'll be as good as gold."

"I'll vouch for her," Althea said with a smile.

I bristled over needing a voucher, but I didn't have the time to make an issue of it. *"One minute,"* she said significantly.

I held my fingers up in what I thought was the sign for scout's honor, and she huffed, but moved off to prep … whatever she had to prep to make me presentable.

"Serena?" I asked Althea quickly, hoping she'd neutralized that threat while the police had held me in custody.

She was shaking her head before the name even left my lips. "Couldn't get to her. She was already with the production people."

"Damn."

"Time's up," the makeup lady said, tapping the spot a watch would be if she was wearing one.

"Tell him," I said to Althea. "I'll—"

"You'll come with me," my new nemesis said, taking me by the arm. I let her lead me away, hoping I'd left our fate in good hands. A petrifying Apollo, me, Pan, and a couple of huntresses against a rising mother goddess who could mesmerize and possess at will ... to say that I was worried would have been a massive understatement.

Then I was in another room and plunked into a chair. My hair was sprayed down with some kind of gunk—probably conditioner to give the stylist a fighting chance to get a brush through it, and then I was combed, curled, twisted, twirled and teased until my head ached. The makeup was less painful only, I presumed, because I'd been pre-threaded and waxed. When the torment was over, all the girls stood round me gaping.

"Wow," Tina said. "I didn't even know you could look like that."

I took in my reflection and ... maybe *took in* was too strong. I saw, but I didn't necessarily accept. The image looked like me, but as Disney might paint me, some idealized version that didn't seem quite real. My hair fell in soft ringlets rather than tangled curls. My brows arched gracefully. My skin was smooth, even and youthful, like I was sixteen again ... only without the acne. I looked ... beautiful.

Except for the dumbfounded expression on my face. I'd been through a lot of crazy crap today, but *this* seemed downright impossible.

"Um ... thanks?" I said to Tina.

I'd certainly steal Nick's breath, but his heart? I had to hope it wasn't already lost to me. I felt selfish beyond all reason even thinking about that in the midst of everything else.

I stood from the chair before I could get too crazy with the new look and start asking the mirror, mirror on the wall whether I was the fairest of us all. It wouldn't last anyway—not past the first sign of humidity or the first course I spilled on myself.

"Let's get you dressed," Althea said, and dragged me off to the room where we'd all hung our gowns. Once she had the door shut behind us, she dropped my arm and said, "We're still working on plans for Rhea, but Serena's going down. Don't sweat it."

"How?" I asked.

"She's a water divinity, right? Apollo said it happened when she walked in on him in the shower. That's because she needed to catch him in *her* element."

"Okay, how does that help us?"

"Apollo's the sun god."

"Yeah," I said, not following.

"It's not in his nature to change. He's not fluid like water. He's centered, steady, that around which things revolve."

"Or so he'd like to think," I muttered.

"That's why he hasn't petrified already. His own attributes fight against the transformation. That means this is an ongoing spell and they're still battling it out. Serena's not strong enough to do this on her own, I wouldn't think, which means she's got some kind of help, a talisman to enhance her power or an effigy she's constructed to work sympathetic magic. All we have to do is find it. Junie and I have already tossed her room and it's not there."

"Which means she has it on her."

"Bingo. And we're going to get it. If not us, then Hector or Apollo. We've got it covered."

It was the first good news I'd heard since I'd seen the tabloid back in LA. But it wasn't a done deal yet, and there was still the matter of Rhea. I knew Hector had told her about the goddess rising. I wondered if he'd filled her in on the rest, like the fact that Rhea could ride me like the city bus. I made sure to tell her, figuring she and Junie would be close enough at the wedding to take me down if I started to act out of character.

"Hector told me about that. But he also says that you saved Apollo's life. Junie and I will keep an eye out for trouble. If we have to, we'll stop you, but we'll do our best to use non-lethal means."

She grabbed my gown and changed gears so quickly I got whiplash. "Okay then, let's get you suited up."

There was a knock at the door, followed immediately by

Tina's voice. "Hurry up in there. We're taking a few quick pics, then we're off to the church!"

Althea held out my dress, and I carefully unbuttoned my shirt and dropped trou to step into it and shimmy it up my body, careful not to disturb a single curl. Althea zipped it for me, and I searched for my shoes. Golden sandals with straps that crisscrossed my ankles and tied at the back. Thankfully, they were flats, so that Tina could almost level the field when she donned her four-inch heels.

When I caught sight of the full effect in the mirror, I had to admit that the dresses maybe hadn't been such a bad choice. The green somehow set off the amber of my eyes and my dark curls contrasted nicely, tumbling over the draping. I felt weirdly powerful. Almost goddess-like, only a lot less bloodthirsty than those I'd met so far.

"Do I have time to make a quick call?" I asked Althea.

"Really quick. I'll cover for you."

I went to the phone in the room and was especially careful putting the receiver up to my ear. I dialed Nick's and my room.

"Tori?" he answered.

"It's me."

He let out a huge breath. "Thank God."

"Want to walk me to the church? We're headed down to the lobby in just a minute." I needed to see him. Everything else was such a mess, but Nick … he was my touchstone, my normalcy in the midst of chaos. I was only just realizing how much that meant to me. He was straightforward, direct, by the book. With Nick, I never had to worry about ulterior motives, what game he was playing, or who he really was. Unlike, it seemed, everybody else … including me. I didn't even know who I'd be from one moment to the next.

"I'll meet you down there," he said.

Tina appeared in the doorway, hand on one hip. "Come on. The photographer wants to take some candid shots before we go down."

I bit my lip rather than point out that they couldn't exactly be candid if they were planned.

"See you in a few," I told Nick and hung up.

Out in the main room, Tina posed facing a huge mirror with me pretending to adjust her veil. We all posed around her, admiring the ring. There was another candid of Tina holding the curtains back, looking wistfully out the room's picture window at the view. There were a dozen or so more poses with a zillion shutter snaps for each before the photographer let us go. To her credit, they were quick. She set them all up and knocked 'em down.

I tried to focus on Tina and her day rather than the bodies, police investigation and impending doom. I hoped my smile looked natural, sure the photographer would have told me if it was too hideous. She'd already told us how to stand, where to look, how to cock our heads and stick out our chins and chests, lean in and generally contort ourselves into the world's least comfortable positions for the sake of the "candid" camera angles.

Then we were on our way down. One of the primping people had gone ahead and caught us an elevator. I picked up Tina's train and held it so it wouldn't be caught in the doors. Her dress was a ruched, sequined fit and flare ball gown with the bling concentrated toward the top, getting scarcer and simpler toward the bottom. In her four-inch heels with her hair bigger than everyone else's—more Marie Antoinette than Grecian goddess—she looked like Bridal Barbie. It was the first time since we were eleven that she could stand and almost look me in the eye.

"Thank you," she said, as the elevator closed on us. "For being here, for finding Uncle Christos to give me away."

I admit it, I got a little choked up.

"No problem. You'd do the same for me."

"You look beautiful."

"So do you," I said, blinking away the tears in my eyes before they could dissolve the glue on the false eyelashes they'd given me.

We smiled at each other, and I could *almost* forget everything going on outside this elevator. Then it hit bottom, dinged and opened up, and I realized there was at least one thing I didn't *want* to forget. Armani. Nick.

He stood there in a silver-gray open-necked shirt with no tie beneath a dark blue suit. He had actual product in his hair, it seemed, so that for once it didn't flop over his amazing eyes that were just a shade lighter than his suit. He looked good enough to eat. Way too good to take to a public place where I'd be expected to keep my hands to myself. I wanted to drag him back into the room and rip the rest of the buttons off his shirt.

He licked his lips as he looked at me, those incredible eyes growing darker as they did when he wanted to drag *me* off somewhere private. I didn't know if we were okay yet, but it was clear that at least we weren't finished with each other. That was something.

I forgot to pick up Tina's train as she exited the elevator, instead going right to Nick. I waited for him to open his arms, to take me into them and hold me so that I could apologize and … but he just stood there, arms at his sides.

My heart fell until he said, "I'm afraid to touch you. You're so perfect."

"Oh no," Tina cut in as I was about to tell him he was being ridiculous, "No touching. Not until after the ceremony and the pictures."

Nick looked amused and offered me an arm instead of a hug or a kiss. Apparently, *that* was okay, because Tina didn't protest when I slid my hand along his forearm and held on.

Uncle Christos stood a few feet away with his date, Detective Beverly Simon of the LAPD. Clearly, we Karacis investigators had a type. He kissed her warmly on the cheek and left her to offer his arm to Tina, since he was standing in for the parents she'd lost.

Tina looked sad for a moment, maybe thinking of them, but then Uncle Christos smiled that infectious smile he had and said, "If I had a daughter, I'd want her to be just like you. You look beautiful, m'dear. Like a cake topper."

"Or Bridal Barbie," I said, out loud this time.

Christos laughed so loudly that everyone stared. "Bridal Barbie, only better, because you are Greek!"

"Hear, hear!" a voice agreed wholeheartedly. I recognized it as Hermes, and looked to see Christie beside him in a dazzling silver sheath dress.

Another person to protect. That was what ran through my head. My heart started to pound, and I didn't know if it was pessimism or precognition—fear or knowledge that something would go wrong.

I looked for Jesus, wondering what *he'd* say about my transformation, but I didn't see him. Clipboard guy stepped up to block my view of the others assembled and clapped to call us all to places in the procession. We were walking to the church. Tina had told me about this bit. Paper lanterns—luminaries—had been lit and placed all along the sidewalks of the short walk to the church, and the hero and heroine of the film were to first catch sight of each other in the candlelight, which meant that Apollo and Serena were here somewhere. It also meant that Nick got pushed aside in favor of my matching groomsman, Jason's cousin Ernest, who had the most pronounced Adam's apple I'd ever seen and who turned pink every time I looked at him. I thought he was going to have a stroke when I had to take his arm.

Uncle Christos walked almost at march, standing every centimeter of his five-foot-nine height, looking like a proud papa as he escorted Tina out of the hotel. Lining the streets were luminaries, light diffusers, roving cameramen and others high up in a cherry picker for the overhead shots. I did my best not to look at any of the cameras, which was fairly easy because the paper lanterns were so beautiful. Like something out of a dream or, yes, a romantic film. I wished it was Nick's arm I was holding.

"That your boyfriend back there?" Ernest asked, nodding behind us toward where Nick and everyone else followed.

"Yeah," I said, wondering whether it was okay for us to be talking. Tina hadn't said, but I doubted the cameras would do more than pan past us, so I wasn't too worried.

"He going to kill me for laying a hand on you?"

I laughed at that thought, and suddenly the image of a sword slashing and blood flying rose up to choke me and I stumbled.

Ernest caught me with a hand under my elbow. "I'm sorry, I was only kidding. I didn't mean for you to take me seriously. I'm terrible at small talk, as you can see."

I fought down the bile that had burned its way up my throat, leaving it stripped and raw. "It's okay," I rasped out. "I just … I'm no good at it either." I worked to put a smile on my face. "No, he won't kill you. He might even thank you for preventing me from falling on my face."

"But it was my fault you stumbled. I shocked you."

"Oh, it takes a lot more than that to shock me. It's just been a long day."

"I heard about your concussion. That's probably it then, you're still a little dizzy, between the altitude and the knock to the head—"

Oh gods. I hadn't been looking or thinking beyond the lanterns. I hadn't been thinking about the height … until then. Panic started to rise.

"Ernest, um, I don't think we're supposed to be talking. Maybe I should just focus on putting one foot in front of the other?"

His face went from pink to red. "Oh, yeah, sorry."

He looked miserable and embarrassed, and I swore to make it up to him as soon as I could breathe without hyperventilating.

If they sat us together at the reception, maybe I could give him my cake … if the ambrosia munchies allowed.

We made it to the oversized oaken doors of the church without incident. No Rhea. No quakes or men in black. No police or portents, except for the vague queasiness in my belly.

In a more orthodox ceremony, Tina's groom would have been waiting for her at the church doors, ready to receive her hand from Uncle Christos so that they could proceed down the aisle together. But the director had decided he wanted a more familiar-to-some ceremony with the bridal party procession and the hand-off in front of the altar.

The church doors opened before us, as if by magic, to reveal the inside of the church, lit by more of the paper lanterns. Branches had been laid along both sides of the white runner that led toward the altar, heavy with deep green leaves and red berries. Straight ahead, the set designers had created a bower from a white trellis strung with climbing vines of what appeared to be poppies, only I didn't think they grew that way, and little white mini-lights that glowed like fireflies. The altars were decorated with more of the berry-laden branches and blazing with candles.

All I could see was doom. The place was a fire hazard, and the sickness in my stomach grew.

Clipboard guy hustled the women of the bridal party into a small anteroom, mercifully candle-free, and sent the men off to seat the guests.

I smiled at Ernest as he bowed to take his leave. Old fashioned and charming. He dashed away, and as the doors closed us off from the guys, Tina suddenly folded like a subway map. I caught her before she could fall.

"Chair, someone!" I ordered, looking around for one myself.

Junessa was there in a flash with a folding chair from the stack against one wall. I lowered Tina into it. Her eyes were wide and shocky. "I can't do it," she said, her gaze meeting mine in appeal. "I thought I could, but I can't. The cameras—*on film.*

They say the camera adds ten pounds. What if I look huge? What if I stumble over my lines? What if they call 'cut' in the middle of my wedding?" Her voice rose with every word. *"What was I thinking?"*

"Get her a glass of—something," I said to whoever would listen. Althea and Junessa exchanged a look. There was clearly nothing in this little room where they kept vestments and extra odds and ends. Althea let herself out of the room to find something, and I squatted in front of Tina and took her hands.

"Breathe," I said. "Just breathe."

The vision hit me like a two-ton truck. Tina gripping Jason as the earth lurched beneath their feet, screaming, fire erupting, panic and pain.

I let go of her hands with a gasp. "What? What is it?" she asked. "Tori?"

I shook my head, trying to erase the vision like the lines from an Etch-A-Sketch, but it wasn't that easy. Not nearly.

My heart pounded, but I made myself put on a show for Tina, starting with a smile. "Nothing, just … your hands are so cold."

Tina gave a little laugh. "Only because yours are so hot. You're burning up!"

Probably my body trying to fight something off—like a body-stealing mother goddess.

Althea came rushing back with a flask.

"Whose?" I asked before I'd let her pass it to Tina. All we needed was the bride hooked on nectar or something to really kick this crisis into high gear.

"Spiro."

I took the flask from Althea, who protested, and tested a drop myself. "Whiskey," I said.

"What did you expect?" Althea demanded, swiping the flask from me and handing it to Tina, who took a huge swig.

Althea grabbed it back. "Enough. That ought to warm you up." Tina coughed and nodded.

Althea dropped to her knees in front of Tina.

"It's not too late to back out. Say the word and we'll have you out of here."

"What?" I pushed Althea out of the way and squatted down to Tina's eye level. "You love him, right?"

Tina looked apologetically at Althea and nodded back at me.

"You want to marry him?"

She swallowed hard and brushed away at tears that threatened to fall and undo her perfect makeup. "Yes," she said.

"So don't let the cameras stop you. Don't let *anything* stop you. The important thing here is that at the end of the day, you're married, right?"

Tina sniffled.

"Right?" I asked again.

"Right," she echoed.

She took a deep breath and smoothed down her dress as she stood. "I'm ready."

"Good, because so are they," Junessa said, peeking out through the door. "Let's go."

Tina went first, leading the way back into the small foyer where Uncle Christos and the groomsmen waited to escort us in.

She smiled transcendently and took Christos's arm. I looked away, wishing I could appreciate the moment, but trying to spot whatever it was tying my stomach in knots. Nothing seemed out of the ordinary, but my inner alarms wouldn't cease. I was wired. I wished I'd had more of that whiskey to settle *my* nerves.

Ernest held out his arm for me to take, and as I did he whispered, "Everything okay?"

"I hope so," I whispered back.

Then we were walking down the aisle—slowly, as we'd been taught. Step. Pause. Step. Pause. I forced myself to smile at everyone, looking for particular faces in the crowd. Apollo with Serena right there beside him, Jesus, Hermes and Christie, Uncle Hector, *Nick*, looking handsome and alert, as though he sensed something as well. Spiro, Mom and Dad, Yiayia and Fergus …

Everyone I knew and loved in one place. Disaster *could not* strike. If the prophetess Cassandra had been cursed with the inability to change the futures she could see, it meant that changing them was a possibility in the normal course of things. I had to hang onto that thought.

I just prayed I'd be part of the solution and not the problem. I put Rhea out of my mind and hoped she'd stay out.

We reached the front of the small church, and Christos kissed Tina on both cheeks before surrendering her to Jason. Then everyone turned toward the priest. I fixed Tina's train as she took her place beside her groom and then she handed me her bouquet. It took a superhuman effort to turn my back on the congregation. An entire church full of potential trouble, and I had to face forward.

My back itched. My nerves jittered. My stomach danced the *syrtos*, at least staying in the wedding theme, but as each second ticked by and nothing happened, the constriction around my heart started to ease.

Behind the altar, the candles flickered, but no more or less than they should. The happy couple stood gazing into each other's eyes, hands clasped, bodies straining toward each other. Tina was beautiful. Her veil, sequined along the scalloped edges like the bodice of her dress, caught and reflected the light, which didn't even come close to matching the luminescence of her eyes. Jason looked at her like they were the only two people in the world, and seemed to pull himself out of a trance each time a response was demanded of him.

It would have been perfect, if not for the nettling sense of doom pricking at each one of my nerves. I waited through the lighting of the bride's and groom's candles with held breath, which I realized only when spots began to form in front of my eyes.

Althea elbowed me in the side like she knew I was in danger of passing out, and I let the breath out in a gasp, sucking more in and then holding that like I couldn't help myself. I stayed tense throughout the prayers, the crowning of the bride and groom, the Gospel reading and their sipping from the communal cup. I was ready to pass out by the time the priest finally gave the benediction.

Then the priest said the words the director had convinced him to add to the ceremony, "You may now kiss your bride." Tina's smile lit the room, and she threw herself into Jason's arms as though she'd barely been holding back. As soon as their lips touched, the earth moved.

Literally.

Gasps sounded throughout the church, even from the bride, but Jason only pulled Tina closer as if he thought she was the one rocking his world. Candles toppled from the altar, and Junessa screamed as one caught her dress. She brushed at it, and it flew into one of the altar cloths, which were already starting to smoke from one of the other candles. I lunged to rip it off the altar, but before I could, it burst into full-on flames. The ground bucked again, more violently this time, and I fell forward toward the blaze. I'd been planning to smother the flames, not snuff them out with my own body, but as I went down, I grabbed at the cloth, which tore free of the altar, falling all around me, along with the branches and berries that had sat atop it. The branches also started to smoke, but were still green enough not to catch … yet. I'd stopped and dropped, now I rolled, desperately trying to smother the flames.

All around there were screams and running feet. Someone yanked at the cloth engulfing me, trying to get me free. It was Junessa, offering a hand to help me up.

We looked quickly around the little chapel filling with smoke, the priest yelling instructions for evacuation, ushering the newly bound bride and groom out and calling to the altar servers to grab holy water and to pray.

Nick dashed to the nave to take me off Junessa's hands, and together we all ran for the door of the chapel. It was bottlenecked by panicked people, including Apollo and

Serena, who was frantically trying to turn *back*, into the church. At first, I thought she was mad with terror, but then I realized she must have left something behind. Something important? Like her purse with the power she held over Apollo. Our eyes met, his and mine, and I mouthed, "Get her out."

He nodded and I stood on my toes to give Nick a quick kiss on the cheek before bucking his grip and promising, "Be right back."

I whirled and pushed through a stunned crowd of fleeing people back into the church. They let me go, more interested in taking my place closer to the door than in stopping the crazy lady who wanted to run *into* the flames.

Smoke clouded my vision as I raced to the pews. The priest yelled at me to get out, but I was on a mission. I ran to the pew where I thought I'd seen Apollo and Serena earlier. I could barely see the bench, but I felt along it. Nothing. Coughing now with the smoke clogging my lungs, I dropped to the ground to search beneath the seats. My hand encountered papers and a pair of shoes—high heels someone had left behind in their haste to escape. I despaired finding Serena's talisman when I encountered something pliable and beaded. A purse! I grabbed it *and* the heels, hoping and praying one held the key, and bolted, wheezing, for the door, which had already spat out the fleeing guests. I had to dodge a fireman racing his way in, but then I was out of the burning building.

More firemen rushed the entrance, one grabbing and moving me away at speed, turning me over to a paramedic who'd just arrived on the scene. I refused medical treatment and went for Nick, who met me halfway, having seen me escape the church.

"Here, stash this," I said, shoving the purse at him.

He gave me a disbelieving look, but grabbed it all the same to conceal under his suit jacket.

Then he grabbed me and kissed me for all he was worth,

which was a helluva lot in my book. I was breathless when he let me go and not because of the fire.

"Don't do that again," he ordered.

"I won't," I promised, leaning into him. "But I think that's Serena's purse and that it may hold the spell petrifying Apollo."

His expression turned grim and I knew then I was losing him. I'd left him and safety to run into a burning building, just like I'd left him aboard the storm-lashed plane. I'd risked my life for a purse, all to help Apollo. I'd have done the same for him or Tina or … but the fact that it was for his rival made all the difference.

In my turmoil, it took me longer than it should have to realize that the tremors had stopped and that no attack had followed, which baffled me. If Zeus Earthshaker and Poseidon Stormbringer had been behind things, surely they'd have brought the church down around us. This didn't feel like them, which meant that it was another thing entirely. The unknown. I didn't like it one bit.

The earthquake had to be a side effect of something else, because Delphi was *not* known to shake, rattle and roll, and the idea that it would suddenly do so while we were on site … too much coincidence to credit.

But what then?

Jesus sprang out of the crowd toward us muttering a string of Spanish that seemed three quarters prayer and half curse, which even I knew didn't add up.

He stopped just short of us and applied hands to hips. "*Chica*, I love Ferragamo as much as the next person, but even I wouldn't have dived back into a burning building for them!"

Ferragamo? Oh right, the shoes.

The absurdity of it all struck me suddenly funny, but my laugh turned into a cough almost instantly.

Yiayia approached as I was fighting it off and I was so glad to see her that I nearly threw myself into her arms … before I saw the look on her face.

"Tori, what the *hell* is going on? That was no natural quake. During your *cousin's wedding* and everything. What have you brought down on us?"

My whole body went cold, frozen out by her words. "Me? What do I have to do with anything? I don't have the power to shake the earth."

I'd gotten loud, and people around us were turning to gawk.

"Trouble always finds you. Or you find it."

It hurt to breathe, but this time I knew it wasn't the smoke. So much for returning to the family fold. Lenny Rialto had kicked me out for turning up trouble. The family had more or less washed its hands of me. I'd thought that finding and rescuing Uncle Christos had won my way back in, but apparently, it had been short-lived. Even Yiayia, who'd always stuck by me, now sounded ready to be done.

The worst part was, I couldn't even tell her she was wrong. With Rhea playing ride-along, I held the potential for destruction inside of me. Despite what I'd said, I *could* shake the earth. Or *she* could, and had back at the police station.

Rhea. Could it be? Wouldn't I have known? Or did it somehow have to do with that head-nodding from my fellow prisoner back at the jail? Was it possible I wasn't alone in my possession? That somehow, like disaster coverage, Rhea could show on multiple screens at once? If so ... if so, she could be anywhere. In anyone. And if this was like a multiplication dance where I tag three people and each of them tag three people ... how long before the possession or mesmerism or whatever this was spread like an infection? I'd been worried about Zeus and Poseidon, Hermes and his addiction schemes, but an invasion from within ... how did we fight that?

"Tori!" Nick snapped—literally and figuratively—in my face. "Tori, come back to us. What's the matter?"

"Only everything." I looked for Uncle Hector in the crowd and spotted him not far away, watching us. "I think it's time to rally the troops," I told him. "So far we've been reactive. I think it's time we change that." I grabbed his hand and started for Uncle Hector ... Pan. That was going to take some getting used to.

"Wait," Yiayia said with a hand to my arm that wouldn't have stopped me if I'd been really determined to get away. "That really wasn't you in there, was it?"

"No. I'm sorry you didn't know that." I took my hand back. "I really didn't start this, any of it, but I'm going to finish it."

"How can I help?" she asked.

I looked at her and at Fergus standing behind her. How much did he know about Yiayia's crazy beliefs? Did it really matter?

"For now just see that all the wedding guests get back safely to the hotel."

I turned for Uncle Hector again, to find Apollo, Althea, and Junessa converging as well.

"What was *that* all about?" Althea asked, but it was a general question, not directed at me. The knot in my chest didn't loosen, but I could breathe through it.

I had a horrible fear I might even know the answer, though saying it out loud seemed to somehow make it real.

I looked at everybody, weighing my words. "When Rhea was in my head she ranted about the time for the Olympians being past and about it being time for the Titans. The last time I felt the earth shake like this a dragon had awakened ..." from its slumber at the peak of Mount Lee in LA. Its rise had knocked the Hollywood sign askew. "Do you think she could be awakening the Titans?"

Silence met my question. I'd been hoping someone would tell me I was crazy, that the Titans had died out ages ago, but I could tell from the looks on their faces that no one would be laying my fears to rest.

"Where's Serena?" I asked Apollo, like he was her keeper.

"She's trying to convince the firemen to rescue her purse," he said with a grim smile. "I made sure she left it behind when I dragged her out."

Nick and I exchanged a look. "You mean this purse?" he asked, letting it peek out from beneath his jacket.

Apollo's eyes widened. "You couldn't have just let it burn?"

I stared at him. Nick stared at me, and I got a sinking feeling. "You mean fire would have done the trick?"

"Maybe. Hector told me about your theory. If whatever she's using to fuel her spell is inside, fire should have cancelled it out. It's anathema to water."

"Gah!" I poured my frustration into that one word, but it was inadequate for the job.

"Never mind," Apollo said, amusement trying to twitch the petrified planes of his face into a smile. "Now that we have it, I know just what to do."

"Good," Nick said, handing it over. "Then it's all yours. Goes much better with your outfit anyway."

Althea looked over her shoulder to where clipboard guy was heading for us. "I'm supposed to be rounding you up," she said. "Andre wants us to stick to the schedule. The fire department has things under control here, and we're due at the Tholos for pictures."

"But—" I said at the same time Nick said, "Tholos?"

As Althea started to explain, "Well, the guidebooks call it the Sanctuary of Athena, but really it was designed to celebrate some old military victory …" Apollo walked over to one of the glowing luminaries and passed a hand over it. The candle inside flared and started to engulf the paper. Before anyone around could react, Apollo reached into the purse and pulled out a little stick doll, an effigy, and dropped it onto the flames. Off to the side, Serena screeched, but it was too late. The little stick figure caught fire instantly, and as Andre arrived, Apollo stomped out the tiny bonfire, crushing the effigy beneath his feet. Instantly, I could see his face relax. The smile he turned in Serena's direction was chilling.

"Come, come," Andre said, bustling up, oblivious to everything. "We've got to keep to our schedule. The fire department has things well in hand here."

As the others started to move, I said to myself, "Yes, by all means, let's go film a movie, *then* stop the Titans, and save Greece."

There was a sudden gasp, and my head whipped around to see that Hermes and Christie had reached us and that she'd just heard me loud and clear. I was looking straight into her widened eyes, her gaze willing me to deny what I'd said, turn it into a joke. I'd kept everything I could from Christie thus far, but she'd seen things that were hard to explain away and it was clear that all the pieces were suddenly falling into place for her.

But Andre was shepherding us toward the limos waiting back at the hotel with a nudge here and there from his clipboard. I could have avoided the accusation in her eyes if his herding hadn't pushed me closer to Christie, who hissed quietly, "*Save Greece?* What's going on? How could you not tell me?"

"I was trying to protect you."

"You're not my mother, and you're not my keeper, so cut it out."

Beside her, Hermes grinned, but it faded when she turned on him. "And *you*. You knew too, didn't you? That's why you locked Jesus and me away in that bathroom in San Francisco, isn't it? To protect us?"

Hermes didn't look a bit cowed in the face of her anger. "You needed protection. You don't know what you're dealing with."

"What about you? *You* didn't need protection?"

Hermes met my gaze, and I bit my lip, not willing to lie to Christie anymore and not quite ready to rock her world.

"No, I didn't."

Christie waited, trying to dig in her heels but being pushed along by the crowd.

The ground shook again, like an aftershock, and we all grabbed each other to steady ourselves. I felt something pass to

Christie when she gripped me, an electric shock that arched between us, zapping us both. She looked at me, startled, and then Andre pushed us on, talking into his Bluetooth. "But the Tholos is still standing? The quake didn't—No, no, you tell them it's already been approved. The tremor is over, and we have insurance. What we *don't* have is a lot of time in the production schedule. Yes, ten, twenty minutes. Make sure it's all ready."

"Do you feel all right?" I asked Christie, worried about that zap.

"Perfect," she answered. It was too serene to be reassuring. She should still be angry at me. Or hurt. But she sounded strangely calm now. I thought about my fellow prisoner back at the jail and started to pull away, to try to drop to the back of the group. What if I was like patient zero, spreading Rhea's infection? What if Christie's calm was every bit as unnatural as it seemed?

But Andre pushed me again and nothing happened this time but an overwhelming urge to deck him, which I was pretty certain was all mine.

Back in the hotel parking lot, the makeup staff waited to touch us up as Andre directed us toward our limos, all the better to drive to the Tholos and the stunning vistas with the Delphi temple complex in the background. They could do remarkable things in post-production now, including, I hoped, smooth over any still-smoking or singed wedding finery. I envied the regular guests who got to stay behind at the hotel and drink away the horror of the wedding chapel going up in flames during the cocktail hour. I just hoped the shoot would go more smoothly than the wedding and that when we returned the bride and groom would make a triumphant entrance and put all the rest behind them.

I grabbed Nick's hand and kept him close to my side, dragging him into the limo with me before the primping posse could get their hands on me. Andre started to protest, but I stopped him with a look. I must have put some kind of freaky force behind it, because he let it go. I'd been able to stop men in their tracks before, flash freeze them temporarily, but never make them compliant. If this was some new thing Rhea or nectar or whatever had awakened inside me, I was glad for it.

It was a tight squeeze with Nick in the limo with the wedding party. When it came time for my escort, Ernest, to climb in, he offered to catch the next limo, the one with the talent, but we pushed in and made room for him.

Then we were off. Andre slammed the door on us, still talking nonstop into his Bluetooth. He slapped the side of the limo like a trail horse, and it bucked forward, taking us to the peak of Mount Parnassus.

I squeezed Nick's hand. "I'm sorry," I said. "About ... just everything." I wasn't going to go all George Bailey in *It's a Wonderful Life* and say he'd have been better off if he'd never met me. He was a big boy and could make his own decisions. Unlike Christie and Jesus, he'd *known* what he was getting into with me, almost from the start. But the fact remained that if he'd stayed away from me, he wouldn't constantly be in any crazy kind of danger.

"Stop," he said. Not *it's okay*. Just *stop*. "I'm a policeman. I accepted trouble a long time ago. Hell, crossing the street in LA can be dangerous enough, and it doesn't come with any of the perks."

Great, so I was trouble with benefits—friends with benefits only with more potential for bloodshed. Go me.

Still, I smiled. "What about—" I couldn't say it. Not in a car full of people. Maybe not at all. *What about me killing people and leaving the scene of the crime?*

But he seemed to know what I'd left unsaid. "We'll ... get past it. If the options were you dead or you alive and the bad guys taking your place, I don't see that you had any choice."

It hadn't been my choice at all, but he was so close to acceptance I didn't argue. Maybe he'd forgive, but I wondered if he'd ever be able to forget. And he hadn't even seen me in action.

I hoped he wouldn't get a second chance. I had a very bad feeling about heading back toward Rhea's place of power with the people I loved all around me, with Nick at my side. What if Rhea manifested again and decided they were in her way? What if I was right about the Titans rising? What if Nick got to see my possession up close and personal?

Nick pulled me closer, as if he thought from my shiver that I was cold. Instinctively I pulled away, like that little distance could save him if something happened.

My gorge rose, and the limo stopped just in time. I popped the door open and climbed over Nick to get out. I stumbled off only a few feet before the contents of my stomach made a reappearance, burning their way up and out.

Everyone else exited on the other side of the car, as far away from me as possible, except for Nick who, like a good boyfriend, came to hold my hair.

I was gasping by the time my stomach was empty, still too horrified even to be embarrassed.

"Who has that flask?" Althea asked.

Junessa handed it over and Althea rounded the car to make me drink.

"Usually, I don't agree with spirits, but every once in a while, they have their uses," she said. "In moderation." As if I might take it as a license to party. Gorgon Girls Gone Wild. It was both the nearest and farthest thing from my mind.

I took a decent swig from the flask, more to kill the taste in my mouth than because I thought it would do any real good, and then tried to breathe through the nausea as the whiskey hit my stomach.

"I'm fine," I lied. "Thank you."

I handed the flask back to Junessa and saw that everyone was staring at me as if I might grow a second head or start clucking like a chicken. "Really," I added, smiling to show conviction.

Andre got out of the second limo with the others, passed a disapproving look over me, by which I knew he'd seen everything, and then made flapping motions to move us toward the Tholos. Two other cars were already parked on the shoulder of the road near the site—I assumed the production people that Andre had been chatting up on his Bluetooth.

Apollo hung back, refusing to be wafted toward anything. He scanned the area, looking up to where his defiled sanctuary could be seen on the pinnacle of Mount Parnassus overlooking the Tholos and everything on down.

There was an official car parked up there, but we were too far away to see what was going on. Apollo scanned downward, toward the Tholos and across to where I was lagging behind. Nick stayed with me, maybe sensing like I did that there was a verdict to await.

Apollo met my gaze, caught Nick's, and then looked back to me. "Something's wrong," he mouthed so the others couldn't hear.

I felt it too. In the churning pit of my stomach, in the way that the place was plucking at my nerves.

Something wicked this way comes.

I looked toward Althea, who nodded to me before I could say a word. She'd seen Apollo's warning and moved off to talk to Junessa. It was hard to be prepared when you didn't know what to be prepared *for*.

A car pulled up behind ours as we walked to the Tholos, a small site practically within the shadow of Apollo's temple complex, which rose in the background to dwarf the much closer Tholos.

The newly arrived car didn't have lights flashing, but there was no mistaking it for anything but a police cruiser. Andre signaled someone to go talk with the cops, and I wondered whether they were some kind of security for the ancient site … or whether they were coming for me. But my precog warning signal didn't point me in that direction. No, I sensed trouble beneath us, as if we were standing on the danger, and above, from the direction of Apollo's sanctuary, but not from the road.

I couldn't keep my gaze from being drawn up the mountain, as if the spirits of those I'd killed might rise up and accuse me or descend to take their revenge. It was stupid, I knew. The bodies would have been removed, and I didn't believe in ghosts, but *something* was up there still. I could feel it. Maybe it was the center of awareness for the goddess we'd awakened. Maybe it was something more. Either way, it was trouble.

Nick pulled me gently along, watching our footing while I, less helpfully, watched the cliffs above.

"Keep an eye out," I told him.

He nodded, stopping with me when Andre put a hand out signaling that we should all halt. Ahead of us, Tina huffed, "But *I'm* the bride."

Clearly, since we only had the site for a limited time, and since the production company had arranged it, Andre was going to make sure they got their film shots first.

Up ahead, the director, who none of us hoi polloi had been introduced to, staged Apollo and Serena, who pretended the sound, lighting and film equipment all around them didn't exist. Serena couldn't quite do the same with her costar, though she didn't seem to know what *to* do with him. The fire of hatred burned in her eyes, and I didn't think it was going to do wonders for their romantic scene or her film career. If she wasn't careful, *she'd* be the one getting replaced. I had a hard time concerning myself about that. Apollo alternated between looking at the mountain and making enough eye contact with the director to feign attention.

They were positioned in the center of the Tholos, on the raised platform ascended by stairs and loomed over by the three columns still standing. Or restored to standing, anyway, since I was pretty sure from the mottled dark and light stone that parts of the column weren't original. But they *were* huge and impressive, especially with the field of white sprinkled with purple flowers and other felled columns lying all around them. It was striking from any angle, whether the skyline peeked between the pillars or the ruins of Delphi rose behind them.

Andre gave us a short "silence or death" speech, and we all stood around gawping as Apollo and Serena acted out a romantic comedy scene about why each had sneaked away from the wedding and what each would have asked the ancient oracles at Delphi. It was amazing how they'd gone from enemies one moment to potential lovers the next. It was a shame Serena was a sociopathic siren. There was no debating she had talent. Together they managed to spin an entirely illusory web of magic and romance.

The first half dozen times anyway. Once the director had stopped and restarted them, moved them and the cameras into different positions and made them go through it ad nauseam, the scene had lost its charm.

Tina began *tap-tap-tapping* on Andre's shoulder, ending more on a thump than a tap. I could see an argument brewing, when the director finally turned and smiled through his scraggly beard. "And now for the bride."

I let out a breath, praying we'd be done and gone before whatever tension I felt building sprung on us like snakes from a can.

Someone snapped in my face, and I blinked at Andre's fingers an inch from my nose. I thought about breaking them, but I was pretty sure it would piss Tina off and, anyway, the police were watching.

I settled for glaring and going where he arranged me. We all stood at the steps of the Tholos, apparently not cleared, like the famous people, for use of the platform. A photographer and videographer both moved in to shoot us. Traditional poses first —boys on one side, girls on the other flanking the bride and groom. Then variations. Just the girls. Just the boys. Guys holding the bride vertically and her looking exasperated. Girls gathered around the groom, all leaning in to kiss his cheek. And then the wedding party was off the hook and it was just the bride and groom in the spotlight.

Tina was gazing up into Jason's face, looking like she'd just won the lottery when my precog kicked into high gear. I looked around at every face, including the face of the mountain above us, searching out the danger. But my vision jerked suddenly as a tremor started up the mountain, radiating down the side. Rocks began to cascade down, knocking larger rocks loose and starting a shearing. The stones sounded like gunfire as they struck, broke apart, and ricocheted down the mountain toward us.

"Back to the limos!" Andre yelled to be heard above it.

No one needed to be told. Already, Tina clutched Jason's hand and was running blindly away from the Tholos, back toward the road. I lurched for Nick just as the whip end of the tremor hit us like an explosion, sending me skyrocketing into him. He rocked with the impact of my body blow but managed to keep us upright … until the ground bucked beneath us again, harder this time, like the earth was a bed sheet being snapped out of its orderly folds. Nick and I were knocked apart. I fell hard, striking my butt bone in a spine numbing impact with the ground.

I lay momentarily stunned, until something began to rise from the ground before me and true fear kicked me in the gut— a monstrous snake with fangs the size of steak knives. The head was triangular, which somewhere in the back of my jibbering mind I knew meant that it was poisonous. Its yellow-green eyes gleamed with intelligence and malice.

Around us was chaos. There were screams and running feet. Someone clutched clumsily at my shoulders, and I looked up into Tina's terrified face, but she had eyes only for the snake— hence the clumsiness—and when it darted its head at her, fangs fully extended, she shrieked and ran. I didn't blame her. I gave her props for coming back for me at all.

The upheaval of the snake's eruption from the earth upset one of the huge stones atop a Tholos column and it came crashing down. I shouted a warning to anyone still in its path and covered my head, as if that would do any good against a two-ton stone, but for one brief shining moment luck was with me. It missed, falling onto the stone platform in an explosion of sharp projectile fragments. The snake's head whipped around at the crash, and I seized the moment to roll away toward Nick.

He reached for me too, a "What the hell!" coming out of his mouth, but I presumed it was rhetorical, because even if I had the answer, I didn't have the breath to offer it.

Gunfire started up around us, and Nick pulled my head down to the ground, covering me with his body to protect me from doing anything stupid like trying to get into the line of fire. I'd forgotten about the police officers and their weapons, but I blessed them now.

I squirmed enough in Nick's grip to be able to see what was going on … and to be very, very afraid. The snake barely rocked with the impact of the bullets. Instead of recoiling, he sprang at one of the officers and bit down hard before the man could even cry out. I flinched my eyes shut as the officer's blood spurted and his gun fell to the ground.

Within me, deep within as if it had burrowed there, an alien part of me reveled, glad to see the serpent rise again. The Pythian serpent resurrected? Rhea's avatar that Apollo had fought for control of the sanctuary back in his glory days? Would Apollo have the power now to do it all over again? I couldn't imagine it. The thing was bigger than a football field—not end-to-end, but circled like a boundary line. It was twice as thick as a person, too thick to wrap arms around and too deadly.

The other officers fell back toward their cruiser, emptying their clips into the creature, which spat their compatriot to the side and went after the next.

We *had* to do something.

Suddenly, an arrow lodged in the roof of the serpent's mouth, catching it in mid-strike. It seemed to shriek as it spasmed in pain, looking around for the source of its torment.

I did the same, and found Althea and Junessa poised by our limo, its trunk open, making it clear from whence their weapons had come. They closed on the serpent in unison, as if they'd been hunting together forever, stopping to fire arrows, advancing again as they reached for another.

The other limo was on the move, carrying everyone who'd piled in to safety. But as it made the turn to head back down the road, a door was suddenly flung open and Apollo bailed out, flying past the hands trying to grab him back inside.

I pushed at Nick, desperate to get up and join the fight, but before I could do a thing, the serpent launched itself at the new moving target, its tale lashing into Nick and I, sending us rolling over the ground, skinning arms and legs, tearing up my bridesmaid's gown something fierce. It blew past the officers still standing, slamming its oversized body right over them to get to Apollo and the girls.

The girls? Women. Huntresses. Right now, our best hope.

The belt radios of the downed officers all came to life at once, and I didn't know the code coming through, but I recognized the address involved. Something was happening back at the hotel.

What in the holy hells was going on?

I rose up and dove after the snake with no real plan but to end things. Thinking only to launch myself on top of it, distract it long enough to keep it from eating Apollo and to allow Althea and Junessa to finish him off. I landed on top of the tail. Beneath me, bands of muscles worked, terrifying in their power, but the snake didn't so much as swivel at my extra weight. The tail *did* flick, and I couldn't find a handhold on the smooth scales. I went flying. My vision went cloudy with a chance of blackout.

Someone called out and suddenly, instead of going dark, the world lit up like from a massive lightning strike, only there was no electricity in the air, and when I blinked the now gold-limned clouds away, I saw that it was as though a beam had shot straight from the sun, a laser-like solar flare targeted on the serpent's face. The smell of ozone and burning flesh filled the air. The snake made an indescribable noise, thrashing and coiling back on itself like a spring that had bounced back, trying to escape the burning light.

The beam seemed to follow it, and the snake's tongue darted out, started to smoke, and flicked back. Blindly, it sprang again, striking in Apollo's direction, but it didn't come even close.

"Now, aim for the eyes!" Apollo shouted.

Arrows arced through the air, striking the serpent again and again. Left eye, right. Everything about it screamed in pain, its contortions like the desperate throes of a worm that's been hooked, and I actually felt sorry for the creature. If I was right, it was following Rhea's compulsion, no less than I had the other night. It was blameless. It didn't deserve this.

"Stop!" I ordered, before I knew it was coming out of my mouth. "Just stop. He's retreating."

And he was—drawing back and back. I'd never seen a snake move that way before. It was spastic and terrible to see, but the arrows halted and the world went back to its former lighting, which now seemed impossibly dim, maybe because I'd burned out some rods or cones or whatever in my eyes.

Momentarily, silence reigned, as we all watched to be sure the monster didn't renew the attack, and then one of the downed officers said, "What the *hell* was that?"

Another rolled over, struggling to his feet. "We called it in. I don't know why help isn't here yet."

"I'm not sure we're getting our backup," said the first. "There's some kind of disturbance back in town."

"Damn." The second officer plucked the radio from his belt and started talking into it as he squatted beside his two compatriots—the one the serpent had attacked and the other who hadn't gotten up after he'd been crushed when the snake went for Apollo. The one who'd been bitten was swollen up around the face, his skin the color of a bruise. It didn't look like he was breathing. The other groaned when his fellow officer put a hand to his neck to check his pulse.

"Ribs," the hurt officer gasped, face contorted with pain.

"ETA on the ambulance is less than five," the other officer assured him, but he exchanged a worried glance with the other cop still standing.

If there were broken ribs, and if one of them had punctured a lung …

"Don't move," the officer said, as if the downed officer had seemed at all inclined. Then he looked around at all of us … all of us still there—minus the director, film crew, Andre, Serena and most of the bridesmaids and groomsmen who'd gone in the other limo. "None of you go anywhere. We're going to need to take statements."

"But the hotel," Tina cried. "I heard—"

"We've already got officers on the scene," the first cop said. "Nothing you can do there but get in the way."

"Hell with *that*," I said. "Who's with me?"

Our limo still waited, and I raced toward it, not bothering to see who might be following. I could guess at some. As for others … well, the cop was right. They'd only be in the way. But stopping them would take time I wasn't sure we had, and anyway, they had the right to make their own decisions and do what they could. It wasn't like I could guarantee their safety anywhere; that was clear enough.

I hit the car and yanked open the driver's side door. Our driver Viggo was still there, but looked to be in some serious shock. "Move over," I ordered him. He didn't have to be told twice. I don't know if he'd heard from across the way and knew we'd been ordered by the police to stick around, but it didn't seem to matter to him as long as someone else took control. Doors opened all around us as I quickly adjusted the seat and mirrors. Nick, Apollo, Althea, and Junessa piled in, Tina and Jason tumbling quickly after.

"What are you waiting for?" Tina asked as she slammed the door behind them. "Go!"

I *went*, wishing I'd stolen a police car so that I could have peeled out with lights and sirens clearing our way, but whether it was the quakes or whatever that kept people off this part of the road, we had almost a straight shot down the mountain. Well, straight but for the crazy switchbacks. Luckily, adrenaline or ambrosia had my reflexes reacting better than ever and I didn't have anything left over for panic.

Our driver felt differently, based on the way he kept trying to stomp on an imaginary passenger's side brake. He crossed himself and started muttering a prayer as I took another corner in a way that a roller coaster car might have envied.

"Tori, what the hell?" Tina asked from the back seat.

"What the hell, what?" I asked back. We weren't far from the hotel. I'd had plenty of interrogation practice with Armani. I could avoid a direct answer for far longer than our drive.

"The *snake*," she said. "And *you girls*"—She turned on Althea and Junessa—"*bows and arrows*. How the *hell*—"

Hell was getting a lot of credit here.

"I thought maybe that was part of the movie," I said. "I missed the rehearsal, remember."

She looked confused for a second, as though working through whether I might actually have a valid point.

"No," she gasped, still shell-shocked. "No way. Phone," she said, holding a hand out to the car at large, waiting for someone to hand her one. Apollo obliged, and immediately she was dialing. "Uncle Hector?" she asked, voice sharp. Then, even more sharply, "Uncle Hector!"

There were screams coming from the phone, and we all heard him yell, "Stay back," before the call ended.

Tina looked terrified.

"I'm, uh, I'm sure everything's fine," Jason said, convincing no one. "The cops said police are already there."

She gave him an *"are you crazy?"* look as we pulled up in front of the hotel … but not into the parking lot. We couldn't. Something had destroyed it. The center had been blasted out like something had exploded up out of it. Chunks of asphalt lay like volcanic rock in the road, denting car hoods, piercing windshields.

Tina was out of the car before anyone could protest, dodging the worst of the damage in a mad dash toward the reception, toward everyone we loved who wasn't already with us. Jason took off after her.

I cursed and did the same, vaulting the debris and trying to catch them. There was a sick, sharp feeling in the pit of my stomach about what we'd find inside, but as it turned out, I'd had no idea. None.

I caught up to Tina, who followed the path of destruction toward the banquet hall. As we burst inside, I didn't know what to process first. Tables were overturned and wedding guests were hiding behind them, using them as oversized shields. That was the upside. The down was that the center of the room was taken up not by one giant snake, but three—two of them in human form. *Zeus* and *Poseidon* … both larger than life, grown as much as they could with the high ceilings and facing (and facing and facing …) off with more heads than I could even process at first. Not the hydra. That serpent had only nine heads, one of them immortal. *This* beast had dozens, maybe a hundred, a seething mass of dragon-like heads on neck stalks bent to fit the room, all deadly as hell and spitting fire. I'd been so distracted by the heads that I only just now noticed the legs—far too many of them. So, not a serpent then. More like a militant millipede.

"Typhoeus," Apollo said behind me, voice hushed in awe.

"You *know* him?" I hissed back, not wanting any of those heads to swivel our way.

Flames shot toward Zeus and Poseidon, and suddenly water burst forth from the sprinklers in the ceiling and wedding guests shrieked anew. The central combatants didn't seem to notice. Except for Poseidon, who was doing something … grabbing the moisture out of the air as quickly as it fell around them and using it to create Super Soaker blasts back at the spitting heads. Where fire met water, the dragon-thing hissed, and the air grew thick with steam. In seconds, no one would be able to see to fight.

"I know *of* him," Apollo said. "Gaea sent Typhoeus after Zeus during the rise of the Titans. Zeus won."

"How?" I asked, still trying to wrap my head around what I was seeing.

"I don't know, but he was at full power then."

The ... Typhoeus gave up on the flames and lashed out with its many heads, coming from every angle. Zeus cried out—or Poseidon, or both—and I could no longer see them, covered as they were in the serpent-head swarm.

A sense of triumph bubbled up from within me that I knew wasn't mine. *Two down*, Rhea crowed. *More to come.*

"Do something," Tina cried.

She was right. Even knowing exactly what Zeus and Poseidon had come for, I couldn't let them die like that. I didn't know that Rhea would stop there anyway. Her anger seemed bigger than that. If they went down, I didn't know that she'd call off the monster rather than turn it on the rest of the guests.

I whirled on Apollo. "Nothing we need to know here, right? If we cut off a head, it won't grow back?"

"No, I don't think so."

Hell's bells, I was risking it all on a *guess*?

"Get back," I told the others, knowing they wouldn't listen. I summoned my inner loudmouth and all the power I could draw. I sensed something deep within ... some hole that had been drilled or some dimension that had been tapped when Rhea moved in. I dove into that too, thrusting her aside as I sensed her try to get in my way. She was so stunned, she didn't react in time, and I dipped a toe into her power stream. The torrent of energy that flooded me was uncontrollable. I let it overwhelm me and screamed at the top of my lungs, stomping and waving my arms to get the attention of the Titan's many hideous heads, "Hey, *you*. *Worm*. Come and get me!"

Some of the heads turned. Not all, not by a long shot, but I'd take what I could get and hope they'd drag the others down. I swept the faces with my gaze—those I could see through the steam—and screamed, *"FREEZE!"*

The power blew out of me in a bomb blast, and the heads looking my way *froze*, dropping like stones. But the other heads, by far the majority, now knew that something was off. Others began to turn toward me. Althea and Junessa, now that I'd entered the fray, took up positions to either side of me and began to fire off arrows. I knew when they hit by the recoil of some of the heads, but there were too many of them, and they were coming on too quickly.

I prepared to freeze more, when inside me Rhea revolted, throwing herself on the power I'd tapped and cutting me off, wresting control back to herself. My body seized up at the struggle like my brain had short-circuited. My eyes rolled up into my head and then …

A Rhea reboot.

My vision righted itself, only I was no longer in control of it. I watched in horror from within and without as I turned and stuck my hand right in the path of the latest of Althea's arrows. She saw it too late, already releasing the bowstring. The piercing pain hardly registered as the bolt went right through my hand, fletching shredding my flesh on the tail end. With my good hand, I reached for her bow and yanked it away, only Althea hung on with a huntress's power. While they fought, Junessa turned her bow on me, but hesitated to shoot it.

With one monumental tug, I/Rhea freed the bow from Althea's grip, whipping her aside with the force of my torque and wielding the bow like a bat, straight at Junessa's head. My heart clenched, hoping she'd duck in time. I saw the indecision in her eyes—fire or duck. At the last possible second, she dropped out of position and tossed her weapon aside, now in too close for it to do any good. Instead, she recovered and went for a flying tackle, aimed at my midsection. Rhea pivoted me out of the way, right into Althea, who'd recovered and showed it with a sucker punch to my solar plexus. I didn't know if Rhea felt it any more than I did, but she didn't let it stop her. She grabbed for Althea's head and was, I was afraid, about to snap her neck, but the serpents got there first, going for her throat and coming up with mouthfuls of hair that had fallen in their path. They yanked Althea by the hair, dragging her toward them, the better to bite her.

But Nick had grabbed Junessa's discarded arrow. I could feel his torment. He couldn't bear to use it on me, but the monster ... that was another matter. He lunged forward like a Maori warrior and thrust the arrow hard, right into the closest dragon's eye.

It hissed back, and another head swung around to its aid, biting the shaft and snapping it in half. Other heads went straight for Nick.

I tried to jump in front of him, but Rhea had complete control. Apollo darted in to grab the bow in my hand, shouting, "Tori, if you're in there, *let go!*"

I tried, but there were no signals getting from me to my body. Junessa grabbed a handful of my hair, yanking my head back suddenly, and I snarled as Apollo swept my legs out from under me. I landed hard on my back with Apollo on top of me, but I didn't surrender the bow. He had to knock the upper curve of it into my chin so hard I saw stars before that would happen.

When he had the bow, he rose up, getting it far, far away from my grasp, "Hermes, you coward, get out here and keep her down!"

I couldn't see what happened next—whether Zeus and Poseidon were still alive, whether Nick had escaped the hundreds of fire-shooting faces he was far too close to with no defense. My heart pounded like it would explode and still my body wouldn't obey.

My brain seemed to spin, and my stomach rebelled with the nausea of vertigo, and then, somehow, I was seeing the room from another angle.

Typhoeus still struggled weakly, a handful of heads trying to get the rest of the body moving. The heads I'd frozen were waking again, sluggishly, about to rejoin the fight. But Rhea must have decided he'd had enough, because I let out a high-pitched whistle that meant something to the beast. He jerked to attention, listening, and then sprang toward Tori ... *me* ... knocking me down like a bowling pin.

And that was when I realized that I wasn't *me*. I'd forgotten in the insanity that I was looking at the world through someone else's eyes—someone who hadn't been brought low by Apollo and the huntresses. I was trying to think who I'd seen hiding where around the room when a voice called in shock, "Christie!"

My sight swung toward the one who'd called out—Hermes, staring in horror at the eyes through which I was seeing—and I realized that Rhea had gotten to Christie and that somehow we were now linked.

But as the serpent withdrew, racing toward his tunnel, so did Rhea, with a final proclamation in Christie's voice. "This isn't over. The Titans are coming. Your time is *through*."

My vision snapped back to my own body, retracting with a force that left my brain bruised. The world was fuzzy and purple, but I fought through it, needing to know who was still standing and who could be helped.

CHAPTER TEN

"Better to have love and lost? Oh, screw that!"
—Tori Karacis

S omehow, I battled back the dark clouds obscuring my vision, only the first thing I saw was even darker ... Nick down. And not in the way that someone falls who has any control over it. He was lying pretty much on the left side of his face. The right side was so swollen and blackened that I could only tell it was him from his suit.

I crawled to him, but when I got to his side I hesitated to touch, afraid to hurt him. Distantly, I was aware of sirens and commotion, but all I could see was Nick. My hands quaked as I held one in front of his nose to see if I could feel him breathing. My heart was in my throat, choking me. I couldn't tell. Dammit, I should be able to *tell*.

In that instant, I understood Apollo entirely. I'd have dosed Nick right then with ambrosia if I had any on me, to spare him pain, to bring him back to me and heal him up. I'd slit open my own wrists and let him drink if I had vampiric blood or if I thought there was enough ambrosia still running through me to help. I'd pay any price to save him.

Could it be? Did I have enough ambrosia running through my veins to heal him? Was it even safe to give a person human blood? I didn't know his blood type or how important that might be. I didn't know anything.

The EMTs arrived and pushed me out of the way before I could give in to temptation. I moved back, still squatting there, though, as close as I could. Part of me was furious that they'd pushed me away when I could have helped him, but the other half knew they'd come just in time. If I'd helped Nick with ambrosia, I'd be making him an addict. I was almost certain he'd rather die.

Still, my heart broke at the missed opportunity, and I let out a sob that had been building.

I forced myself to turn away, to see if there was anywhere I was needed. Off to the side, Tina cried uncontrollably, a puddle in Jason's arms, both collapsed together on the floor. Wedding guests were coming out of hiding. Paramedics were helping others who'd gone down—one figure with a prodigious beard among them. Fear filled me that it was Yiayia, and I felt terrible about being relieved when I looked beyond and saw her wringing her hands, watching Fergus with the EMT much the same way I'd watched Nick. She seemed to sense my gaze and met it from across the room. She looked desolate. Neither of us mouthed a word.

The EMT working on Nick got my attention and asked if I was his wife. I nodded, lying in silence, willing to admit to anything if it kept me by his side.

"Want to ride along? He's alive, but badly burned. It may be touch and go. Decisions may be to be made."

Hope and dread warred. Alive, but badly burned. Decisions? I wasn't actually authorized to make any medical decisions on his behalf. What if it came down to—? I ruthlessly clamped down on that thought and nodded again.

Our EMT signaled another to help him get Nick onto a gurney. I felt a hand on my arm as they started to count in order to synchronize the lift, but I didn't turn.

"I'm sorry," Apollo said. He sounded sincere, but I didn't know if he was sorry for Nick or for taking me down earlier when I was possessed. I nodded again. It didn't matter.

"We have to plan," he continued. "Let them care for the wounded."

I turned now to stare at him, shocked that he'd even suggest it. "I can't leave him." He tried to pull me aside and I dug in my heels, but he was stronger, and I owed him, even if I was only just realizing how much. I moved off with him, but only far enough for the EMTs not to overhear. Then I repeated. "I can't leave him."

"You can't do anything else," he countered, eyes soft with understanding. "You can't do anything for him, and if Rhea comes back—" *I won't be able to control myself.* He didn't need to finish the thought. He seemed to sense it and moved on. "If Rhea really is raising the Titans it's a world-ender. Truly. No one will be safe. The best thing you can do for him and everyone else is to help us stop it."

"How?" I asked. "So far I've been part of the problem, not the solution."

"Even more reason for you to be with us. It's safer for Nick, and I keep thinking there must be some way I can use our mind link to get through to you when Rhea's in residence, or at least piggyback on her thoughts so that we can learn her plans."

"What if there isn't?"

"Then we're no worse off than we are now."

I knew in my head that he made sense, but my heart—the pieces that remained—didn't agree.

"Give me an hour," I said. "Let me get him to the hospital.

Let me be there in case he wakes. After that, they'll probably have him on sedatives and in surgery. But for now—"

Apollo's eyes were indescribably sad. "Go. I'll get everyone together."

I looked around suddenly. "Where are Zeus and Poseidon?"

We both looked to their last known position, but we couldn't see them with the EMTs in the way. At least one was alive enough to refuse treatment and have the EMT argue with him over the extent of his burns. I didn't hear any more after that and could only assume that the belligerent one had either passed out or been knocked out by some kind of painkiller.

"Seems they'll be going to the hospital as well," Apollo said. "Maybe you can talk to them."

"*Talk* to them?"

He gave me a very serious look. "If the Titans are rising, we can't do it alone. I'm not even sure we can do it together. When Zeus beat the Titans before he had help—the Cyclopes and Hecatoncheires. It wasn't a battle, it was a war."

This kept getting better and better. "Fine, I'll talk to them, but I have to go."

The EMTs hadn't waited for me, but were wheeling Nick out on their cart. I ran to catch up with them.

He didn't moan or shift as they hoisted him into the ambulance and bumped him into place. He barely looked alive.

And *I'd* done this. Or at least I'd been too weak to stop it from happening, to stop Rhea from taking me over, using me to commit human sacrifice and awaken her fully into her power. This was the second time Nick would be in the hospital because of me. There wouldn't be a third.

I had to quickly get out of the way as another EMT came through with another stretcher and they loaded that into the ambulance as well. I couldn't tell who it was with his face as blackened as Nick's, but from the suit it looked like another wedding guest. Poor man.

The medic got up into the ambulance; his partner motioned

me in as well, then slammed the doors behind us. There was barely room for me and the medic between the two stretchers, and he had to shift back and forth between patients, starting IVs, checking heart rates. I tried to stay out of the way and prayed to anyone and everyone—Christ Pantokrator straight through to Rhea herself—with everything I had for Nick to be okay. For *everyone* to miraculously be okay. And for them to send Nick home where he'd be safe. He had no part in this war, but I couldn't see him accepting that. If people were in danger he'd fight until his last breath to save them. That's exactly what I was afraid of.

The medic fired questions at me as he worked on Nick, and I did my best to answer, remembering that I was supposed to be his wife. It was amazing how woefully ignorant I was. Finally, I patted him down for his wallet and pulled out his blood donor and insurance cards, which answered some of the questions I couldn't.

As soon as we hit the hospital, I was sidelined again, shoved off on someone with a computer and a no-nonsense attitude to answer questions, many of them the same as I'd already been asked, and to fill out paperwork that seemed endless. I asked every time I could catch a break whether I could see him, but I kept getting, "Just one or two more things," until I wondered how the data entry lady had ever passed kindergarten math.

Finally, I was allowed into the emergency area waiting room. No further. When I tried to ask the nurse who'd occasionally call someone in what was going on, she insisted that someone would be out to talk to me.

I tried to wait. Really, I did. But it didn't take. I'd told Apollo I'd be back in an hour. After twenty minutes had passed, I glanced around at my fellow waiters—reading magazines, playing on their smart phones, worriedly pacing the floor. All wrapped up in their own stuff. No one was concerned with me. I got up out of my seat and without rushing or doing the "casual saunter" that never looked anything but suspicious, I approached the door that would take me into the treatment area, turned the knob, and simply walked through. No one was there to stop me. I dodged doctors and nurses, desperately willing them not to see me … or at least not to care if they did. Whether it worked or whether the craziness of the ER was on my side, I didn't know. I peeked behind curtains and dodged into and out of treatment areas with impunity. But no Nick. No sign of him. At a guess, he'd had to go straight into surgery or some super-sterile area because of his burns and exposed flesh.

Tears welled up in my eyes, and I would have let that last curtain fall, seeing only the barrel chest and gray mane of hair, knowing it wasn't Nick, but a voice lashed out with venom, "Gorgon-spawn."

I froze, torn between ignoring it to continue searching for Nick and stepping inside. I recognized that voice. *Poseidon.* He'd spoken to me once—threatened me, really—through the mouth of a singing fish I had mounted on my office wall … just before he attempted to drown me and succeeded in flooding my office. And that had been *before* he'd tried to explode a charge in an offshoot of the San Andreas fault to set off the quake to end all quakes, dropping LA into the ocean to announce his (and Zeus's) second coming. Oh yeah, and he'd tried to kill me then as well when I got in the way.

Talk to them, Apollo had said. Yeah, right.

I stepped inside and let the curtain drop behind me. "Poseidon," I said, as neutrally as possible. "You're looking … well."

Part of his silvery mane had burned away, and that lovely smell of burnt hair clung to him. Oxygen hissed softly as it fed through a tube up into his nose. His face was blackened, but miraculously not too burned. Possibly there was some protection against fire in being a water god. But a dry, wracking cough overtook him as I approached his bedside. It continued for the better part of a minute, which wasn't such a long time in the grand scheme of things, but when you're listening to someone cough up a lung, it seemed like forever.

"What have you done?" he asked when he could talk again. Why was everybody always asking me that?

"Me, nothing. Why don't you ask Zeus what *his priests* set in motion at Delphi? No, wait, I'll tell you. Their attempt at human sacrifice woke Rhea, your loving mother. Apparently, she's not happy to see you."

Poseidon glared. It hadn't been *him* she'd saved from Kronos, after all. She'd let him be devoured, along with the rest of her children. It had been Zeus alone she'd saved. Talk about mommy issues.

"I should kill you," he growled, which set off another, longer coughing fit, which ended on a wheeze and a rattle in his chest.

"You tried that," I answered when it died down enough that he could hear. "You're welcome to try again, of course, but I don't recommend it. Right now I'd say you have two options. You can keep threatening me and I can raise holy hell, bring people running and alert them that they've got an international fugitive on their hands. A *terrorist*, no less."

He snarled.

"*Or* you can agree to join forces with us to put Rhea back in her place. She's already come after you once. If she and the Titans make a triumphant return, I'm going to be the very least of your problems."

Poseidon was silent but for the rattle in his chest. "Think about it," I said.

"Have you talked to Zeus?" he asked gruffly.

"Does he speak for you?"

He started to growl again and had to stifle another bout of coughing. "Up this high," cough, "he's the one with the power."

The cough that burst out this time went on for so long I thought he'd break a rib. Poseidon was left gasping like a fish out of water, his barrel chest working like a bellows, trying to make up for the deprivation of air.

"Think about it," I said again, turning to go. "You're with us or you're on your own."

A man in scrubs with some kind of breathing machine on a wheeled cart nearly crashed into me as I exited, and I moved quickly away to let him do his job. Poseidon was right—this far from the oceans and his base of power, he was probably pretty near human in his abilities, but the Titans weren't just land creatures. If this thing got out of hand, if Rhea got down off the mountain, or if she was able to move through followers who could, we'd have a worldwide awakening on our hands. We'd need an army. And even that might not be enough.

I stood there trying to figure out how I'd missed Zeus and where to find him. A pair of hands clamped down on my shoulders and yanked me into one of the treatment alcoves. The hold shifted, and I stomped down on an instep, threw an elbow back and then pivoted out of reach—or out of reach in a perfect world. In a cramped treatment room, I pivoted into the bed and rolled myself up over it instead, coming down on the other side. The bed between us, I now faced my grabber, staring into the crazed and hate-filled eyes of the king of the Olympians, Zeus Earthshaker.

"You called my mother?" he asked.

I was so stunned that it took me a second even to laugh. But as soon as I did, I realized it was the wrong move.

Zeus, enraged, shoved the bed at me. Luckily, the casters were old and clunky and the bed didn't go far.

"Maybe you didn't notice, because you were so far over your head, but we saved your ass back at the hotel," I spat back. "I'm not sure why. But to answer your question, no, we didn't 'call your mother.' Your priests did that."

He was breathing hard, looking from the hospital bed to me, as if he might give up trying to shove it and just lift and launch it instead, but that caught his attention.

"What?" he asked sharply.

"When your priests tried to gut Apollo in that stupid ceremony, the power unleashed with his blood woke her up. And I think she got up on the wrong side of the bed."

He fell back a step, like I'd slapped him, and man did I want to.

Anger bubbled up at that thought, but it wasn't his ... wasn't mine. Inside I was like a boiling pot with the top about to blow off.

No, no, no.

I gasped, trying to release some of the pressure, trying to fight Rhea down. "What's wrong with you?" Zeus asked.

I tried to answer him, but it wasn't my voice that came out. *"My son,"* Rhea spat. I listened helplessly, mentally clawing at my own throat. "Your days are over. Typhoeus was a warning. The Titans are rising. You couldn't even hold your world against the humans. How will you hold it against us? Your time is through."

I braced for another quake or explosion, but none was forthcoming. Rhea's serpentine minions were off licking their wounds or whatever giant mythological beasts did when they'd been beaten. At a guess, she didn't have any more tricks currently up her sleeves. I imagined it would take time to gather more monsters. There couldn't be too many in the immediate vicinity. Which meant we had time. But how much when a Titan could probably chew up the landscape like a *2 Fast 2 Furious* car in a no-holds-barred race?

Zeus stared into my eyes, but I wasn't the one glaring back. "I defeated you once," he said. "I'll do it again."

"You and what army?" Rhea asked. "The giants have largely faded from the world. The Cyclopes haven't been heard from in ages untold. Your allies are no more. Your strength is no more. If you'd been alone tonight, Typhoeus would have destroyed you. You can't stay surrounded forever."

Zeus's eyes blazed like one of his infamous bolts. "If you're so sure you can defeat me, why waste time talking about it? Do you expect me to concede?"

"No," she responded calmly, my mouth forming the words. "If you did, I could hardly use you as a rallying point. I expect the promise of vengeance will overcome anyone's reluctance to awake. I've only come to say goodbye, my son."

He lunged for me, straight across the bed between us and I fell right into his hands as Rhea suddenly withdrew from me and Zeus latched onto my throat, thumbs digging into my windpipe, cutting off my air. I stared, terrified, up into his bloodshot eyes, struggling to tell him that she'd gone. I wasn't sure it would matter, and anyway, I didn't have the breath. I dug deep for the energy to throw my head forward, crashing my forehead into his. His grip loosened, and I forced my hands in under his forearms and thrust, freeing myself from his grip.

I choked and coughed, my eyes watering, and whirled for the counter, grasping for anything I could use as a weapon. But there were no handy scalpels laying around for just such emergencies. Only tissues, a box of sanitary gloves, a plastic container of tongue depressors …

I spun back around, ready to find him closing in on me, prepared to use my body as a weapon, but he seemed to have gotten ahold of himself. He hadn't rounded the hospital bed, but *was* watching me like a hawk from the side of it.

"You see," I said. It came out, well, strangled. "She's dangerous. We didn't call her, but we're going to have to work together to put her back to rest."

"Work together?" You would have thought *he'd* been strangled by the sound of his voice. "You've got to be kidding me."

"You think you can stop her alone?" His glare was answer enough.

"Talk to Poseidon and meet us back at the hotel. I promise you, we defeat her together or we go down separately."

He didn't say a word as I edged cautiously past him, but neither did he grab me again.

As I stepped out of the treatment room an intercom crackled and snapped, then a voice came over asking for Tori Karacis to report to the ER front desk.

My heart gave a *thump*. Fear and hope battled it out in a

cage match in my chest to see which would win in regard to Nick. I'd lied and told them I was his wife. I prayed they weren't calling to tell me I was a widow.

I rushed back the way I'd come, back toward the waiting area. As I burst out of the inner door to the treatment area, I nearly collided with an orderly, who turned just in time to catch me before I could overrun him.

"Mrs. Armani?" he asked.

Close enough. "Yes," I answered.

"Your husband's out of surgery if you'd like to see him."

"He's okay?" I asked, for the second time today, feeling like I wanted to collapse as the tension went out of me and relief flooded in. Relief was not nearly so rigid as fear.

"He'll need skin grafts and reconstructive surgery, but as long as we can keep infection away ..."

Skin grafts and reconstructive surgery ... and I'd brought this on him. "I'll follow you?" I asked.

He led me back the way I'd just come and used a keycard to get us beyond the general ER area and back to the trauma treatment rooms. Nick was in the first one on the left, and I had to keep from throwing myself on him as I spotted him lying there, looking so helpless. One side of his face was loosely bandaged in white gauze pink with blood. The eye on the bandage-free side rolled to look at me, so blue and perfect in contrast.

I gasped and approached the bed tentatively, as if even displacing the air might cause him pain. My vision went blurry, and I realized there were tears in my eyes.

"I'll give you a minute," the orderly said, "but he may not be awake long. He's on some pretty serious pain meds."

Nick raised a hand, again on the uninjured side. The left, I noticed, which meant it was his dominant side that had taken the hit. I reached gently for the hand and stood by his bed, afraid to perch on it and cause him to shift.

"I'm so sorry," I said. My damaged throat and the tears made it a hoarse whisper.

He shook his head. "Not your fault," he whispered, as soft as spider's silk.

"It is," I insisted, not allowing myself the relief of looking away from his pain.

"Tori—" Saying my name recalled my gaze to his one good eye, and I realized I was lying to myself. I had let my gaze wonder down to his chest where the skin was less angry.

"Yes," I said, wiping tears away from my eyes with my free hand.

"I'm out."

I blinked. "Well, of course. I'm so, so sorry. No one expects you to come back to the fight. I should never—" a sob stopped me, and I had to swallow it down before I could continue. "I should never have drawn you into any of it."

He started to shake his head and stopped as it sparked pain that flashed across his face and made his body nearly arc off the bed. He breathed shallowly through the pain for a minute before his muscles untensed and he relaxed back onto the mattress, looking smaller than before somehow.

"No, I mean I'm out of everything. I can't be ... part of this." He sounded like he was drowning on his words, and I could see a single tear welling in his good eye. "I'm not ... equipped for these battles, and now ... can't even fight for those I'm meant to fight for, back home."

He wasn't a god ... or a gorgon. Hell, *I* wasn't equipped for this and that was with ambrosia and my gods-given gifts. But I suspected he was saying something more ... something I desperately didn't want to hear.

His eye kept closing, and it looked like it took more effort each time to reopen it, like the medicine was dragging him down into sleep. I wanted that for him, the freedom from pain, but he squeezed my hand to hold me there as he sensed me start to pull back to leave him in peace.

"Come with me," he said, finally letting his eye shut and stay that way. "Not your fight either. I'm not sure …" He trailed off, and for a second I thought he was finished. Then his lips moved again, though his eyes stayed shut. "Not sure you're helping the situation. Not sure things aren't worse." My heart stopped beating. I wondered if it was the medicine talking. Or confusion from the pain. But deep down I knew. He meant every word. I knew it, because he was voicing my very own doubts. Only, he was my touchstone. *He* was supposed to believe. And he'd cracked under the pressure.

I was so torn up and tangled up in my own pain that it took me a second to realize he wasn't quite finished. "If this is … your path … can't walk it with you."

His hand went slack in mine, and I checked to see that he was still breathing. He was, and I struggled to feel something at that, but I'd gone numb with the stopping of my heart. I didn't know what to process first—that he blamed me as I blamed myself or that it sounded like he was cutting me free.

Because that's what he was saying. I couldn't turn my back on the fight that had begun. I *couldn't*. My responsibility was here. Now. With my friends and family and this mess I hadn't started but had been sucked into nonetheless. His responsibility, his job, his *identity* was back in LA with the people he'd vowed to protect and serve. And because of me—I'd said it myself—because of *me* right now he couldn't even do that. All he could do was hurt and heal. He couldn't stay and I couldn't go. After all I'd put him through, that felt like a betrayal. Yet I couldn't see any other path.

I walked out of there like I was walking the Green Mile, already dead inside.

The tears didn't start until I was in the limo Uncle Hector had sent to collect me, and then they wouldn't stop.

Viggo looked at me in the rearview mirror and asked, "The man, he's going to be okay?"

I wiped the tears out of my eyes. "Eventually. Nothing skin grafts and time away from me can't cure."

He looked sad, like he could read between the lines. "Back to the hotel?"

I thought about asking him to go by way of a liquor store, but I needed my wits about me.

"Yes," I said finally. "Thank you."

"It'll be okay," he told me.

I wished he had the power of prophecy.

I was too emotionally exhausted to fear the hairpin turns on the way back up to the hotel … or maybe I was getting used to them. Exposure therapy.

Like before, we had to stop short of the actual parking lot that looked like an explosion site. I thanked Viggo and raced out, ready to find the others and plot away my sorrows. Nick had pulled away from me. I didn't think it was just his painkiller talking. My touchstone was gone. That voice that told me *not* to do the crazy things I usually did anyway had given up on me. But more than that … I hadn't said as much, not even to myself, but the truth was that when Nick and I finally got through the bantering and dancing our way around our relationship, I thought we'd … settle down sounded too tame. Be together forever sounded too romancy. But somewhere in there lay the truth about what was slipping away from me.

The lobby of the hotel was all but deserted when I entered. One lone receptionist was holding down the check-in desk. I realized I didn't know where to go. The banquet hall would be a crime scene, although what crime the police could prosecute I could only imagine. I headed for the elevators while I pulled my phone out to call Apollo, feeling stupidly guilty as I did it, even though this was hardly a social call. Anyway, I wasn't sure I *had* a relationship anymore to worry about. The thought didn't cause me anything but pain.

I was *not* going to cry again. Big girls don't cry. I'd heard it in a song once. The wisdom of Fergie.

I heard a phone play out the first few bars of "Black Magic Woman" in the elevator coming into the lobby and knew I didn't have to look any further for Apollo. I'd found him. He accepted the call just as the doors opened, and then dropped his hand to his side at the sight of me.

"What happened?" he asked immediately, stepping toward me. I took a step back. "Are you okay?"

I looked at the hand reaching out toward me, the phoneless one, and he stopped. "I'm fine," I said. "I'm not the one hurt."

"Then what was all that I sensed?"

Damn and double damn, I'd forgotten our weird, unwanted bond that meant he'd had a front row seat for the breakup. But he could sense emotions, not read minds. He might guess, but he couldn't know anything I didn't tell him for certain. And I wasn't about to tell him. He'd been wanting me to break up with Nick since we'd met. I wouldn't give him the satisfaction of knowing it was done or appearing pathetic because Nick had been the one to end it.

"Zeus is a douchebag, so what else is new? But I think I talked some sense into him and Poseidon both. I don't think they can fight Rhea without us."

"Without Zeus and his idiot priests, we wouldn't have to fight her at all."

"Where is everybody?" I asked, before he could whip out any more questions of his own.

"Strategizing," he said, "in the bridal suite."

"Oh, Tina must love that."

"She volunteered it. She's pissed that 'that bitch goddess' ruined her wedding. We had to fill her in. Pretty hard to keep her in the dark after everything."

I felt oddly pleased. If she knew the full story, she'd have to know that none of this was my fault. Oh sure, Rhea would never have awakened if Zeus and Poseidon hadn't come after me and Apollo and bolloxed up the whole thing, but I hadn't put them up to the vengeance. As far as incurring their wrath to begin with … what was I supposed to have done? Let them drop LA into the ocean? Maybe some day she and I could sit down over a pint and I could tell her about my heroic adventures when I wasn't possessed by a mother goddess.

"Lead the way," I told him.

Inside the elevator I stood as far away from him as humanly possible—toward the front while he stood in the back—but I could feel his gaze on me. He hadn't bought my explanation for the emotional turmoil for even a second.

I was out of the elevator the instant the doors opened, but then I had to wait for Apollo to catch up.

He led me to a room at the end of a long hallway. I could hear even before we reached the door that we were in the right place. There were a lot of voices talking over each other. I would have thought "party" if I didn't know better.

Apollo knocked, and the voices hushed. It was Hermes who answered the knock, looking from me to Apollo with sharp eyes that seemed to catch everything and guess the rest.

"Come in," he said soberly. I didn't know he could do sober. It made the whole situation seem that much more dire.

Hermes stepped aside, and we entered. Everyone stared at me as if I might go on the offensive again. I couldn't blame them.

"What's the news about your young man?" Yiayia asked from across the room. Fergus, I was shocked to see, was still at her side, singed but whole. Christie was conspicuously absent.

"He's burned and hurting, but he's going to be okay."

"Zeus and Poseidon?" Hermes asked.

"Healing. Not all fired up to join us, but I don't see that they have much choice. I'd guess it's a matter of time." I looked around the room. "What have you come up with so far?"

Everyone stirred uncomfortably, swapping glances, meeting each other's gazes, but not mine … until I got to Althea. She looked me right in the eyes and said, "We can't tell you. It's like talking to the enemy. Tori, I'm sorry."

I felt it like a blow to the chest. Nick didn't want me. Now neither did they. And I couldn't convince them they were wrong when I was sure they were right. But I also couldn't stay side-lined. There was a battle brewing of epic proportions, and I knew with that sixth sense I had that I was part of things. I had to be.

I swallowed down my first response and reconsidered my second. *"Fine,"* I said. It came out tight but strong. "I understand. A quick suggestion. Yiayia's been keeping track of who's been doing what with whom and where for at least a decade. If you're looking to recruit allies, I'd start there."

"Egona—" Yiayia began, stepping forward as if she'd embrace me and make it all better. I held up a hand to stop her. It was the only way I could stay strong.

"Let me just ask—who's going to approach Hades? With or without Zeus and Poseidon, we'll need him on our side."

No one spoke.

"Fine," I said again. "I'll go. I'm expendable and he knows me."

He didn't *like* me. The last few times we'd met he'd actually tried to kill me. But he knew me. Maybe he'd marvel at my audacity in approaching him long enough to listen.

There was something wrong with my vision again, and I fumbled for the doorknob. A strong hand, warm like someone had been soaking up the sun, came down on top of mine and twisted the knob for me. I didn't thank him. It felt too much like he was coming to the rescue of some kind of damsel in distress, and that wasn't me.

He followed me out into the hall. "You're not going alone," Apollo stated.

I whirled to confront him and found him way too close, but I refused to take a step back.

"You gonna stop me?"

"No, I'm going *with* you."

"You're needed here."

"I will be when things heat up again. For now, I need to be with you."

"Why?"

"I sense it," he said, his turquoise eyes burning like sunlight reflected off the Mediterranean.

"A vision?" I asked. "What do you see?"

"I see you coming into your own. I see you having a pivotal role to play, and I know you have to survive."

Not *I know you* will *survive*, but *you have to*.

"What about you? *You* have to survive, to fight. At my side doesn't seem a terribly safe place to be lately."

"Well darn, because you know how I like things nice and safe. Crossword puzzles, warm milk, in bed by nine," he smiled.

To my shock, I started to smile back.

"You realize that if I get you killed, your sister's huntresses are going to have my hide."

"At the very least," he agreed. "So don't get me killed."

"Sir, yes, sir." I clicked my heels together and saluted, and his smile got wider. "You think they'll help us out with some weapons to aid us in not getting slaughtered?"

CHAPTER ELEVEN

"Wit is educated insolence."
—Aristotle

I t turned out that it was Apollo and not Yiayia who had the intel on nearby entrances to the Underworld. Apparently, we'd already been within spitting distance of the nearest one. A cult of the dead had operated around the Tholos tomb where the Pythian Serpent had attacked. It seemed logical, I guessed. A monument commemorating a military victory would probably also involve honoring the dead. If Hades's influence had been particularly strong there, it made sense that this would be a link to his domain.

Outfitted with a bow and a brace of arrows (Apollo) and a huge hunting knife (me), we stood in front of the Tholos now. No guns allowed. Althea didn't have any because, in her words, "they weren't sporting." Neither was my bridesmaid's gown. I'd changed into something a lot more practical—jeans and a heather-gray, long-sleeved tee and hiking boots.

Viggo and his limo would have been too conspicuous, a cab would have left a trail, so Apollo and I walked, counting on the dark to hide us from watchful eyes. Because the Tholos was still a crime scene, just like the Sanctuary at Delphi. Site by site, we were taking out tourist destinations and millennia of history, just what Uncle Hector and his movie had hoped to bolster. It had to stop. *We* had to stop it.

"Where do we start?" I asked.

There was crime scene tape blocking off the access path to the Tholos, but no police here or up at the sanctuary site. We'd spread them too thin. Those who weren't wounded or dead were probably down at the hotel, where structural damage caused by Typhoeus kept the danger level high.

In answer, Apollo ducked the crime scene tape. I followed, trying to avoid flashbacks to the Pythian Serpent crunching down on the officer who didn't make it, the monolithic stone tumbling from the top of the Tholos and nearly crashing down on our heads ...

Apollo stopped at the edge of the crater caused by the serpent erupting from the earth and shined a flashlight down into the depths. I stepped up beside him and stared down into it. And down ... and down. It was more an impression of depth than an actual visual, since the beam didn't penetrate the whole length of the tunnel. Or maybe it was the way air seemed to be trapped in there, moaning to be free. It was eerie.

"What are you thinking?" I asked him.

"What do you think's more likely," he asked back, "That the serpent made all new tunnels coming after us or that he used existing pathways?"

The man was more than just a pretty face. "Existing," I answered.

"That's what I thought."

He put the butt of the flashlight in his mouth to have his hands free for disentangling our climbing gear—harnesses, ropes, carabiners, anchors that he'd borrowed from Spiro, who'd apparently planned on a little adventuring after the wedding. He'd given me a knowing look when I'd asked for it, as though climbing were code for something a lot more horizontal than vertical, but he relinquished it with the demand that he wanted it back in good working order. I heard the shower going in his room when I went by for the equipment, and figured that he was otherwise occupied for the time being anyway. I wondered if it was Jesus and instantly realized I didn't want to know.

"Do you know how any of this works?" I asked, looking at the twisted-up ropes like I would a string of hopelessly tangled Christmas lights I'd never put up. With my fear of heights, I hadn't ever had the occasion to ascend or descend anything more challenging than stairs.

He took the flashlight out of his mouth and handed it to me so that he could answer. "Of course."

Of course, I mimicked under my breath, wiping the flashlight off on my jeans. I had a bad feeling about this. I didn't want anyone else hurt because of me. The Underworld was supposedly booby-trapped so that mortals could get in but they couldn't get out. And gods … they weren't even supposed to get in. Hades wasn't crazy about how he'd made out in the dominion lottery, but he *was* crazy dedicated to guarding what was his.

"Apollo," I began, ready to voice my concerns.

"Stop," he said firmly.

"But—"

"No."

Now he was just pissing me off. I was going to say my piece.

"Yes," I said adamantly. "You make whatever call you're going to make, but listen first."

He looked up from messing with the lines, straight into my glare. "Okay."

"When the Titans were defeated, weren't many of them banished to Tartarus?"

"Yes," he said, brows furrowed, wondering what I was getting at.

"So there's a good chance that if they're rising, Hades has his hands full." He nodded.

"That could mean that he's too busy to take any notice of our approach or that he's already on high alert for trouble, which will make this infinitely harder. Even if he's fully occupied, I'm not sure that sneaking up on him is our best idea ever."

"I don't see what choice we have. There are no cell towers in Hell."

"I'm just saying … this is your chance to change your mind. Show me how to use this junk and get back to the others. I won't …" My voice broke. "… I won't be responsible for your death."

Apollo's whole face lit with … something. I turned away. It was too much. Like staring at a solar eclipse. I felt rather than saw him rise and take the few steps toward me. When he grabbed my chin, I looked up at him reluctantly, and he pulled me toward him with his free hand. I expected him to come in for a kiss and shook my chin out of his grasp, ready to turn aside, but he just wrapped that arm around me and hugged me to him. My arms were trapped at my sides. My face pressed to his chest, and I felt … warm, safe, and disappointed all at the same time. I'd been ready to avoid that kiss, but on some level I'd wanted it … or wanted him to try it, anyway. Screwed up, that was me in a nutshell.

He rested his chin on top of my head and we just breathed together for a minute. "Tori, I'm a big boy. I can make my own decisions. You're not responsible for them. What's more, I'm a god, and that comes with certain responsibilities … it's in the handbook."

I pulled back enough so that I could see his eyes. "There's a handbook?"

"Sure. I wrote it. It's in graphic novel form. I figured more people would read it that way. I've even got a small cult following."

"You're kidding me," I said.

He shrugged, his eyes glimmering with mischief. "Maybe. You'll have to live through this to find out."

I stuck my tongue out at him, feeling better, respecting him for not trying to kiss me while I was vulnerable.

A graphic novel as a reason to live. Well, why not?

"Come on," he said, eyes still shining. "Let me hook you up." He paused for a second, then added, "Huh, I always thought that when we got to play around with ropes we'd be having a lot more fun and wearing a lot less clothing."

And there went that respect, evaporating into the evening air. Or not, because I couldn't help but smile, which I'm sure had been his intent. If nothing else, the banter was keeping my mind off my fears and recriminations. Someday I'd thank him for that. If we lived that long.

"Ready?" he asked, holding open a section of harness that I guessed was supposed to be a leg hole. I gave it a dubious look and stepped through. He repeated the procedure with the other leg and then buckled something around my waist, tugging a section at my back to make sure all was secure.

"I feel like a marionette," I said.

"Trust me, you are much too pretty to play Pinocchio."

"You say the sweetest things."

"You're very inspiring."

I snorted, and he left it alone, though I wouldn't have minded if the banter lasted a little longer, postponing our descent into the abyss.

I winced as he drove an anchor, or whatever they called it in mountain scaling lingo, into the ground. I knew the site had already been violated and that we weren't exactly standing on undisturbed ground. Still it hurt to deface an ancient site this way. Like kicking over a standing stone.

He looped a rope through the anchor, tested things out, did some voodoo with the equipment and a harness of his own, and we were apparently ready to go ... way too soon. I wondered if his harness cut into him the way mine cut into me. Or, maybe not in the *exact* same way. I wondered if I was wondering to keep my mind off the amazing stupidity of what we were about to do—descend into the Underworld, hotbed of Hades, restless Titans, Thanatos and Hypnos and Cerberus—oh my!

"Let's go," he said, when he decided all was in readiness.

"I liked our last date better," I said, before I could consider my words.

"Duly noted. When all this is over, I'll buy you a nice dinner at a beautiful upscale restaurant. You can wear that wrap dress again ... and maybe something other than a scowl this time."

I scowled at him. It was nostalgic. "I'm taken," I said, even though I wasn't so sure it was true anymore. It was still true in my heart.

He shrugged. "You're the one who brought it up." But his expression wasn't nearly as casual as his words.

"How do we do this?" I asked.

"I'll go first," he said. "That way I can get to ground level, make sure it's all clear and hold the rope so that you can rappel down. Just like climbing a rock wall."

Right. Just like that thing I'd never done. But, hey, I'd seen it on TV, so that was the next best thing, right?

"Bombs away," I told him. He looked at me funny from his perch on the edge of the abyss, but I was used to that. If I took exception every time someone looked at me funny, I'd spend my life in righteous indignation. Sounded exhausting.

"A kiss for luck?" he asked.

"Yeah, 'cause I've been so lucky so far. Look at Armani. Um, Nick." He held my gaze a moment more, letting me know he'd caught that.

"Right," he said. "You'll miss me when I'm gone."

And then he was. He pushed off the side and was sliding down into the abyss, holding his own rope with gloved hands. I watched him go, but with the sun now set, it wasn't long before he disappeared.

Yes, I missed him. But more because I was squatting on the

edge of a big black hole, waiting for my own journey to the center of the earth.

When he yelled, I learned over the abyss, got vertigo and stopped. "What?" I yelled back.

"Slide down. I've got you." It seemed to come from a long, long way away. If I hadn't been straining, I'd never have heard him.

The shakes set in. My pits grew damp. It was like ambrosia withdrawal, only without the fun hallucinations. The horror before me was real.

I took a deep breath, counted to ten, let it go. I'd seen people do that on television too, or maybe in infomercials to calm stress. They were full of shit.

"Tori?" he called.

"Coming," I yelled down impatiently. *Geez, give a girl a chance.* "Okay," I said for my own sake. "Here goes."

I sat down on my butt and scooted myself toward the edge, shaking the whole way. Terror rose up, choking me, making me feel like I couldn't catch a breath or let one out. My heart was pounding so hard I expected my chest to explode. But I didn't stop … until I hit the very edge and small rocks started to skitter out from under me, raining down into the abyss. Probably coming down on Apollo's head. He'd flinch. I'd fall.

"Are you *sure* you've got me?" I yelled.

Suddenly, something started to fill me, like a humming in my head. Soothing, calming. My heart rate started to slow again. I wanted to panic at the invasion, afraid Rhea might be taking over again, that she might use me to close the tunnel behind Apollo—bring it down on his head. But—

"Better?" Apollo called up.

"Are you messing with my head?" I called back.

"I'm inspiring peace."

"Well—keep it up." *Cut it out,* the fiercely independent part of me wanted to say, but she was vetoed by sanity. Not a frequent visitor to my world, so we tended to listen when she spoke. Yes, *we*. Me, myself, and Rhea. One more personality and we'd make a blockbuster film … or at least a made-for-TV movie. Ah, there, I knew the sanity wouldn't last long.

I took a deep breath, swallowed hard and let myself go. I didn't drop far. A body length, maybe, and then the rope pulled taut.

"Good girl," Apollo called, making me wonder if there were cookies in this for me at the end, or a good ear scratch. "Now, I'm going to let you down easy."

Easier than Armani. No, no, I wasn't going to think of that. Now was no time for distractions.

Hand over hand, Apollo lowered me down into the darkness while I tried not to think of Nick, creepy crawlies or falling to a deadly death. Yes, I knew it was redundant. But any scenario where I didn't just go quietly into that good night at a ripe old age struck me like that.

When the hands reached me, I shrieked.

"Tori, it's *me*. I've got you."

Apollo. I wanted to hug him and squeeze him … and call him a bastard for scaring me like that.

"Your hands are cold," I lied.

"Uh huh."

I heard his clothing rustle and then realized that I still held the flashlight, so illuminating our surroundings was up to me.

Apollo gently angled my hand to shine the light on the climbing ropes so that he could release me. "If they weren't so awkward to move in, I'd suggest we stay in the harnesses for a quick getaway, but—"

He found the release. When the harness fell away, it felt like a weight had been lifted off me. Finally, I could breathe.

Apollo took the flashlight back from me and moved the beam slowly around the space. The snake's tunnel continued downward at a slope, the floor of the tunnel smooth and almost polished, as if countless scales had slithered over it during the course of ages. It was creepy, and the way was going to be slippery, especially if we came across any wet areas.

"You got another of those for me?" I asked, nodding toward the flashlight.

"I have a cell phone with a flashlight app," he answered.

"Never mind."

Apollo kept the light and led the way, figuring, not wrongly, that if he slid from behind me with his greater bulk, he'd take me down with him, but if *I* slipped and he was in my way he had some chance of stopping the slide.

We moved slowly, and at the first branching stopped to consult our precog. It seemed counterintuitive to head *toward* the danger, but the right path was clearly more ominous, based on the mule kick my precog landed on my solar plexus.

"Right?" Apollo confirmed. I nodded.

The tunnel leveled out almost entirely and the walls grew as smooth as the floors. Water dripped from the ceilings, though, and when I shone the light up toward them, it became clear that the drips were coming from the end of dark stalactites that looked like petrified icicles.

There were other branches leading off, though not many. Still, our guts kept telling us to move straight ahead and after a while—monotony tended to mess with my concept of time—there seemed to be a glow from up ahead, as if we were getting somewhere. I got the sense, too, that things opened up ahead, and the phantom mule gave me another kick to the gut, as if in affirmation.

Apollo felt it too. He put a hand back to slow me, silently, and together we crept toward the end of the tunnel … the *light* at the end of the tunnel. Hadn't I heard somewhere *not* to go into the light? Unfortunately, I didn't see that we had a choice.

When Apollo stopped, I nudged him aside, unable to let him discover anything before me. The light was coming from some kind of florescent moss covering the stalactites. Spiro would have loved it, but my attention was caught by what the light revealed. The smooth floor of the tunnel led down to a shore of equally smooth rocks, and beyond that, a slow-moving river on which sat a weathered skiff and a skeletal ferryman. Or, at least, as thin as he was there couldn't have been much more than bones beneath his tattered cloak.

Charon. Ferryman for the dead.

If he knew we were here, then Hades …

And yet my precog hadn't kicked up full force—bells and whistles and migraine-inducing klaxons.

Charon turned as he sensed our approach. I couldn't see his face inside the hood and cowl of his cloak, but the bony finger he pointed our way, which I was glad to see was covered in a minimum of flesh anyway (fish belly white) was unmistakable. He crooked it at us in the universal sign for "Come hither." *To your doom,* my brain wanted to add, but I beat it into submission.

I pointed to my own chest to make sure he was really talking to *us* and that there weren't some other lost souls, maybe spirits we couldn't actually see, who he might be signaling.

"Come here," he demanded, his voice as threadbare as his cloak. It sounded like the wind howling mournfully through thick marsh grasses—thin and rank with decay.

Apollo and I looked at each other. "But we're not dead," he said, just to be clear.

Charon sighed like a bubble of swamp gas releasing. "Hades sent me to fetch you. There is trouble afoot."

Well, no shit, Sherlock.

I looked to Apollo for some sign. He knew the old gods better than I did. Was Hades for real? There was no way he could have missed the earth quaking. And if the Titans were rising, he'd no doubt need help. I just couldn't see him asking for it. On the other hand, Charon hadn't exactly been *asking*.

"We don't have the fare," Apollo said, still testing.

"Your fare has been paid."

"One-way ticket?" I asked.

"There *is* no way back. At least, not on my skiff."

We'd have to find our own way home.

"Come, come," he insisted. "I have souls waiting."

Apollo and I shared one last look before approaching the boat. It looked like if you stepped wrong you'd put a foot right through it. Fine for disembodied spirits. Not so for the living.

"You sure this will hold us?" I asked.

Charon stared at me from the depths of his cloak, and even though his face was still locked in impenetrable shadow I could feel his lack of give-a-damn.

Whatever. Maybe my buoyant personality would keep me afloat. Tentatively, I stepped into the boat. It canted crazily beneath me, but didn't scuttle or dump me through, so staying low as I'd been taught once upon a time, I pulled my other foot in behind me. The floorboards creaked ominously. If I were that kind of woman, it would have given me a complex about my weight. But I wasn't, and it didn't. I sat quickly and watched Apollo board. The boat lurched as his weight hit, and I grabbed instinctively for the sides to hang on for dear life. Beneath us, the water flowed in a slow, viscous way, as if it was more oil than water. It even had rainbow swirls like spilled gasoline floating on top. Or ... not floating, but shifting, like a kaleidoscope, the picture ever-changing. For a second, I thought I caught a memory, and then it was gone, whipped like a rug out from under me. I almost wanted to dive after it.

"Don't do it," Apollo said, putting a hand on my arm. "The River Styx. You go in, you don't come out again. It's like the tar pits."

I looked at him, and then Charon, who laughed, a sound like bullfrogs croaking, as he worked his pole, pushing us across the River before we could change our minds. The River wasn't wide, but now I knew why it took a ferryman to cross.

We bumped up moments later on the opposite shore, rocks scraping the bottom of the bow. I braced for the water to seep up and into the skiff, but nothing happened. Charon used the pole to rock the boat and get my attention. "Out," he commanded.

I considered flipping him off, but I couldn't see what good it would do, so instead I let Apollo disembark first and hold out a hand to me. I accepted it, proud but not stupid. I'd take the steadying influence.

As soon as I was on solid ground, I turned to Charon. "Where to now?" I asked.

But he was already poling the skiff back across the way and didn't even acknowledge me. I was already dead to him.

"Great." I muttered, facing Apollo again. I was about to ask him the same question when my gut clenched with warning, and I saw the three sets of shining red eyes coming at us out of the darkness beyond the glowing moss. *Emerging from side tunnels?* I wondered, as if it mattered *where* they came from so much as their intentions.

I *knew* those eyes. Hellhounds. Quite literally.

Apollo and I moved a little apart from each other—not quite shoulder to shoulder—so that we'd have room to fight and yet be able to protect each other's flanks. Like we'd done this before. Which we had. But as the hellhounds emerged, they didn't seem ready to attack. Their lips stayed down over their teeth, and while they were wary and their hackles raised, they didn't pick up speed as they approached or bunch up like they were ready to lunge … not unless we made a wrong move.

"Our emissaries?" Apollo ventured.

"If he's got an uprising in Tartarus, they may be all Hades can spare," I said, watching warily as the three started to circle behind us and close in, almost as if …

"They're herding us," I said.

"Well, then we let them. For now. But keep watch, just in case we're headed into a trap. This all seems too easy."

It was … until it wasn't.

The hounds kept crowding us, cutting off exits they didn't want us to take, herding us along the paths they intended. I kept vigilant for tripwires and stepped tentatively, worried about anything from another abyss to pressure grenades. But in a place of souls it was hard to prepare for everything—like the shriek of a thousand voices that greeted us up ahead.

Apollo and I gave each other a look and started running full out. We stopped short at the sight that greeted us when the passage opened up. In front of us stood a monstrous pack of hellhounds, Cerberus in all his three-headed glory and a mere handful of gods. I recognized Hades. He'd traded in the pastels of the Miami Vice look he wore above ground for red and black —a loose-fitting black suit with the sleeves rolled up, red T-shirt underneath, Italian leather shoes ... or Greek, who could tell? I also knew his two sons, Thanatos, who looked like the stereotypical Grim Reaper, only wielding a sword instead of the iconic sickle, and Hypnos, all punked and pierced. The woman was a mystery, but her black leather catsuit was rockin' and her hair was wild with some kind of storm that seemed to rage only around her. Hecate, at a guess. She was the only other Underworld god/goddess I knew off the top of my head, though from the other figures gathered, I assumed there were more. Or that Hades's dubious charm had garnered him allies.

But it was what was beyond them that captured my attention. Beyond them was ... it looked like a barrier, a bubble stretched to its limit with arms and limbs and tentacles pushing through. The hellhounds growled, as if they could warn the Titans back. Cerberus snarled and snapped at the air. The gods arrayed themselves against the imminent outbreak, arms out, a miasma or mist coming from their outstretched palms. It flowed toward the near-to-bursting barrier and formed a layer that momentarily pushed back the uprising.

"You going to help?" Hades called over his shoulder, apparently aware of our presence.

Apollo ran forward. I had no choice but to follow, though I didn't know what good I'd do. I had one trick in my arsenal. One. I could freeze people and creatures ... temporarily. But it had never worked on the Olympians, and the Titans were older and more fearsome still, children of the original power couple, Ouranos and Gaea, the progenitors of Kronos and Rhea. They were the oldest of the old. Against them I was a single ant trying to take down a giant anteater.

Apollo took position beside Thanatos, and I stood next to him, my heart trying to pound its way straight out of my chest. As I stared there seemed to be a coordinated attack on the barrier and all at once it burst with the power of a sonic boom. The gods were blown back. I landed hard, right beneath Thanatos, whose elbow caught me on the chin as he fell, making me see stars. I blinked hard, desperate to clear them so that I could at least meet doom head-on. My brain almost went on strike refusing to process what was before me. Some of the Titans were nearly human-looking but for their vast size and the fact that they could have been carved out of mountains. Some had extra limbs or predator's teeth or tusks. Others had tentacles or stingers or far, far too many eyes.

And they were coming straight for us. I pushed Thanatos aside as a tentacle slammed his way and he hadn't recovered fast enough to dodge. As I pushed him, I used the counterpressure to roll the other way, toward the sword he'd dropped. I grabbed the hilt just as something grabbed me—another tentacle from the way it wrapped my ankle. I kicked and bucked to turn myself over onto my back where I could get the leverage and the space to swing the sword. I flopped like a landed fish—inelegant, but effective—and brought the sword down hard on the tentacle holding me. It didn't release, though it did flinch, tightening its muscles painfully, like a constrictor squeezing me so hard I thought the foot would pop right off the end of my leg. Frantically, I swung again, and this time when ink-like blood spattered me, the tentacle loosened, and I realized it was because I'd cut it clean off and yet it was still attached to my ankle. There was no time for a girly gross-out. Another three tentacles were coming for me.

I rolled and scuttled out of the way of them, looking for some distance from which I could strategize a better angle on the battle than one tentacle at a time. I saw that Thanatos had pulled a second sword from somewhere and was swinging about like a madman, severing tentacles and claws, slimy with blood and ichor. Hellhounds were darting in—or being hurled out, yelps cut off in a horrifyingly final manner. Apollo was using a claw from something that could have been the great grand-pappy of all velociraptors to wedge open a gryphon-like mouth that was trying to get at him.

I jumped the latest tentacle lashing out and went in with Thanatos's lost sword, aiming for the soft skin under the Titan's neck. As the sword pierced the skin, the gryphon bugled and thrashed, knocking me to the side. The sword whipped free with me and together we went sliding across the ground in a puddle of something I didn't want to identify.

From my ant's eye view I saw Cerberus facing off with a mega mountain of a man—a Titan, looking almost human but for a second head. It was a death match. The Titan had one of Cerberus's heads locked within his massive arms, trying to choke the life out of it, while the next closest head had its fangs buried in the back of the Titan's neck. Both struggled, both locked on, it seemed, until their power ran out. I couldn't worry about them.

I rolled back to my feet, sword still miraculously in hand. Half my body aching and the other half unable to be heard over those complaints.

Apollo's gryphon was down, and he'd rushed to Hades's aid, now standing shoulder to shoulder with Hecate as she defended Hades, who was chanting with ever increasing furor, something dark and sinister growing between his cupped hands.

A massive club swung by one of the other Titans knocked Apollo aside, sending him flying. I raced to intercept—to cushion his impact, flinging my sword arm out to my side so that I wouldn't catch him with it. Apollo struck me just as Hades let loose with his spell. It crashed into the chest of the club-wielding Titan and exploded outward. The Titan howled as the impact from the darkness seemed to open some kind of miasma in its chest. Not so much a wound as a void, a black hole. Its knees buckled, and the ground jumped, as it fell hard. The darkness expanded, catching another Titan, who looked part crab, claws whipping out toward Hypnos, who dodged them like Jack-be-Nimble jumping over the candlestick. Hypnos kicked off the claw, doing a flip in midair, which would have been completely impressive if an involuntary spasm of pain hadn't sent the claw flailing out and catching him just wrong, striking the back of his legs and unbalancing him in the air. He went crashing into the side of the monstrous, two-headed Titan and slid to the ground.

Catching Apollo had knocked the wind out of me, but that was nothing to the sight of the coming stampede. The sounds of terror—raptor, serpentine, leonine, human—erupted as the darkness spread, and all thoughts of battle evaporated. A single-minded, instinctive flight response took its place. Anything to avoid the miasma. And *we*, all of us, Team Underworld, were between the Titans and escape. I saw it coming on, but there was nowhere to go. Nowhere to escape. Apollo had recovered himself, and faster than thought pivoted us out of the way of the first massive body blasting past us, taking chunks out of the tunnel wall as it went, but then the next hit us like a freight train. We ricocheted off into the next and went down under a set of knife-sharp hooves.

After that, I lost track and, very quickly, consciousness. We'd failed. The Titans were unleashed.

CHAPTER TWELVE

*"We often want one thing and pray for another, not telling
the truth even to the gods."*
—Lucius Annaeus Seneca

My body was on fire, surrounded by it, like I was
sinking into a pool of molten lava. I burned,
mouth open to scream, but nothing escaped. My
eyes were closed, but the lids seemed almost translucent with red
light, as if I could see right through them if only I could focus.
The agony was worse than anything I'd ever experienced. I
desperately hoped to black out again, but the pain stopped and a
voice commanded unsympathetically, "Get up."

He had to be kidding. But Hades, Lord of the Underworld,
was not known for his sense of humor. I blinked my eyes open,
surprised when they actually focused and I *wasn't* surrounded by
a pit of fire. Beside Hades, Hecate stared down at me, her face
all angles, like a top model on a diet of air. It wasn't just the
catsuit that made her striking. Sure, you could cut glass on her

cheekbones, but her eyes were sheer obsidian—shiny black, the same shade as her wild hair. Wilder than mine and snapping with electricity, as though it were made of live wires.

"If hairs be wires

Black wires grow on her head"

What a time to remember my Shakespeare. I wondered if he'd met our darling 'Cate. "I healed you," she said, her voice deep and rough, a la Kathleen Turner if she'd gargled razor blades.

Oh, was *that* what "get up" had been all about—healing. It had felt more like torture. Eyeing her dubiously, I tried my arms and legs. She was right. They worked, and the burning sensation had faded away. They still felt ... singed ... but maybe that was from massive regrowth of tissue or reknitting of bones. I didn't know how bad off I'd been. And everything itched like a sono-fabitch.

"Which way did they go?" I asked.

"It's too late," Hades snapped, even as Hecate pointed ... not the way we'd come, but in the opposite direction. It made sense; the Titans couldn't cross the River Styx, even if Charon would allow it. There was no way the skiff could carry their weight and no way across on their own.

"They're gone," he continued. "But you will help us get them back."

I stared at him in disbelief. "Yeah, because I was so much help this time."

"You brought this trouble on. You will help us end it."

It seemed fair enough in theory. In practice ...

"How?" I asked.

"You know where they're going?"

I bolted upright. "We have to warn them. Everyone at Delphi—"

There was a masculine moan, and Hecate and I looked to see Apollo, still unconscious, his head ... I couldn't look. It was misshapen, as if a tremendous weight had squashed it, stepped on it in the escape. Hades nodded to Hecate—permission to heal him, I could only hope, and the mother of witches knelt beside him, her hands aglow in that red fire as she lifted them to his head. I watched his eyelids flutter and saw only white beneath them as his eyes rolled up into his head and he curled into a fetal position, trying subconsciously to shield himself from the pain I knew all too well.

"Delphi?" Hades prompted me.

I told him the whole story, from Zeus's priests through Rhea's rising and her threats to return the Titans to their former glory.

He cursed long and floridly in Greek, but an older form, it seemed, because I only understood one in five words and they were enough to blister my ears.

"Then those at Delphi already know they're coming," he concluded, boring into me with his crazy Manson-eyes.

I swallowed a ball of acid that had burned up my throat and nodded.

"And once again I get to clean up my brothers' messes." He sighed dramatically, even for him. "Let's go see which way they've gone. Perhaps we can cut them off or perhaps they've already dead-ended themselves. Many exits. Most of them are illusions."

He showed his teeth in a psychotic smile, something like the Cheshire Cat might give after picking his teeth with White Rabbit bones. I wondered what kind of horrors those illusions hid.

"How do we find out?"

Hades approached a wall and put his palm to one of the stones. I was shocked to see a smart board light up in front of him. I'd expected magic, some kind of all-seeing eye. Not a high-tech screen he could tap and wave his hands at—almost like magic—to reveal different sections of his domain. I rose to follow him, expecting it to be painful, still shocked when it wasn't. But before I went, I looked toward Hecate and Apollo.

His head had rounded out again, and his color was good. Much better than it had been. He was still in the fetal position, but was now snoring gently. It was almost ... cute.

"Head injury," Hades said. "He's going to need to sleep for a while. That kind of thing will take a lot out of you."

I considered planting a kiss on Apollo's head, but decided against it. There were witnesses, and anyway it would be just my luck that he'd wake up and make something of it.

Thanatos and Hypnos were rousing the wounded and Hecate went off to help others. I went to see what Hades had in mind.

When I stepped up beside him, he was studying a schematic on his smart board, all lit up with red dots in one area. "Ah," he said, not bothering to expand on that for my benefit. He tapped the screen, made an opening motion with his hand, brought in a second image and suddenly we were watching the escapees from two different camera angles. Security cameras ... in Hell ... who'd've thought?

Then I spotted something. "Right there," I said. "Expand that." He shot me a dark look at the order, but he gestured the screen to zoom in on the section to which I'd pointed. I thought I'd seen a person-sized figure running ahead of the crowd. On expansion, I saw that I'd been right. What's more, I *knew* that figure.

Christie. It occurred to me now that I hadn't seen her at the meeting in the bridal suite. But ... how had she gotten *here*? How had she paid the ferryman? However she'd gotten in, how would she ever get *out* alive? Hades, so far as I knew, had a one hundred percent success rate. Souls checked in but they never checked out. What would that mean for Christie? Or me? Something I'd carefully *not* thought about on my way down. But Hades had sent Charon for us. Apollo and I were invited guests now. That had to count for something.

Beside me, Hades froze the screen on the image of Christie. "I recognize her," he said ominously. "A split second seen in a certain hotel room in San Francisco." He turned on me. "A friend of yours?"

I met his gaze dead on. Oh, poor choice of words. There was no use in pretending. "Yes," I admitted, "a friend. But not acting on her own. Rhea's got to be controlling her."

"First you steal my bride Persephone away from me. Then your friend breaches my security and leads an escape." He lashed out on the last word and grabbed me by the throat. I never even saw it coming before I was on my tiptoes trying to ease the pressure on my neck to breathe.

I hated to think how the king of the Underworld would collect. My soul forfeit? Condemned to Tartarus in place of the Titans? My innards pecked out every day like Prometheus or like Sisyphus forced ever to roll a boulder uphill only to have it slide back down again.

"Let go of her," Apollo demanded, rising from behind Hades. My distress must have reached him right through his unconsciousness.

Hades swiveled his head, owl-like, to look at Apollo with a leer, and then pointedly turned back to me, dismissing Apollo as less than a threat, which, given the way he was swaying on his feet, still weak from his own destruction, wasn't unreasonable.

"The two of you owe me," he said, his eyes burning like hot coals. He took a minute to savor the situation. "I have it. *If* I help you stop the Titans and defeat Rhea, you will watch over my kingdom while I take an extended vacation. Oh, the things I could do."

I couldn't have heard right. Oxygen deprivation had to have me hallucinating. He could *not* have just blackmailed us into housesitting. He shook me like a dog shakes its favorite chew toy before loosening his grip just enough for me to gasp the air to respond.

"What about them?" I asked in a whisper. Even that hurt. I indicated *them* with a flick of my eyes—Thanatos, Hypnos, Hecate.

He didn't follow my gaze, but brought his face in close to mine and then murmured in my ear, "*They* might not return my kingdom. *You,* on the other hand …"

"We'll do it," Apollo said for us both. "Just … let her go."

Hades's hand opened, and I dropped to the floor with the sudden release, coughing as each wonderful breath seemed to saw at my throat. As grateful as I was to breathe again, I didn't trust Hades. I thought about Atlas tricking Hercules into accepting the weight of the world onto his shoulders and then refusing to take it back, but if Hades was worried about a coup in his absence, surely he wasn't going to stick us with the Underworld for keeps.

Anyway, Apollo had already agreed. My throat ached as I took in air too greedily. "Done," Hades said.

Apollo rushed toward me, and I went into his arms, so glad to see him recovered and to be alive myself that I wasn't worried about signals, mixed or otherwise.

"But no sitting on my throne," Hades said, fixing us both with a glare from those coal-burning eyes.

Now that he mentioned it, I was a little tempted to play with his things. I could have a ton of fun with his helmet of invisibility on the off chance he left it at home.

"Fine," Apollo said, though *I* hadn't made any promises. "Now, what do you bring to the table?"

His eyes glittered. "Only all the heroes of old."

Apollo smacked his head. "The Elysian Fields, how could I have forgotten."

"Paradise sounds great until you have an eternity of it. Truthfully, the heroes have been growing restless. If I don't do something, like let them out to fight an epic battle, they'll start fighting each other."

I was dumbstruck. The heroes of old! Hercules, Perseus, Odysseus, Achilles, Theseus, Jason and the Argonauts … Was I really about to come face to face with them? It was funny that the gods didn't make me geek out—mostly because I hadn't even believed in them at first—but the *heroes*, normal mortals facing overwhelming obstacles … (Okay, maybe some had Olympian parents, but the others …)

"You look like a fan girl," Apollo said, a little grumpily, I thought. "I'd know, I've seen enough of them in my time."

"Women interested in your onscreen attributes," I teased, letting my gaze drop so that he'd have no question about the attributes to which I referred. Rumor had it that Apollo had started out in adult films before transitioning to more mainstream theatre.

"Exactly. Maybe if I showed you—"

"*Children,*" Hades snapped. "Focus."

He pressed a button on his smart screen and then enlarged the thumbnail picture that came up … The Elysian Fields. Fruitful, lush, perfect, like the concept of the Garden of Eden. Butterflies chased each other in a meadow, and when Hades swept a hand across the screen, the image panned to show two young men wrestling nearly naked in a field—and looking very enthused about it.

A smile lit Hades's face, and he clicked some kind of link. Then he cleared his throat and the sound seemed to carry through the screen and out across the fields, based on the sudden pause in the wrestling match. "Gather in the Hall of Heroes as soon as possible. Full battle gear. This is not a drill."

"Drill?" Apollo asked.

Hades's smile widened. "Keeps them on their toes. Plus, Cerberus likes the workout. Come on."

"What about the Titans?" I asked, looking at a moving picture Hades had relegated to the bottom of his smart screen, the one with Christie and a whole host of monsters who could crush her with a flick of their fingers or … whatever.

"They're already at the Archeron."

"The Archeron, but—" Apollo started.

"You see the conundrum," Hades said.

"I don't," I cut in.

Hades turned his burning eyes on me. "Archeron was a god, son of Gaea. He aided the Titans during their first battle against Zeus, and as punishment he was cast into the Underworld and turned into a river. The question is, will he offer them aid again, or has he learned his lesson?"

"He's got nothing left to lose by helping them," I said, horrified. What was it with the ancients and their crazy punishments? Who turned someone into a *river*?

"You'd think that," Hades said, "but never underestimate the power of sulking. He's had time out of mind to regret his decision and to blame others for the consequences. It will be an interesting experiment, no?"

"Experiment?" I asked, horrified.

"Yes, it all starts with a theory of mine ..."

"We don't have time for this," Apollo said. "They're waiting in the Hall of Heroes." Hades's eyes burned, not with the fire of suns, but with a much more infernal glow, like the molten core of a volcano ready to explode.

"Someday," Hades told him, "you and I will have a reckoning."

"I'll look forward to it. Now, let's go."

If Hades had laser vision, Apollo would have been cut in half, but since he didn't, he had to settle for a glare. Then his gaze swept past Apollo, and he rapped out, "Thanatos, you're with us. Hecate, you hold half back with you to repair what damage you can and prevent further escapes. Hypnos, you take the rest and meet us at the Archeron. One way or the other we'll defeat the Titans. Either we'll stop them at the river or if they're beyond, marching on the gods, we'll sandwich them between the two armies."

Armies. Right. I hoped the others' recruiting efforts had been successful and I hoped that Rhea had been quiet while we'd been gone—other than possessing my best friend, which she was so going to pay for, and unleashing the Titans. Come to think of it, that probably would have kept her pretty busy.

Hades turned back to us and ordered, "Follow me."

He barked an order at the smart board and then made a gesture like he was closing it up between his hands. A door opened even as the smart board closed—part of the stone wall of the echoing space sliding out of the way. Beyond was a dark passage that Hades illuminated by clapping his hands. A Clapper? Seriously? Along the walls of the tunnel, torches seemed to flicker, but when I looked more closely, it was just a trick bulb. Electric torchlight.

"Nice effect," I said wryly.

"I think so," Hades answered.

I was eerily aware of Thanatos bringing up the rear of our party. He'd already tried to kill me more than once in our short acquaintance. Sure, those attempts had been at his father's orders and we were temporarily on the same side, but if his father was worried about a coup, how much weight would that really hold? He could do away with his father and blame it on us without breaking a sweat. If we were killed in the assassination—if Thanatos killed us in supposed retribution—who could contradict his version of events?

Apollo, apparently picking up on my tension through our link, reached down and squeezed my hand. He let go almost immediately, to have both his hands free, I guessed, in case of trouble, but it was reassuring. Right now, the odds were stacked against Thanatos. He had to know that. And anyway, who wanted to inherit a kingdom in the middle of crisis? Much better to let someone else do all the heavy lifting of putting things back in order.

It was a long corridor, and the walk was uneventful except for the gnawing in my gut, my precog trying to tell me what I already knew. *War is coming. Hurry, hurry.*

When we hit the end of the corridor, marked by another sliding slab of stone, we stepped out into another desolate cave. Skeletal trees stood on rocky ground, bearing no fruit and only the most occasional leaf, looking like carcasses dotting the landscape. As we followed Hades's lead, though, moss and lichen started to cover some of the rocks. Then grass. Then, slowly, flowers started to appear within the grass. Teeny, tiny white flowers, sometimes interspersed with purple. Just like above ground. The light in the tunnels had changed too. Though I couldn't spot the source, weak sunlight seemed to sift down from above.

And then … and then we reached them—the Elysian Fields. The diamond gates gave it away. A hundred million facets glittered in the sunlight that had grown progressively stronger. It should have been gaudy, like a Miss America crown. Instead it was … Heaven. Or one incarnation of it, anyway. Because beyond the gates the sunlight shined, butterflies chased each other, the whole world was in bloom. The peace and beauty of the place called out from beyond the gates, beckoning, making promises I was pretty sure it could keep. I *wanted* with an ache that was almost physical.

"Tori?" Apollo asked.

"Why would anyone ever leave?" I gasped, awed.

"Maybe you should wait here," he said gently.

That swung my startled gaze toward him. *"Like hell!"* I answered, catching the irony only as the words left my mouth.

"Fine, but don't eat or drink anything. And for gods' sake, don't fall for Theseus's sloe-eyed look," Apollo warned.

I gave him a startled glance. "Do I seem like the swooning type?" I asked, giving him the stink-eye.

He shrugged. "No, but then he doesn't necessarily wait for the swooning. He's more the grab and go type." He looked to Hades. "Sounds like someone we know. Surprised you two aren't best buds."

Hades glared.

We followed him toward the gates, but he stopped a distance before them to mutter a spell to let us pass through the invisible barrier, like the one we'd seen explode outside of Tartarus. Once we'd stepped through the barrier, the glitter of the gemstone gate was almost blinding. It was a wonder the Underworld wasn't awash in thieves. Then again, maybe it was. But Hades's realm was like a roach hotel. You no sooner checked in than you checked out ... permanently.

Hades put a hand to the ornate gates that rose to triple our height and they began to swing inward, so silently that we could hear the buzz of the bees beyond and the wing beats of fireflies. Or maybe that was my imagination, but there was a music to the place, and a sweet breeze that wafted out toward us, scented with flowers and the smell of dew drenched grass.

I breathed deeply as I passed through the gates, taking in the barely traveled path before us and the orchard all around, trees heavy with every kind of fruit imaginable. I wondered if the Elysian Fields had been modeled on the Garden of Eden or vice versa or ... What did it matter? The thoughts flitted away along with all my cares. If I could just stay here in this heaven then no one else could ever get hurt because of me. No death, no destruction. No mystery, motives, or murder.

Apollo pinched me. I yelped and jumped, then punched his arm. Hard. "What did you do that for?"

"The Elysian Fields, they're making you peaceful, yes? Complacent? It's something in the air here. It's like a drug. Get over it."

"You get over it," I said stupidly. I rubbed my butt where I still felt his pinch. "Next time I pinch you back."

He flashed a smile at me as lethal as Typhoeus. "I'm ready to turn the other cheek."

I stuck my tongue out at him. But he *had* broken the spell. For now. I still felt the pull and the peace of the Elysian Fields ... and most compelling the release from responsibility. But now I could remember that there were people who needed me, even if *they* didn't think so. And those people were waiting for our help.

"Any way you can crank down on the happy hormones?" I asked. "I think rallying the troops for battle would go a whole lot smoother."

Hades muttered yet another spell so low that I could barely hear it, and in a language I couldn't understand. The breeze stopped. The sound of wingbeats and the buzzing insects no longer carried toward us. Everything seemed dead still, as though perfection had been trapped in amber. No longer a living, breathing thing.

As we walked through the orchard, I spotted a temple up on a hill. Classic architecture, built on the highest point, looking down. It had the typical pillars, pitched roof, and triangular pediment at the pinnacle. I couldn't see the relief carvings, but at a guess they'd be Hades's greatest hits. I wondered what those would be. On the upside, he wasn't the philanderer that most of the gods were. On the downside, he'd kidnapped his wife and impressed her into marriage against her will and he wasn't exactly known for his heroism.

"The Hall of Heroes?" I asked, looking up.

"Precisely," he answered.

It wasn't as far off as it looked. Once past the orchard, we came to a grassy area that led into what looked like a temple complex or market square, similar to a Roman agora. Half-clothed children played hide and seek among the pillars, and a few women lay about in a grassy area nearby, drowsing, only half watching the children. No one else was about. I guessed everyone else was already at the Hall of Heroes.

The women began to sit or stand as Hades approached, but he motioned them down and smiled with almost a fatherly beneficence at the children. Could it be the Elysian Fields worked its magic on Hades as well? It was the first time I'd seen anything but a sadistic smile or out and out rage on his face. He directed us beyond the agora to a path that wound a little as we climbed, our view of the temple above, and the agora below, obscured from time to time by the trees in the way, some of which rose straight into the air, almost like Christmas trees that had never been cut out of their restraining mesh. They were that narrow and concentrated. Just like some actual trees on the actual Greek landscape. In fact, Elysia was so much like home, no one could possibly get homesick … except for the lack of monsters to fight, wars to win or other heroic pursuits. We were about to change all that.

As we took a turn of the path and it opened up onto the leveled grounds surrounding the hall, a child spotted us and flew into action, yelling that we'd arrived in Greek so ancient I barely understood.

We were met at the propylaea, the grand entrance to the temple, by a gaggle of men, some of them covered in the traditional drapery, some much more exposed. One wore not much more than a huge golden lion pelt thrown over his shoulder with the lion's own teeth used to clamp the cloak shut. I struggled to remember which hero that might be. Didn't Hercules have some labor involving a lion? He was definitely hero-sized—as if Andre the Giant and Arnold Schwarzenegger at his biggest had borne some bizarre love child with thick black hair and a manly beard coming to a neat point over his heart. The others were equally intimidating—young men with flowing hair and bodies that encouraged overpriced gym memberships. Or with tight black curls and arms of steel, stomachs going to paunch. All clearly men of action, even if that action was a distant memory.

They all looked at us with wary, barely leashed hunger. "You called us," Lion-man said, stepping forward.

I remembered now. That had to be the famed Nemean Lion cloak from Hercules's first labor. It was said to make him invulnerable, though if that was true, how had he ever ended up here?

"I did," Hades admitted. "But I will not discuss it with you on the steps of the hall. If you've forgotten how to treat your host, then perhaps you have forgotten too much to be of use."

He was riling them up, giving them something to prove, working the crowd before we'd even begun. It was cleverly done.

An even larger man elbowed Hercules aside, and said heartily, "The upstart forgets his manners. Come, come, please, we have brought enough for a feast."

"Ah, Perseus," Hades said, clamping a hand down on his massive shoulder. "That's more like it." He sent a glare Hercules's way and proceeded into the hall with Perseus as the others closed around us and followed. I was getting *way* more attention than I was comfortable with and realized that I was still in my makeup artist war paint with my hair all dramatically pinned and curled. You'd think after all the action I'd seen that it would have fallen, but it was shellacked to within an inch of its life. Short of Cerberus and his foul and vaporous doggy breath, I didn't know if anything would wilt it.

I glared all around me at the attention, but it seemed that heroes were not so much cowed by dirty looks. In fact, two young men only seemed encouraged—one with twinkling golden eyes, the other with rare green, but alike enough otherwise to be twins.

The green-eyed twin sidled up to me. "Hello," he said with a "come here often?" implied.

I rolled my eyes, but that only brought me to the golden-eyed twin, who said, "Want to tell us what's going on?"

"I'm sure Hades will fill you in."

"Well then, want to fool around?" the green-eyed one asked, moving in closer. Apparently, come-ons hadn't changed much since ancient times. I didn't have the least bit of trouble understanding *that*.

I upped my glare and he turned up the wattage on his smile from lewd to lascivious.

I looked to Apollo in amusement. He was eying the twins as if he'd like to bash their heads in but wouldn't deny me the pleasure. Somehow, it put the devil into me.

"Maybe later," I said, letting my face relax into my best coquettish look.

"Really?" green-eyes said. He hit his twin. "Hear that, Castor?"

Apollo growled and moved in.

"You two had better beat it for now," I told them.

The golden-eyed one gave me a wink and a half bow before grabbing his twin by the cloak and pulling him into the sea of men. Mostly men, anyway. Here and there was a woman or a child, but overwhelmingly the Elysian Fields—or at least the Hall of Heroes—seemed to be populated by men. Darn sexist ancients. Where would Theseus have been without Ariadne's ball of string to find his way out of the labyrinth? And Achilles's heel was only famous because that was where his mama had held him when she dipped him into the River Styx to make him invulnerable but for that one little spot. Gah.

Apollo must have sensed my agitation. "Don't worry, you're twice the hero of anyone here."

"Yeah, how do you figure?"

"You successfully resisted the charms of Castor and Pollux, a Herculean task, I'm sure."

I grinned. "That only puts me on his level."

"Well, then there's the fact that you've resisted me all this time. Oh, and fought Zeus, Poseidon, and Hephaestus, and lived to tell about it. You've faced down Dionysus, Hades, and his hellhounds. Need I go on?"

"I didn't do any of those things alone," I protested.

"And you think they did?"

He had a point. Jason had his Argonauts; Odysseus had his fleet.

And then I spotted a group of warrior women off to the side ... Amazons? Had I been wrong about their existence? The previously unknown fan-girl in me geeked out at the thought. Most were easily as tall as the male warriors, and they were dressed much the same. They weren't one-breasted that I could tell, but their chests did seem to be bound flat and their hair short-cropped or tightly woven to keep it from being gripped in battle. One of them gave me a nod as she caught my eye and I nodded back.

We crossed into the temple proper, and the huge chryselephantine statue at the front of it made me catch my breath, and then spin around as I noticed others in less well-lit alcoves. Apollo closed my mouth for me.

"But—but that's—" I began, pointing at the statue that had first caught my eye, a huge ivory and gold representation of Athena Parthenos that had once stood in the Parthenon, if histories and the scale model in the National Archaeological Museum were accurate. Was it a reproduction or—

"It's the real thing," Hades said, turning to see why we'd stopped. "The Turks looted it once upon a time. Hermes actually helped me steal it back, along with the statue of Zeus that once sat in his temple at Olympus."

I didn't remember ever reading about the statue that held the place of honor—Hades on his throne, Persephone at his side—but he didn't comment on that one and neither did I. In fact, he couldn't even bring himself to look.

Instead, he turned in a circle, surrounded by the heroes of old, making eye contact with as many as he could. "*Men*," see, sexist, "I've called you all here because a new threat menaces the world. Many of the monsters you've faced and defeated in the past have escaped Tartarus. *Rhea* has awakened and has called them to her. The time for heroes is once again. Hermes and Pan"—he looked at us to confirm—"Zeus and Poseidon wait to do battle with them. They need an army. Will you supply it?" This last he yelled, pumping a fist in the air to crank up the crowd.

"Yes!" came the shouted reply, but it wasn't unanimous, and there was some hesitation.

Hades looked around again, assessing, studying, piercing right into their hearts. "I said," he rumbled, "WILL. YOU. FIGHT?"

The roar this time was almost deafening, as the men thumped their chests or beat on their nearest neighbor. The smell of testosterone was in the air.

"Then come!" Hades strode to the foot of his monumental statue and stopped at the base of the throne to mutter a spell and carve symbols in the air. A door appeared in the base, and he pushed it in with a solid blow. The panel moved in and over, revealing such a stockpile of weapons I wondered what Hades had been stockpiling them *for*. "Arm yourselves," he ordered.

There was a bottleneck in the doorway as all the heroes tried to rush in at once—the Amazons, I was glad to see, near the head of the pack.

I pushed my way through as well. I didn't want to end up with the picked-over remains—a barbeque fork where only a trident would do and that sort of thing. I immediately went for the wall of projectile weapons. Hades didn't have guns, oddly enough, which were the only weapons I was trained to use, but crossbows worked on the same principal—load, point, and shoot. I could handle that. Apollo was right beside me, choosing a more traditional bow and two quivers of arrows. *Finally*, armed and fully dangerous.

Clangs rang out as some heroes tested their steel against others, until Hades called a halt to it. "Follow me!" he called by way of a war cry. His voice bounced all around the room, and a cheer went up, drowning it out. Swords were raised in exalta-tion, and Hades looked oddly regal, his goth Don Johnson look replaced now with a bronze breastplate sporting a hydra's heads decoration in raised relief. He'd chosen a sword nearly as big as he was, but he made it seem light as he swung it in a full loop and then pointed forward in the universal sign for "Charge!"

We all marched after him as he led us from the Hall of Heroes, down the winding path and back through the agora. Some men stopped to kiss women or children—or remove swords and helmets from children who thought they'd come along. By the time we reached the diamond gates, only the warriors remained. The heroes and me, headed to face the monsters and men at least triple our sizes with bronze-age weaponry and a few gods for good measure.

CHAPTER THIRTEEN

"You can laugh or cry in the face of danger. Laughter is far more disconcerting for the enemy."
—Pappous

We met up with Hypnos and the others at the Archeron ... or at least a riverbed with not much more than a trickle of water left at the bottom. The remains of what looked to recently have been a mighty river were splashed about the banks, wetting the barren rocks all around and slowly slinking back into the earth. Whether there had been a massive battle, the Titans had drunk it dry, or we were seeing the result of hundreds of feet, claws, tentacles and hooves crossing in a frenzied rush, I couldn't tell. One way or another, the Titans had bypassed the barrier and were headed into trouble.

Hades stared in horror at the destruction of the Archeron, and when he looked to his son and the reinforcements he'd been able to gather, there was a fire in his eyes. Literally hellfire, and he gave off the stench of brimstone like he bathed in the stuff. Hypnos had managed a dozen or so hellhounds and a few unassuming gods in house black who I presumed to be relations based on the family resemblance. Now that I thought about it, myths had Hypnos breeding at least once—his son Morpheus, the Shaper of Dreams. But beyond that, my knowledge failed me.

"They *will* pay for this," Hades growled.

He whirled, giving us the back of his hydra armor, and led the way through the nearly nonexistent river to the other side.

The ground started to climb and the walls narrowed in as we passed by it, until we were moving only about four across. Part of the ceiling had come down where the larger Titans had knocked their heads, so that smaller stones turned ankles and made the way somewhat treacherous, but no one went down. No one complained.

The tension in my stomach ratcheted up with every step. I didn't like this setup at all. A huge rockfall ahead or behind … or *both* … and we'd be cut off. Surely the Titans would expect pursuit and leave us with a nasty surprise somewhere along the way.

Apollo had slung his bow over his back in favor of another, more modern weapon.

He had his cell phone out and was fussing with it.

"I thought you said there were no cell towers in Hell," I said, nudging him to get his attention.

"There aren't, but the way we've been climbing, I keep hoping we're close enough to the surface to get messages in and out. We need to know what's happening up there, and they need to know the situation down here and that help is on the way."

"Anything yet?" I asked.

"No, dammit. I'll keep trying."

Someone tapped my shoulder, and I turned to see the twins. "How 'bout now?" the green-eyed one asked. He seemed to be the ringleader.

"Might be your last chance," said the other. "We might not survive the battle." Wow, were they the princes of romance or what?

"I thought you were already dead," I said wryly.

"Do we *look* dead?"

I really didn't know how to answer that.

A huge rumble up ahead saved me the trouble. The ceiling seemed to jump, like an ancient elevator finally hitting its floor, and then it buckled right overtop of us. I screamed like a girl and from the choral effect, I wasn't the only one.

A man lunged forward to catch the center of the dipping ceiling, his muscles bulging where his lion pelt exposed them—Hercules, once again taking up the mantle of the earth as he had from Atlas. I hoped he hadn't gone soft in the intervening millennia.

"Go!" he grunted at the rest of us. "I'll hold it up. Just go!"

"You heard him," Hades said. "Go!"

The army moved around Hercules. Sweat was breaking out across his brow, and I could make out not only every muscle, but every vein and artery.

"Can you hold out?" I asked with no clue what I'd do if the answer was, "No."

He must have gotten the gist of what I was saying, "Don't worry about me," he answered. "Just get out of here. The sooner you go, the sooner all I have to worry about is me."

"We'll be back for you," I promised. I hoped I lived long enough to follow through.

He nodded, as though another word would break him, and jutted his chin toward where the others had disappeared, signaling us to go.

Apollo grabbed me, and I ran after the others, trying to ignore the creaks and groans of the stone ceiling above, the jagged shards of rock still falling here and there like icicles to shatter on the ground.

I almost jumped out of my skin at the sound of a phone

ringing. Apollo grabbed it out of his pocket and answered on the run. "Yes?" He listened for a second. "We're on the way. We should come up behind them. And for Olympus's sake, tell Zeus to stop shaking the earth—at least until we're above it."

He hung up. I guess whoever was on the other end already knew the Titans had broken free.

"Who was that?"

"Hermes. He says get there as fast as you can and that it's not Zeus doing the shaking."

"Great."

A rock pinged off my head, but I hardly registered the pain with all the adrenaline flooding my system. Ahead of us, people were calling out warnings and slinging boulders, pulling them away from the cave-in at the exit. We were already one hero down, but the others had it covered. All Apollo and I could do from the back of the field was stay out of the way of flying rocks.

When they'd cleared enough room to crawl out, Thanatos insisted on leading the charge, his sword raised before him to skewer anyone in his way. With a great cry, he pelted up out of the ground, the heroes echoing him as they followed.

Apollo and I climbed over the rocks in our way and blinked into the sudden sunlight, our sight clearing onto chaos. We were on the field of the Pythian Games that capped the sacred site of Delphi at the very top of Mount Parnassus. My natural fear at the height clashed with my precog alarm klaxons for a sickening, blinding panic attack that threatened to take me down, but I didn't have time for any of that. The battle was already in progress, the Titans towering above our force of Hellenic heroes who'd rushed into the action, weapons drawn.

I couldn't see our allies—gods and goddesses, my friends and family—all the way across the field, opposite our titanic foes, but I could feel the electricity in the air. I desperately hoped that meant Zeus and Poseidon had joined our team. I wondered who else had been recruited.

Something at the edge of my vision caught my attention,

and my head swiveled as a figure rose into the air, great black wings unfurling, batlike in construct, but feathered along the struts where on a bat there might be fur. But at its core was something very familiar ...

Hypnos? It looked like him, all punked out with spikes and piercings, but the wings ... they were new. Or maybe there just hadn't been cause to reveal them in the cavelike Underworld. But now ... he was magnificent. He flapped the wings just enough to hover above the battleground, and as he did, he began to sing, something atonal and ... not flat, but bottomless. I blinked again as the air began to ripple, like a Hollywood intro to a dream sequence. His wings beat the rippling air toward the Titans. Those closest began to sway, as if he were sending them to sleep. Then there was a raptor cry from within the melee and a second winged figure rose up, this one from among the ranks of Titans—a flying female, half woman, half bird of prey.

She flew at Hypnos, and as they grappled in the air, his waves ceased. The Titans shook off their strange effect, and renewed their attacks with double their ferocity. We couldn't stay on the sidelines. I just had to figure out where we'd do the most good.

"There!" Apollo said, as if he'd read my mind. He pointed to a spot of high ground that would have been a spectator section during the Pythian Games, where the Amazons were already spreading out for a good clear shot at our enemies.

I nodded, took two steps in that direction, and seized up as something took control of my body. No, not something ...

Rhea.

I cried out a warning to Apollo, but it came out just a strangled sound. He whirled, though, in time to catch me as I fell forward, fighting Rhea for control. Losing.

And then suddenly I was pushing Apollo away with a strength not my own and swinging for him in a way that would snap his head around ... and maybe a few vertebrae. He caught my fist before it could connect, but in that instant my other hand lashed out, aiming for something a lot more vulnerable. My hand like a talon, I caught and gripped Apollo's bait and tackle, twisting mercilessly. His eyes got big and betrayed, and he started to buckle to the ground. I let go and used the fist he'd been holding to knock him aside. Even as he rolled, my leg shot up, ready to stomp down on him, but he did the unexpected. He rolled back toward me, grabbed the stomping leg and twisted. I went down on top of him, but kicked hard as I fell, managing to land a blow on his thigh, very close to those bits I'd already manhandled. His eyes filled with pained tears and I—Rhea—rolled away and shot to my feet, reaching for the bow and arrows strapped to my back.

Rhea loaded a crossbow bolt and pointed it down at Apollo, straight at his heart. Weapon cocked and ready, my gaze zeroed in on the sight, preparing to pierce him through.

Frantically, I fought to regain control of my body, flinging myself against invisible barriers, trying to get through to myself or even just mess up the signals, to save Apollo as he'd saved me so many times. I might as well have been a firefly beating at a glass jar.

Something flew up into Rhea's peripheral vision, but she didn't blow her aim by looking. I started to release the bolt, knowing that this was it—that Apollo's death would break his hold on Delphi, the navel of the world. Rhea would capture the lashing rein, Delphi's power once again hers to command.

My panic meter went to eleven.

The pain struck from out of the blue—a bolt to the chest. So stunning it took a second to register anything but that I had missed the shot, which had gone wide. Rhea looked down in disbelief to see an arrow sticking out of our chest, just inches shy of my heart.

She bellowed in more anger than pain, and immediately wrapped a hand around the shaft to pull it out.

I smashed through with everything I had, knocking her hand away. The shock was all that allowed it, I was sure.

Apollo kicked my legs out from under me as I stood there wavering, my body ready to topple as Rhea and I fought for control.

I went down in a heap and my sight caught on what had moved in my peripheral vision—a winged boy, teenager anyway, all tussled hair and shining eyes, wearing little more than a bow and arrows. Eros, aka Cupid? I'd been downed by *Cupid*?

My vision started to swim as Apollo kicked the bow out of my hand. "Tori?" he asked.

He looked strange from this angle—him up, me down, the rising sun behind him lighting up his hair like a halo around his head. Put him together with Cupid's wings and he'd look like an angel.

Was I delirious with pain?

"She's not my only one," Rhea's voice issued from my lips, and then she was gone.

I was left cold. So cold. Numb. I could barely feel the pain anymore, and I wasn't sure that was a good thing with no Hecate available to heal me.

"Go," I said, faintly. Breath was hard, and I thought I felt fluid in it, like maybe the arrow had pierced something never meant to be pierced. "Fight. Win."

Apollo looked at me for another moment and then threw himself down on top of me, careful of the arrow.

He muttered something against my lips. It tickled. I wanted to breathe in his warmth, but that was getting harder and harder.

Then he kissed me, lips on mine, but softly, no more than a touch. For a second, he seemed to be breathing for me and something passed between us. Something profound. If he was opening up another damned gateway in my mind or another unwanted link, I was going to be pissed … though I didn't see how that would matter for much longer.

When he pulled away, the numbness had spread, and I

couldn't even blink. If my eyes closed, fine. Otherwise, I was going to see the battle through to the bloody end … mine.

He gave a quick caress to my face, grabbed my bow off the ground as a backup for his own and ran off, Cupid flying beside him, firing as he flew.

I was left behind, staring wide-eyed at the battle, helpless.

On the field was chaos. Arrows and crossbow bolts struck the Titans but not with the same success they'd had against me. Meanwhile, hellhounds were being hurled yelping through the air or being crunched between monstrous teeth. Hypnos and the eagle-woman had fallen to the ground, but he was rising again, though with tears in the membrane of his wings. Still, he was able to take to the air, if nowhere near as gracefully as before. Thanatos, Hades, and the heroes slashed again and again, but didn't look like they were gaining ground, except what the Titans gave in their push forward to overrun the Olympians on the other end of the field.

From that far end, lightning flashed, but it was more electric shock than branch or ball lighting, as though Zeus was up too high to gather the full force of his storms. Rhea had chosen her battleground well.

And then my heart went cold. Figures came running toward my high ground. *Human* figures. Female human figures. I immediately recognized one of them.

Christie … still in the dress she'd worn to the wedding, but now with a bow in one hand and an arrow in the other. The women with her … I squinted, it was as much as I could do … my fellow inmates from Delphi prison. Rhea's recruits.

My fault. All my fault.

They lined up along the spectator section of the stadium opposite the Amazons. I tried to get up, to distract them, or fight as they started to take aim at Althea, Junessa, and the others and … nothing … I couldn't move.

I felt pinned to the ground by the arrow in my chest, staked like a modern-day vampire. I knew it was stupid. I knew it was probably the loss of blood making me so weak, but the feeling wouldn't leave me. I had to pull the arrow. It was the right thing to do. Precognition or delusion? What did it matter when I couldn't even move?

No. I was *not* going to let everyone I loved down like this.

My fault.

With a monumental effort, I made my hand move. Just the one farthest from the arrow and just a flop, but I was amazed even at that. It was a start. I focused, pouring every ounce of strength I had into that one arm, praying that my last dose of ambrosia wasn't all used up and out of my system.

Heal, dammit, I thought. *Heal now.*

I'd never been patient. Imminent death certainly wasn't going to change that.

The hand moved. Slowly, painfully. It felt like *I'd* been petrified. No, not just petrified—stoned. Stone weighed more. A ton or so, it felt like. Eventually, the hand bumped up against the arrow, causing an explosion of pain to shoot straight down the shaft and all through my chest.

I coughed hard, and there was a gurgle to it that I knew to be a bad sign. Punctured lung? Drowning in my own blood?

Didn't matter now. Diagnosis wouldn't change a thing.

I labored against the aftermath of the cough, gasping for breath too painful to take. But I forced my hand up again for another try at the arrow, focusing on fine motor skills and actually grasping it this time. The hand moved torturously slowly and when it bumped against the arrow it was too weak to knock it hard. But it did make contact, and I forced it to turn and grasp.

Drawing my next breath took all my concentration for the moment, and it was another after that before I could refocus on the arrow and on pulling it out.

Meanwhile, Christie and her cadre were unleashing arrow after arrow, but with more regularity than skill. They were being controlled, but Rhea didn't yet have the power, the *precision* to make it count.

She couldn't have Christie and she *couldn't have me.*

I gave my last ounce of strength to pulling the shaft from my chest. I almost passed out as it started to slide, ripping through already abused muscle and tissue. Pain blinded me, and I wanted to arch up, my body following the path of the arrow as if I could control the pace, but I didn't have time for slow and easy.

When the tip came free, I collapsed. My hand fell to my side, along with the gored arrow. Blood began to bubble and gurgle up from the wound. Bubbles in the blood—bad sign, I thought, battling back the darkness that wanted to swamp me.

It felt like removing that arrow had removed some kind of blockage. Now the full measure of pain became heart-stoppingly clear—razor-sharp, stabbing shards of crystal being pushed through veins and arteries too narrow to handle them, tearing, ripping and scraping me raw. But behind it … *what* had Apollo breathed into me? The crystal shards of pain felt like unmaking —tearing apart my stitching, doing demolition. But behind that, the feeling that I was being restitched, putty poked into old scars that were then spackled over, base coated, repainted and remodeled. Like I was being remade.

What the hell.

It was unbearable, like my whole insides were crawling with army ants rebuilding me one cell at a time. It was the creepiest, most awful feeling in the world. Worse than ambrosia withdrawal. Worse than being possessed. Worse than the makeover at Christie's upscale spa. I lay in a pool of my own sweat and blood, unable to stop it. Unsure if I'd survive.

And then, just like that, it was over. I thought I died. For a minute, I couldn't feel anything at all. Couldn't hear. Couldn't see. And then I gasped in a breath—a *full* breath with no rasping or bubbling or blood, and it was the sweetest thing in the world. I gulped in more air until I felt my lungs would explode with the fullness, and then they seemed to adapt. The sights and sounds and *smell* of the battle came rushing at me like a flash mob, coming from everywhere at once. Too vivid. Too much, as if I'd been experiencing the world through a bubble all my life and it had suddenly popped. And I felt ... unbelievable. I tested out my arms and legs; they lifted as though gravity no longer had such a pull on me.

The twang of bowstrings snapped me out of my wonder and whipped my head around. The first person I saw was the woman who'd signaled me outside the jail, who I now knew Rhea had touched. I went for her, and my legs seemed to push off the ground with double their power. When I was close enough to spring for her, I sailed through the air, knocking her to the ground before she could get off her next shot. She writhed under me, trying to throw me off. I grabbed for her bow, yanked it from her hands and broke it in half, throwing the pieces and myself to the side in order to roll to my feet and go for the next girl. I rushed her just as she released an arrow. With no time to stop it, I leapt in the way and caught the bolt in my bare hand.

Her eyes widened, but she couldn't have been more shocked than I was. She backed away as I started toward her, but then straightened and held her ground as if she'd received a new directive from Rhea. She reached for another arrow, but I was on her before she could nock it, driving the one in my hand into her leg. She dropped the bow in pain. I picked it up and ran for the next archer ... only to come face to face with Christie.

She saw me coming and turned her loaded bow my way. I'd been shot once today. It wasn't going to happen again.

"Christie," I called, giving her the chance to snap out of it. "It's me." She didn't even blink, but let fly the arrow she was holding back.

I used the bow in my hand like a bat to swat the arrow out of the air, shocked when it worked, and leapt for Christie, even as she reached for another. I landed on top of her, knees to her stomach, hands on her shoulders, riding her to the ground. She hit with an "ooph" and for a second I saw my friend Christie flash in her eyes. Then they were cold again—dry ice cold, the kind that burned.

"You dare?" Rhea asked.

She reached Christie's hands up, not for my neck, as I expected, but toward my face. Her icy eyes went wide as she touched me. "But ... that's not possible ... I can't reach you."

I didn't know what Apollo had breathed into me or what the long-term effects of the ambrosia or nectar had made me, but if it included being impervious to mesmerism, I'd take it.

Still, now that I had Christie down, I didn't know what to do with her. She was my best friend. I couldn't leave her behind to hurt me or anyone else on the battlefield, but I couldn't hurt her. Rhea stiffened Christie's hands like claws and I had less than a second to decide what to do as they came for my eyes.

"Sorry," I whispered, sucker punching Christie on the temple, just hard enough, I hoped, to send her to sleep. Her head fell to the side, eyes closed. I felt for her pulse, found it and moved on, stealing the bow and arrow from her unconscious body. I immediately nocked one arrow and sent it flying for the last archer on my side of the field—the final woman from the prison. I went for her bow hand, hoping to hurt her as little as possible.

With my crazy bolstered vision, it was no problem at all to hit my target, and she dropped her weapon, going down clutching at her hand.

I turned my stolen bow toward the battlefield, but it was too much of a melee, everyone engaged together. Even with my new acuity, I couldn't trust that no one would shift and my arrows wouldn't strike friend instead of foe.

Cursing, I threw down the bow and ran toward the field. The mother of all earthquakes hit between one step and the next. I went down watching the fighters on the field fall like bowling pins, barely catching myself on my hands, smacking my nose on the ground as the earth continued to convulse.

Mother of all quakes was right. From the center of the field, a figure started to rise, massive and female. I didn't wait for her to fully emerge before pushing myself to my feet and starting to run again. I knew who it would be—Rhea—and I knew that if she was rising it was because she'd become strong enough to take us all on.

I don't know what I thought I could do about that. I wasn't thinking. I was only feeling—the need for vengeance against her for hurting Nick and Christie, for controlling me. She was going down.

Cupid and Hypnos circled her in the air, like the helicopters around King Kong on top of the Empire State Building. Only Rhea was a *lot* bigger and only slightly less hairy. She had a fountain of black hair spilling all around her head and eyes the color of hard earth. If I'd thought the Titans were big, Rhea was humongous.

Just the thing you wanted to say to an angry mother goddess … "Hey, lady, your bazongas are the size of my laundry room." Yeah, that would go over well. Clearly, however I'd been remade, my snark had survived.

As I ran toward her, something started to burn at my back. I felt tearing, and it was more than my shirt. I stumbled as I tried to twist and run at the same time, to see if someone had stuck a knife between my shoulder blades, and then almost fell on my face as I saw wings rising out of my back instead of the knife hilt I expected. The wings—*gargoyle* wings, black and leathery and *attached to my freakin' back*—flapped as I started to fall, righting me and then raising me up to hover just above the ground.

Had Apollo somehow activated some dormant gorgon genes? I thought about Perseus's gorgon shield—the crouching gorgon with her monstrous tusked face, wings half furled. *This was not the time for vanity*, but still I had to touch my face and hair to make sure there were no tusks or snakes rising out of it. Although, right now they'd really come in handy.

As far as I could tell, my face and hair were as they'd always been, which was a good thing, because I didn't have time for a breakdown over any sort of reptile dysfunction. Rhea already had her upper body entirely free and was pushing off the ground to get her hips loose as well. If we had any shot at her, it was going to have to be now.

I darted in, still with no plan. With all the static electricity Zeus's pyrotechnics had unleashed in the air, Rhea's hair was rising alarmingly, and it gave me ideas. I knew I couldn't see a thing when my crazy hair flew in my face. It was a start, and I had to do something quickly, because the arrows being sent her way via Althea, Junessa, and Apollo were only pissing her off.

I willed myself to fly toward her, hoping my wings would obey, having no idea how to work them. I jerked back and forth as they flapped, trying to work out how *not* to do that and real-ized pretty quickly that I just had to relax and go with it. It was like I had some ancestral muscle memory. The wings knew what to do, even if I didn't.

Rhea tried to bat me out of the sky as I flew in, but I dodged instinctively, flitting like Tinkerbell in the face of Captain Hook. Proportionately, the description was apt. I dashed in closer, rather than dancing out of reach and grabbed hard for a handful of her hair. It was too thick, though, and too heavy for me to grab enough to make any difference, and I realized it as soon as she shook her head hard and all that hair whipped around, lashing me a thousand times and sending me flying.

From across the battlefield Zeus saw what I was trying to do and yelled, "Stay back!"

He whipped up the winds and sent them in a tornado cone toward Rhea. Her own hair whipped up around her, blinding, restraining. Maybe we could lash her up, net her in her own tresses.

Rhea raised her face to the sky and sucked in a breath. It was like the suction of a black hole; the winds roared down into her open maw. Her hair fell still about her head and shoulders. And yes, in front of her face, but it didn't seem to even give her pause.

I saw her prodigious chest expand until I thought it might bust ... no pun intended.

Then she blew out the breath again in a gale force wind that knocked everyone to their knees. I went head over feet, wind-milling through the sky until I crashed into something and crumpled to the ground.

CHAPTER FOURTEEN

"Screw diamonds, self-agency is a girl's best friend."
—Tori Karacis

My vision wasn't just double, it was Ferris wheel—an image in every car, all circling around, making my stomach lurch along with the ride. Blinking just seemed to send the wheel spinning faster. I closed my eyes and focused on breathing.

Three calming breaths were all I could stand. I had to know what was going on. I had to get back in there.

My stomach gurgled as I opened my eyes once again and the images shifted, slowly coming together into focus. I was laying on top of a behemoth chest, very human except that the hair covering it was more like fur, bunny soft. It was ... disconcerting. I sat up in a shot, anxious to make sure the Titan wasn't about to squash me flat, but it looked like he'd gone down badly. His head was at a funny angle and his eyes gazed up unseeingly at the sky. No one who'd seen death could ever question how you could tell. There wasn't just a stillness. There was a light that went out of the eyes, almost a film, or a shade drawn across them. They just looked *dead*. There was no poetic way to describe it. Not that I could think of.

I didn't even know him. Likely, if he'd been alive he'd have been trying to kill me. But, oddly, he reminded me of Pappous —my grandfather, the strongman with the weak heart. Maybe it was that the Titan was so massive and seemingly strong, yet the bunny fur and the bad fall made him seem so vulnerable. So dead.

Bile burned its way up my throat, and I quickly slid off the Titan's cooling chest toward the ground before I could lose it.

I knew what had to be done. Separately, we were vulnerable. Each part of this battle from Zeus on down was so used to being powerful in his or her own right that they weren't thinking about working together. Not really. Zeus had seen what I'd been trying to do with Rhea's hair and played off of that. It was a start, one we'd have to build on.

We were going to need a strategy. A coordinated plan of attack.

I was still in shock over my wings, didn't know what to feel about them or how I'd get them home on the plane, but they were good for getting a bird's eye view on the battle. I rose, keeping a watch on Rhea, who had now completely risen out of the earth and faced off with two bearded figures, Zeus and Poseidon, who'd managed to pull themselves up off the ground. Serena, who'd clearly joined up with her lord of the deep, wasn't so lucky. She lay beside them like a doll who'd been tossed aside. I could tell she still breathed, but she hadn't yet regained consciousness. Hermes hovered beside the brothers in his winged sandals. My movement caught his eye as Rhea swept downward with an outstretched hand to swat them like flies. With no hope of stopping her, he zagged out of the way and flew to my side, staring at my wings.

"Tori—what—when—how?"

I shook my head. "No idea. We need a plan."

"You got one?" he asked.

"Maybe. How do I know I can trust you?"

"Tori," he said, a hand to his heart. "How can you ask?"

I gave him my best gorgon glare. "I know, okay? I figured out about the thing you've got going with Eterné. 'Where's the real money?' you asked. I'm going to say pyramid schemes and youth serums. What's in your product? Nectar? Ambrosia?" I don't know when I'd guessed, but suddenly it was all crystal clear. "It doesn't matter. Whatever it is, it ends. You promise me. If I save the day, no more trying to hook humans."

Hermes's eyes blazed, and for an instant, I could see his relationship to Hades. "And if I don't agree?"

"Then I'll do this without you and let the whole ancient world know what you could have helped and didn't. If that's not enough, I'll come after you myself."

He eyed me sourly, but we didn't have the time for a battlefield sulk. "Yes or no?" I asked, staring straight into his eyes, looking for a lie.

"Yes," he spat.

"Swear."

"Swear? What are we, five? Swear on what?"

"On something you care about, beyond mischief and mayhem. Swear on your blood and your balls."

"*My balls?*"

"Do it."

"Fine," he said, quickly. Rhea was swinging around toward us now, Zeus and Poseidon clutched in her fist. I presumed we were next. "I swear by my blood and balls I'll carry your messages faithfully. Happy?"

"Unbelievably." I grabbed his shirt and flew him up, up and out of even Rhea's immense reach, and then I told him. Everything but my part of the plan. He dashed off the second I lowered him back to Earth, and I flew off too, sweeping the battlefield for those I needed. Hades. Apollo. Castor and Pollux.

Three of them—Hades, Castor and Pollux—were in about the same position on the field as I'd left them. Closer in, of course, but bashing it out with two Titans who'd, like them, survived Rhea's blowback. The one Titan, spiderlike, was already down to about half its legs, and as I watched, Castor grabbed one side of its huge, clashing mandibles and Pollux the other, and they pulled with everything they had, cracking it open, breaking its jaw. The spider spit something out of its mouth as it collapsed to the ground in pain, and the something hit me square in the chest, burning like a firebrand, but I didn't have any time to worry about it.

"You two ever play bait and switch?" I asked them. They looked at each other, grinning.

"Good. Think you can do that with Rhea? Distract her, taunt her, make her come for you, see if you can get her so riled she forgets to finish off her sons?"

They exchanged another glance, like they had some sort of mental twin speak going on.

"Where will that get us with you?" Castor asked.

"I'll introduce you to a siren," I told them. "You'll forget all about me."

"Done!" Pollux answered for them. "Come on!" he called to his brother.

They were off like this was the greatest fun they'd had in a long time. Maybe it was.

Maybe peace and quiet was overrated. I'd like the chance to find out.

I turned in time to see Hades leap into the air, slashing his sword for his opponent's throat. The Titan's hand lashed out, and I could see that Hades was going to get knocked on his ass. I swooped in to save him, but Hypnos came out of nowhere and grabbed him up first, taking him to safety with Hades hollering the whole way. I'd have been tempted to drop the ungrateful bastard, but that was me. Anyway, I needed him—needed them both.

I flew to their side and landed as Hypnos did.

"Just the gods I needed to talk to," I said. "Hades, I don't suppose you can access the River Lethe from up here."

"You suppose wrong," he said, with a glare that was more, I thought, about the fact that I'd seen him rescued than that I'd questioned his powers.

"Good. And Hypnos, you've still got the power to send people to sleep? You haven't used it up or anything?" Riling them up just like Hades had riled his troops. Now they'd both have something to prove. Anyway, it was a valid question. I had no idea how these things worked.

"No, I haven't 'used it up,'" he answered. His look asked me why on Earth I was wasting their time with stupid questions.

"Good. Here's the plan."

When I finished, both eyed me dubiously, but it was Hades who voiced it. "Why should we take orders from *you*, who have so far been nothing but trouble."

"Because *this* time I'm on your side, sending my trouble *her* way. Don't you want to see how it turns out?"

They considered. I didn't have time for them to make up their minds. "Anyway, this is all Hermes's idea," I lied.

Their looks cleared right away. "Ah, the trickster god," Hypnos said. "This might just work."

"Good, get with Zeus and Poseidon." The three brothers, together again. Mythologically speaking, there was power in threes—the Muses, the Gray sisters, the Gorgons, the Father, Son and the Holy Ghost, Larry, Moe and Curly.

I prayed it would work, but I still didn't know who I was praying to. "Ready?" I asked Hypnos.

He nodded grimly, and we both stretched our wings, primed for takeoff. It was still strange, but I didn't have time to dwell on that now. I had a goddess to face down.

I flapped my wings and rose up into the air, Hypnos right beside me, and we headed straight for Rhea.

Castor and Pollux had gotten her to drop her sons, but they

were all now running for their lives as she bellowed, trying to stomp them out. Very god-like.

I flew up into her face, startling her, but she was too smart to hit herself trying to be rid of me. Instead, she flapped her hand in front of her face, as if brushing off a fly. It was all I could do to stay airborne when she missed me by a hair, the displaced air nearly enough to send me pinwheeling through the sky.

"Hurry up, hurry up, hurry up," I muttered under my breath. I didn't have the capacity for actual words. Flight was winding, and I wasn't used to it.

Hypnos held back, as he was supposed to, waiting for his cue.

Pest blown away, Rhea ignored me to continue after Zeus and Poseidon, but I couldn't let that happen. I dashed in again, flying just outside Rhea's peripheral vision until she suddenly howled and clamped a hand to her nose as an arrow pierced it for her.

"Ha, gotcha, you old bat!" Cupid said, already nocking another arrow.

The first one didn't look like much more than a splinter given Rhea's huge size, but it seemed to enrage her all the same. Rhea went for him, and I grabbed for her ear, hoping to pull her up short, but I had nowhere near the power. She swatted at me, and this time caught me in a full body slap. For an instant of mind-bending pain, I swore the front of my ribs met the back, and then I was falling, still chanting *hurryhurryhurry* in my head.

There was no air left inside of me when I hit the ground, and for a moment the pain seemed stunted, twisted up somehow and unable to get from my back to anywhere else. I stared up at Rhea's rampaging form, wondering if Apollo was still alive in all this, wondering if my plan would come together, when the sky started to blacken.

Yes, I thought. *Finally.*

I shifted my gaze, the only thing I could move, to track

along the ground, looking for the brothers—Zeus, Poseidon and Hades.

There. Being defended by Castor and Pollux, Hermes and … was that? *Apollo!*

Apparently, my eyes *weren't* the only things I could move. My heart could leap. And did … very quickly meeting the cage of my compressed ribs and nearly shattering against them.

They formed a human shield around the brothers as they pulled together a massive storm, fueled by the River Lethe, accessed by Hades, whipped into a frenzy by Poseidon and molded by Zeus into a funnel aimed like a spear point right for Rhea.

She laughed as she saw it. After all, she'd already turned Zeus's tornado against him. But this was another beast entirely. Again, she inhaled deeply, lungs stretched to capacity, swallowing the storm into herself, only to sputter and choke as it went down. A coughing fit seized her, blowing the brothers down, but the funnel was now a force all its own and was still raging, still on-rushing and—the River Lethe, invading, stealing her memory, her anger, her thirst for vengeance.

Hypnos was up next. He got up right into her face, wings flapping and flapping. That strange distortion where the night seemed to grow darker and deeper emanated outward from him, rolling over Rhea like waves.

She started to sway, shook her head hard trying to clear it and instead grew more disoriented with the motion. I had an instant of fear that she would shake it off, but the head shaking only seemed to make her dizzy. Between Hypnos and the waters of forgetfulness washing away her agitation, she seemed to shrink in on herself, eyes watering from her coughing fit and still trying to rediscover her breath.

"Get back!" I tried to yell as her swaying became frightening. It was either that or "Timber!" but neither actually made it out of my mouth, which wasn't obeying me at the moment, though already I thought I could breathe a little easier—without ambrosia or Apollo's intervention. Like the wings, I didn't know what it meant, but apparently what didn't kill me made me stronger.

And then Rhea teetered my way.

I had just time to think, "Oh, shit!" because my last words *would* be that classy, when someone swooped in out of nowhere and swept me out of the way.

Behind me, the concussion of Rhea striking the earth blew out eardrums and shook stones free of the ruins.

Hermes held me aloft until the earth stopped shaking. When it did, he looked into my eyes and grinned a wicked grin. "Now who owes who?"

I half heard and half read his lips, my ears still ringing from Rhea's impact. I was too relieved to rise to the bait.

"Put me down." My lips formed the words, but I wasn't sure they were understandable.

Hermes flew me jerkily toward Apollo and let me slide down his body toward the ground. Apollo caught me as I started to fall forward.

"You did it!" he said.

Then Rhea started to snore like a buzzsaw.

CHAPTER FIFTEEN

"And now, the end is near/ And so I face the final gerkin."
—Pappous singing Frank Sinatra's My Way

"Uh, Pappous, that's 'final curtain.'"
—Tori Karacis

"Is it? But I've sung it 'gerkin' all my life. What a pickle!"
—Pappous, as Tori facepalms

The wings stayed.

I was able to furl them, bring them in close to my body, but there was no way to vanish them. Unlike Rhea. Together, the three brothers worked to sink her back into the earth where everybody prayed she'd sleep for another few millennia or more.

Some of the Titans had disappeared themselves, escaping into the night. But Hades, Hypnos, and the heroes herded or carried the rest back to the Underworld … just as the sound of police sirens carried up the mountain. Someone or ones had to have noticed the freak storm atop Mount Parnassus and no one within range could have missed the quake of Rhea rising or the concussion of her hitting the earth.

There was no time to clean up the battlefield. Zeus raised a mist that gave us cover as we all slipped off into the night, returning to the hotel in twos and threes, slinking in through side entrances, back up to the bridal suite. I was torn between the hotel and the hospital, where I knew they'd take Christie and the other girls who'd fallen on the field. I felt responsible for them … and besides, there was Nick. Even if we were through, there was history there. He deserved to know the battle was over.

Well, over except for tracking down the escaped Titans.

But first I needed to see everybody safe and sound—Mom, Dad, Yiayia, Spiro … Oh, and I had a certain promise to keep to two heroes who stuck to me like glue. An introduction to a siren. Sure, she was a bit of a psycho and had tried to petrify Apollo. For that, introducing her to the twins seemed a fitting punishment. And if they hit it off, well, she had fought for our side in the end. Maybe the two would keep her too busy to cause any more immediate mischief.

So with a raggedy cloak borrowed from one of the downed Titans wrapped around my body to hide my wings, we approached the bridal suite.

There was a party going on behind the closed doors. I could hear it even from down the hall. Startled, I looked left and right at the twins, who looked back at me with identical grins. Apparently, where I was ready to mourn the dead and wounded, they were more than ready to celebrate the victory.

I knocked loudly at the door, which swung open after a second of loud, drunken debate about who would get it. I wasn't surprised to see that Spiro had won that battle. The door opened to reveal his flushed face, sweat starting to curl his hair along his forehead and neck. His shirtfront was open a button or two beyond the norm, giving him a dissolute look, even before I spotted Jesus on his arm, tie askew as I'd never seen it before. Spiro raked a glance over me and my two companions and grinned from ear to ear.

"Leave with one man, come back with two. Way to go, sis!"

"Don't be a pig," I told him.

"And *togas*," he continued. He opened the door wider to let us in and started chanting, "Toga, toga, toga!"

I glared at him as we passed, not bothering to point out that they wore chitons, not togas. It wouldn't have mattered to him and anyway I was too happy to see him alive to argue.

Jesus, looking not the least bit sheepish, studied me in typical Jesus fashion. "Rough night?" he asked, eying my wardrobe choice.

"Oh, you've no idea. Way to go, keeping me out of trouble. Bang up job."

His eyes widened at that, and I air-scored a point to myself, catching the cloak as it began to slip off my shoulders.

Tina came rushing up the second she saw me, talking a mile a minute even before she was in range. "Hope you don't mind. I couldn't sit around waiting, so I invited people up and pretty soon—*What* are you wearing?"

To her surprise, I grabbed her in for a hug instead of answering and held her tightly enough that she protested. When I let her pull back, she looked me over from head to foot. I was a mess, but all she said was, "I'm so glad you're alive." And then she pulled *me* in for a hug until two throats cleared behind us.

I grinned into the top of Tina's head and disentangled myself to ask, "Where's Serena?"

"Serena?" she said, shocked.

"Is she here?"

"She most certainly is," Serena said from the hallway behind us. The twins and I turned to see her standing with a hand jauntily to her hip, looking none the worse for wear, but for a bruise on her cheek and a scrape along her neck. I was surprised she'd dared show her face again, but the emerald green gown she'd changed into showed a lot more than that, embracing her curves like Jesus embraced GQ or Cosmo. I supposed she had amends to make with Pan … Uncle Hector … if she wanted to stay with the film.

Castor and Pollux stepped forward even without my introduction, drawn by her striking green eyes that flashed as she spotted them.

"Well, well, well," she said. "Who do we have here?"

I performed the introductions and quickly became extraneous, which was just how I wanted it. I left them behind and moved into the suite, spotting Jesus and Spiro. Beyond them Mom and Dad, Yiayia and Fergus, Uncle Christos …

Yiayia caught my eye and tugged on Fergus's arm. I didn't need my precognition to see the future. She'd corner me and make me tell her everything. *Everything*. In excruciating detail. I'd be stuck here all night.

But now that I knew everyone was safe, there was somewhere else I had to be—the hospital, checking on Christie and Nick and all the people I'd failed.

I quickly headed for the door, doing my best not to cause a ripple in the crowd that Yiayia could track.

Apollo was coming in the door as I was leaving. I tried to sidestep him with a muttered, "excuse me," but that wasn't going to work. He grabbed me by the shoulders. "You okay?"

I shrugged him off and looked up desperately. "Step aside or come with, but if we don't get out of here now, we won't be going anywhere."

He looked over my shoulder, saw Yiayia coming our way, and quickly put two and two together.

He grabbed my hand and pulled me toward the door. As soon as we were out and the door closed behind us, he jogged me toward a dogleg in the corridor.

"Come on," he said. "My room's closest."

"But the hospital—"

"You can't go in like that," he said. "Hospital's the first place the police will look for injuries that could have come from tonight's trouble. You can't even ask about Christie. They'll want to question how you knew she was there."

"But—"

"No buts."

"But *Nick*."

He blew out a breath, stopped in front of a door and used his key card to get us inside.

"Fine, Nick, but don't get caught sniffing around the others."

"Sir, yes, sir," I said, saluting him. My cloak dropped and my wings unfurled, nearly knocking over the little decorative table in the room's foyer.

We both froze.

"I thought I'd seen, but … I didn't … are they permanent?"

My heart dropped. I didn't realize how much I'd been wishing *he* could tell *me*.

"I don't know." I was surprised to hear a sob in my voice. After everything that had happened … The wings had been a godsend during the battle, but now … nothing would ever be the same again. "What did you do to me back in the fight?"

Apollo's gaze slid away from mine, and I grabbed his face, pulling him back around to look at me. "Apollo?" I asked.

"It was the breath of life," he said softly.

"The what?"

"I gave you some of my divinity. It was … it was just supposed to save you, but everything I do keeps having unexpected side effects with you. It's like parts of you that have been dormant are starting to awake."

"So today the wings, tomorrow the tusks?"

"I don't know," he said miserably. "This has never happened before. I've never—"

"Can it. Recriminations later. For now, I need to clean up and get to the hospital. Do you have a jacket I can use?" I didn't have to say "oversized," because with the width of his massive shoulders everything he had would hang on me.

Besides, whatever he gave me would do well enough. I had to get out of here and away from the look in his eyes that said there was nothing I could accuse him of that he didn't already blame on himself. Another second and I might be trying to comfort him, let *him* off the hook. I wasn't sure I was ready for that.

Apollo grabbed my chin, gently, and now made me look at him. "Tori, this doesn't change anything about you, you know. You're still you. Still beautiful and amazing and vital. You saved the day. Not the Olympians or the heroes—you."

"Great, pin a big ole medal on me. Maybe it will distract people *from my wings*. I have to get out of here."

I backed out of his grip and closed myself in the bathroom. I was a wreck. Apollo was right, the police would have converged on me the second I set foot in the hospital.

I started with the tear tracks on my face, staining his white washcloth with dirt, makeup and blood. Then another for my clothes ... and another. I rinsed grit from my mouth and brushed twigs, grass and dirt out of my hair, which still, miraculously, fell in waves rather than tangles, a testament to whatever industrial grade gunk they'd put in it.

In the end I looked halfway presentable. Pale and ragged, as one might expect from a woman whose fiancé ... or had I called him husband? ... was in serious condition. I hoped I'd pass.

I stepped out of the bathroom five minutes from when I'd gone in, wearing determination like a shield.

"Give me one minute," Apollo said, stepping in as soon as I was out and closing the door behind him.

It was two, but I used the time to find a blazer of his and roll up the sleeves. I was slipping out the door when he emerged. He caught the door before I could close it and slid out behind me.

"We'll go together," he said, "in case of trouble."

I turned and glared, crossing my arms over my chest, which made my wings want to flare, as if I had feathers to ruffle. "I don't need your help for this."

"You're getting it regardless. Don't worry, I'll stay out in the waiting room."

"Fine," I said, though it wasn't fine at all. I didn't want him there, sensing my every emotion through our strange link. If I broke down ... well, I didn't need an audience. It gave me a tiny sense of the vulnerability people felt when I poked around in their lives. No wonder the Rialto Bros. had kicked me out and my family still had no idea what to do with me. I was a freak. Now I had the wings to prove it.

Apollo swooped in and kissed me hard, his hands going to my hips. The suddenness of it made me catch my breath and made a hot spike of desire start in my stomach and finish up somewhere significantly lower. The shock of it brought me back to myself and I heaved him away, ready to slap his face ... before I saw the look on it—satisfaction.

"What?" I asked. "What did you do that for?"

"You were feeling sorry for yourself. I figured the kiss would either turn you on or piss you off. Either way, no more pity."

"Screw you," I said, giving him my back and starting for the stairs.

"Any time," he said softly.

I pretended not to hear and continued on my way, only stopping when I got to the front desk to ask about a cab. I'd already put Viggo through enough. "Ms. Karacis?" the desk guy asked.

"Yes."

"You have a message. I took it myself."

He grabbed it from an old-fashioned lattice of message boxes behind the counter and handed it to me. It was on hotel stationary, folded in half.

I read it as the hotel clerk tapped away on his keyboard. Apollo sensed it the second my heart stopped. "Tori?"

"He's gone," I said. No inflection, no emotion. Dead.

"Who's gone?"

"Armani. Nick. He's gone."

I had to hold tightly to the counter, my knuckles white. "Gone where?"

"Home. He wants to be treated and heal at home. Without me. I didn't even get to say goodbye."

Apollo opened his arms, and this time I stepped into them willingly. "Do you still want the cab?" the desk clerk asked.

Apollo shook his head. I could feel it through our hug. Then he guided me back toward the elevators.

"What do you want?" he asked. "A drink? Bed? The comfort of your family?"

"You," I said. It slipped out before I could think, but I realized I meant it. "I want to be with someone who understands."

The elevator came and he was so stunned he didn't move until I did. "Just hold me?" I asked as the door closed behind us.

"I can't make any promises," he said, more truthful than he had to be.

"That's okay too," I said, not knowing if it was true. I wanted him—had *always* wanted him, from that first second he'd walked into my office. But Armani'd had prior claim on my heart.

But now, without that, I realized I couldn't make any promises either. If Apollo were to kiss me again, I couldn't answer for where it would lead.

ABOUT THE AUTHOR

Lucienne Diver does not actually come from circus folk, though you'd never know it to meet her family. She is, however, in no particular order, a wife, mother, literary agent, book addict, sun-worshipper, mythology enthusiast, travel-junkie and crazy person. In addition to the *Latter-Day Olympians* series, she writes the *Vamped* young adult novels (*Vamped, Revamped, Fangtastic, Fangtabulous* and *Fangdemonium*) as well as YA suspense. Her short stories have appeared in the *Strip-Mauled* and *Fangs for the Mammaries* anthologies edited by Esther Friesner (Baen Books) and *Kicking It* edited by Faith Hunter and Kalayna Price (Roc). Her essay "Abuse" is included in the anthology *Dear Bully: Seventy Authors Tell Their Stories* (HarperTeen).

More information can be found on her website at luciennediver.com. You can also follow her on Twitter @luciennediver.

IF YOU LIKED ...

IF YOU LIKED RISE OF THE BLOOD, YOU MIGHT ALSO ENJOY:

Battle for the Blood
by Lucienne Diver

Unnatural Acts
by Kevin J. Anderson

Knight of Flame
by Scott Eder

OTHER WORDFIRE PRESS TITLES BY LUCIENNE DIVER

Bad Blood

Crazy in the Blood

Battle for the Blood

Blood Hunt

Our list of other WordFire Press authors and titles is always growing. To find out more and to see our selection of titles, visit us at:
wordfirepress.com